MERCY HOUSE

MERCY HOUSE

ALENA DILLON

THORNDIKE PRESS
A part of Gale, a Cengage Company

Copyright © 2020 by Alena Dillon.
Thorndike Press, a part of Gale, a Cengage Company.

Thorndike Press® Large Print Core.
The text of this Large Print edition is unabridged.
Other aspects of the book may vary from the original edition.
Set in 16 pt. Plantin.

LIBRARY OF CONGRESS CIP DATA ON FILE.
CATALOGUING IN PUBLICATION FOR THIS BOOK
IS AVAILABLE FROM THE LIBRARY OF CONGRESS

ISBN-13: 978-1-4328-7884-9 (hardcover alk. paper)

Published in 2020 by arrangement with William Morrow Paperback, an imprint of HarperCollins Publishers

Printed in Mexico
Print Number: 01   Print Year: 2020

*For Rowen, whose alchemy
set everything in motion
and whose magic continues to delight us.*

*And for all women who recognize
themselves in these pages.*

CHAPTER 1

January 2010

Sister Evelyn knew she was on call that night — it was her turn to answer any knocks or rings after midnight — and so, when she heard the first tentative rap at the door, she groaned and pried one eyelid open just enough to read the red numbers glaring from the digital clock on her bedside table: 2:43 A.M. An ungodly hour. Evelyn burrowed deeper into her pillow. She'd answer the door. She would. After thirty more seconds of sweet rest.

The second strike was more assertive.

"Get your lazy bones out of bed, Evie," Sister Josephine cried from the neighboring room. "This is your calling, after all."

Evelyn struggled up onto an elbow. "If you're awake enough to be clever, you're awake enough to answer the door yourself." She was satisfied with that response and waited twenty, then forty seconds for Jo-

7

sephine to stir. When her housemate ignored her, Evelyn sighed, pushed herself upright, and began the painful process of extricating herself from bed.

Ever since Evelyn entered the convent fifty years ago and was required to rise with the sun, she worshipped sleep like it was a false god. But now that Evelyn was sixty-nine, the physical difficulty of making her way from her cot to the ground was a relatively recent development. Her body had thickened, her bones had become brittle, and her joints were stiff and reluctant to bend. Every inch of her skeleton creaked when used, but gouty arthritis precipitated the worst of it: the condition swelled her toe, tightened her ankle, and sent a burning ache through her knee. The slightest movement was a reminder of her nearly decade-long status as a senior citizen.

Certainly when God created man, He knew human life expectancy would eventually extend; couldn't He have designed the aging process to be just a bit more graceful? Even a half century after her formation period, Evelyn could still hear the response of her first Mother Superior. "Who are you, young novice, to question the will of almighty God?"

Hobbling around in the darkness of her

bedroom, Evelyn muttered, "Forgive me, Lord. I am but Your meek and humble servant. But you, Mother Superior? You can kiss my fat Irish ass."

Evelyn tucked an arm through the sleeve of her ratty bathrobe and winced as she laced the terry cloth around her other shoulder. As she slipped her puffy feet into moccasins whose insoles retained her impressions, her bladder stung with fullness. She had to pee; she *always* had to pee. She shuffled toward the bathroom just as another thump on the front door echoed up the stairs. "For crying out loud." She'd have to delay relieving herself, which was just as well. It meant she wouldn't capture a peek in the mirror of the disheveled face she was presenting to this newcomer. Because of her matronly shape and dowdy gray hair, one of her former residents said she looked like Flora, Sleeping Beauty's fairy godmother — if Flora had been fired, lost her wand, and was forced to live on the street. With that in mind, Evelyn braced the thick wooden banister and descended the Mercy House staircase, step by careful step.

Mercy House was a safe haven for victims of domestic violence, founded and operated by Sister Evelyn, Sister Josephine, and Sister Maria, nuns of the order of the Sisters of

St. Joseph of Mercy. Their five-bedroom, hundred-year-old row house in the Bedford-Stuyvesant neighborhood of Brooklyn was almost always at capacity. As Evelyn said, *Good for business, bad for humanity.*

In the entryway, Evelyn pressed the security code into the system's keypad: 0–4–1–6, for Hebrews 4:16. "Let us then approach God's throne of grace with confidence, so that we may receive mercy and find grace to help us in our time of need." Maria had chosen the verse because it contained two of her favorite words: "grace" and "mercy." Evelyn had voted for 2–8–3–6, numbers on the keypad that corresponded with "at em," as in, "Let me at 'em," because revenge was often her sinful impulse when she saw the battered women who arrived at their door. The other sisters didn't think this instinct should be condoned, and her suggestion was vetoed.

When Evelyn pulled the door open, she found a girl whose skin was tan, even in winter, and whose black-walnut hair was rigid with gel and coiled in miniature ringlets over her shoulders. Thick charcoal liner, smudged from crying, rimmed her eyelids.

Her face acted as a history of her relationship with her assailant, and Evelyn's experienced eye — she was trained as a nurse in the convent and practiced medicine for many years — surveyed the girl's injuries. A fresh red welt circled from her cheekbone to her forehead, like a swollen parenthesis left open, to what, Evelyn didn't know; a scab, an older wound, ran vertically down her bottom lip like dried-blood stiches; and her nose took a sudden detour in its center, a trademark break from a previous run-in. No matter how many times Evelyn saw such marks of violence, they still made her stomach turn. Beneath the bruising, there was softness to the girl's face that suggested her features were still developing; God had not yet finished his carving. Based on this and her still-budding form, Evelyn guessed her age to be about sixteen.

"Sorry for knocking so much. I didn't know if you heard me." The words rushed from her mouth, as though she were afraid she'd been followed and wanted to explain herself and get out of sight as quickly as possible. The girl squeezed her full, cracked lips together and then released them. "I heard this was a place for, you know . . ." Her stare darted from Evelyn to the uncertain night at her back. She faced Evelyn again and shrugged. Her eyes welled with fresh tears. "Do you have room or what?"

Sister Evelyn had been doing this long enough to know she wouldn't sleep again for hours, maybe not until the following night. Maybe not even then. She swallowed, opened the door fully, and gestured down the hallway. "There's always room for one more."

Evelyn twisted the cap off the rusty teakettle and flipped on the sink faucet. She ignored the girl while the kettle filled, allowing her time to settle into her new surroundings and some privacy to apply the ice pack Evelyn had nonchalantly deposited onto the table. She'd also set out the ham and swiss that had been sitting in the fridge; she made a sandwich every evening before bed, just in case a resident — current or newly arriving — needed a snack in the middle of the night. Evelyn loosed an unencumbered yawn without bothering to cover her mouth. The burner clicked three times before the flame caught.

It never took long for Evelyn to become endeared to each of their residents — well, to most, anyway. But when they first arrived, she had to remind herself: although this was just an ordinary day for her — just another interrupted night's sleep, just another stranger at her door — it was probably one of the worst nights of their lives.

The girl sat hunched at the table with the ice pack pressed against the left side of her face. Her eyes cast about the kitchen, as if something were about to jump out at her, but she just didn't know from where.

Rage swam through Evelyn's veins and poisoned her heart. *Let me at 'em.* "What's your name, dear?" she asked.

The girl straightened, as if startled to remember she was not alone in that room. "Lucia."

Evelyn reached into the cabinet and brought down two chipped mugs. One read in chunky hot pink letters "Best Sister Ever!" a gift from a former resident of the house. The other read "What Would Jesus Brew?" Evelyn couldn't remember the origins of the second ware, but it was her favorite. She reached back into the cabinet for teabags, but then hesitated over the selection: black, green, or chamomile. This girl didn't seem the green tea type, and who really liked chamomile? Then again, judge not and all that crap. "Black?" Evelyn asked.

"Puerto Rican," Lucia said.

The misunderstanding took a moment to register. "I meant your choice of tea, dear."

"Oh, right." Her chin dipped, embarrassed. "Yeah, black. Whatever."

Evelyn dropped a Lipton bag into each mug. "Lucia is a fine name. Saint Lucia is one of only eight women named in Canon of the Mass. She was a virgin martyr."

Lucia snorted. "Yeah, well, I ain't no virgin."

She was too young to make that remark so offhandedly, and frustration and sympathy for this girl bloomed anew. In all probability, her sexual experience was not voluntary. Evelyn wished she could detect in her traces of her young age: more naivete, more curiosity, more innocence. More joy.

"Virginity is about the only requirement for sainting a woman. Men need to have accomplished something, but women just need to have kept their legs crossed. Otherwise, you're guilty of bewitching a good man into sin," Evelyn said. The kettle hissed and she extinguished the flame. "But, from my experience, the whole virginity thing is overrated." Her stare casually drifted over to Lucia's, and she was satisfied to find raised eyebrows; startling newcomers out of their funk was one of her routines. With Evelyn's coarse silver hair cut bluntly across her forehead and her lined expression permanently set in a scowl, nobody expected the gruff nun to have a sense of humor, especially not a crass one. Evelyn's lips pitched up into a grin to emphasize the gag, and then fell almost immediately. She was at once the joker and the straight man.

Lucia's eyebrows pulled from surprise to suspicion, and an acrylic fingernail wandered up to her lip. She propped it between her teeth. "So, how does this work?"

From years of cooking, cleaning, carrying, and caring, Evelyn's hands were so thick and calloused, she thumbed the metal cap from the teakettle's spout without an oven mitt. Boiled water cascaded into the mugs. "What do you mean?" Evelyn asked. She pinched the paper tags and bobbed the teabags until they were saturated with water and began to seep sepia.

"I mean, like, what do you do here? What do you do for someone like me?"

"What do you want us to do?" Evelyn asked. Lucia worked her lips together and then shrugged. Her eyes began to water and she blinked her lids quickly to pat the tears down. "Do you need medical attention?" Evelyn glanced up at Lucia, again assessing the damage to her face and wondering what hurt might be lurking beneath her clothing. Lucia shook her head. Evelyn knew not to press this early. She spooned sugar into each cup. "Do you want to pray together?" Lucia again indicated no. Girls very rarely responded to that suggestion from the onset; prayer was too hokey, or perhaps too intimate. Prayer was something they agreed to only when they were ready, and often never at all. Evelyn pulled open the refrigerator, heaved out the jug of milk, and plunked a drop into each mug. The milk swirled independently in the tea and then blended, a foreign body assimilating. "Do you want to talk about why you're here?" Evelyn asked, and Lucia stared into her lap. Her chin jutted to the side. Evelyn stirred the cups, knowing the ceremony of tea — the boiling, brewing, mixing, and heat of the ceramic between her hands — would be a comfort all its own.

She gripped the handles and shuffled toward the table. Her knee cried out with each step, and her square body rocked atop her limp. She placed one mug before Lucia, who appeared grateful for something on which to focus her attention. Then she dragged a chair out, clamped her teeth, braced herself, and lowered her body into the seat. She exhaled a groan and closed her eyes against a sear up her right leg.

A resident had once offered her marijuana to treat the pain, but that was a slippery slope, and Evelyn knew from experience she had trouble maintaining her footing.

"You all right?" Lucia asked in a tone that was more a comment on how Evelyn was, so obviously, not all right.

"Just another Tuesday morning." Evelyn swallowed and then reopened her eyes. "Want some advice? Don't get old," she said, only afterward realizing, from that angry lump that would last for weeks, Lucia was already well acquainted with pain.

Lucia's finger skimmed the edge of the plastic plate that held her sandwich. She didn't meet Evelyn's eyes when she asked, "You got potato chips?"

Evelyn straightened. Hunger was a good sign. A very good sign. "I have pretzels. Would you like some pretzels?"

She shook her head. "I put chips in sandwiches. I like the crunch."

"Well I hope this doesn't affect our Yelp review," Evelyn said, but she made a mental note to pick up some potato chips from the corner bodega later in the morning. She sensed that this girl, like so many, was in need of simple, healthy love, the kind without agenda or ulterior motive. And she prayed the girl would find it there.

When Evelyn was four years old, she was bartered into the sisterhood by her father, a scrawny Irishman who lived on a diet of

17

sausage, eggs, and whiskey. He promised God, if his oldest son returned safely from the invasion of Normandy, he'd commit his youngest daughter, Little Evie, to His eternal service. The name Evelyn came from the Irish Aibhlín, meaning "wished for, longed for child." When Sean returned in one piece, without even a hairline fracture — except inside his mind, her daddy said, "Little Evie, look what you did. Look what wishes you keep making come true."

Evie, who worshipped her gregarious daddy, accepted her fate.

Lucky for her, she loved everything about being a Catholic. As a child, instead of having tea parties, she practiced serving Communion to her dolls. Since she always knew she'd become a nun, she viewed her family's house of worship as a home. The nuns, who glided around the halls of her church and school like a robe-swishing, rosary-clanging army, were aware of her pact with God, and, when they were allowed to speak, discussed her future in "whens," not "ifs." Priests were paternal figures — so much so that when she had a more serious sin to confess, like stealing bubblegum, she walked an extra mile to a different parish so none of her priests would recognize her voice.

She liked the ceremony of her religion,

and felt secure in the predictability and order of the Mass as well as in the familiar words of the liturgy. She appreciated the solemnity with which the priests lifted a chalice from the altar, the way they whispered the Eucharistic prayer, as if murmuring directly into God's ear, and the elegance of the thick gold stole draped around their necks.

Evelyn felt she belonged in church, often more than she felt she belonged in her own house, where all her siblings were over a decade her senior and treated her like the spare sibling who was leaving, and her parents frequently forgot they still had one last daughter to raise.

But then there were times when she watched her high school English teacher, Sister Angelica, gaze out the classroom window, mournfully, as if trying to recapture a precious memory that slipped away. And in those rare moments, she wondered if the fate awaiting her was a happy one — if there were better lives to live. Like the ones her high school peers prepared for by taking training courses and dressing for dates at the drive-in or sock hop. But boys never took an interest in Evie. She suspected it was because she wasn't very pretty with her bristly auburn hair and wide, flat nose. Her biggest insecurity was her neck. It didn't elongate, and was barely thinner than her face. She wished it were more delicate, as a woman's should be, but instead it was as sturdy as a redwood. Maybe it was best that she had a groom in Jesus.

If the Dodgers could leave Brooklyn, she supposed she could too.

She entered the Hudson Valley convent when she was nineteen, in 1960, at the tail end of Vatican I, when the sisters still abided by the Code of Canon Law, two thousand restrictive regulations to keep nuns reverent, including no newspapers, magazines, radio, or television; letters were censored and not delivered during Advent or Lent; no personal belongings or spending money; female visitors only once a month and none during Advent or Lent; daily silence, except for forty-five minutes of conversation allowed after both lunch and dinner, with total silence on Sundays; and clothing limited to the habit, a head-to-toe wool uniform marked with her assigned number — 106 — that was only washed four times a year. Maintain custody of your eyes, meaning don't let your stare linger anywhere for too long. No chewing gum or swinging of the arms. No razors or sweets. No congregating in groups of fewer than three to

20

prevent intimacy. No tampons or eating bananas, because both were suggestive. No classical music by Claude Debussy because it was too racy.

Inside the convent, the women knew little of the cultural and social evolution occurring outside their walls: Beatlemania, the Space Needle, *West Side Story*, Marilyn Monroe, the Cuban Missile Crisis, the Vietnam War, Spiderman, Bob Dylan, Muhammad Ali, LSD, the civil rights movement, and the first breast implants. To them, the 1960s didn't look very different from the 1860s.

Although the convent was a short hour-and-a-half drive from Brooklyn, Evie wasn't allowed to visit home, and she rarely heard from her family. She felt used up and spit out, like she'd satisfied her role, paid her debt to God on their behalf, and now they had no use for her. Suddenly her Irish name, Aibhlín — longed for child — seemed cruel in its irony.

In her more melodramatic moments, she likened herself to Jesus on the crucifix, abandoned by His father. She stared at the single photo she was allowed to keep of her family and asked, "Why have you forsaken me?"

There were dark days. Once, when Mother

Superior caught Evelyn sneaking a scrap of turkey before dinner, she made Evelyn lie down in the doorway so all the other nuns had to step over her on their way into the kitchen. Some days were darker still.

In fact, one of the few times she laughed in those first few years was when one of the older sisters stood too close to a prayer candle and her veil caught fire. While the smoldering sister and several other nuns flailed about, slapping the side of her head, trying to swat out the flame, the priest, Father Stephens, continued with his service as if they weren't squawking like a brood of hens at the back of the room.

Evelyn wouldn't have survived her formation had it not been for Eloise Harper. Eloise entered the order shortly after Evie. Eloise taught her to read body language when words were forbidden, to hear God in the silence. Eloise taught her to want to be a nun, not just because of her father's promise, but because the vocation suited her, made her better. She began to find comfort in the communion of sisters, peace in prayer, and purpose in the commitment and sacrifice. Her habit (with the loose white veil of the novitiate years) made her part of a higher calling. It gave her a new family.

Her father died of liver failure before Evelyn took her vows — what she once thought of as his vows. But by the time Evelyn sheered her hair down to its fuzzy roots in order to fit into the guimpe that hugged her face and held the black veil like a crown, they were indeed her vows — mostly, anyway.

When Evelyn opened her eyes the next day, it took several blinks to orient herself. She was slouched in her rocking chair in the Mercy House living room, her olivewood rosary beads still laced through her fingers from her prayer the night before, and Mei-Li, a nineteen-year-old resident of the house, clasped Evelyn's shoulders and rubbed her hands up and down to generate warmth.

"You're shivering," she whispered. Having been there six months, Mei-Li was the house veteran, and so Evelyn knew her better than the other residents. She'd learned she worked at a theater concession stand so that she could escape her reality by watching movies for free, including *Twilight* seven times; she was almost always smiling, but was rarely happy; and although she appeared shy and compliant on the outside — her uncle had trained such a demeanor —

when overwhelmed, she held her breath and didn't release it until she was on her own and could emit the exhale along with a deluge of profanities spat in three languages: English, Russian, and Mandarin. The first time Mei-Li returned from one of these private outbursts, Evelyn said, "If you want to curse so only God can hear you, that's between the two of you. But there's no need to censor yourself for anybody else's sake; don't hide your fire under a bushel."

In the rocking chair, Evelyn gathered her beads into a fist and shifted, a call for a status update from her body. She was answered by severe stiffness in her back and would pay for this restless night's sleep all day long.

"You should stop giving up your bed. It isn't right," Mei-Li said, straightening. Her skin was pale and smooth, her nose was set on a sturdy wide base, and her eyes danced with the complex joy of teardrops in a paisley pattern. "Bring new girls into our rooms, even if it is three in the morning. This isn't good for you, *popo.*" Evelyn was told the Mandarin phrase was one of respect for an older woman, but she liked Mei-Li so much, it could have meant "trash hag" and Evelyn wouldn't have wanted her to stop using the endearment. Mei-Li began to leave the room, but then hesitated in the doorway. "How is she? The new girl?"

Evelyn twisted in her chair despite the pinch she knew the movement would trigger in her back. She loved Mei-Li for asking about Lucia. She loved her in the way she grew to love all of her residents, women who had been broken by men, but who put themselves back together, who asked after others despite what was stored up inside themselves. Evelyn forced her voice to be tender through her pain. "You remember what it was like."

CHAPTER 2

MEI-LI

When I was a girl, my father played paper dolls with me every evening after work, and when he cut out the dresses and hats for my little paper girls, he worked cautiously around their edges so they'd be just right. His eyebrows bunched together like two hairy caterpillars. His scissors closed slowly, millimeter by meticulous millimeter. He worked like he wasn't a New York taxi driver who shared his cab with his terrible older brother and two other Russian men in our apartment building who smelled of gasoline and borscht. He worked like *this* was his living. He was a paper tailor — and a good one.

I was careless. Too eager to get past the tedious preparation and down to the business of playing. I sliced through an abdomen without looking, or cut off a sleeve. And when I realized what I'd done, I'd collapse against the kitchen table and wail. (This was before I learned sharing my emotions was a disadvantage to survival.)

"Zolotse," my father would say, his hand on my back. "My gold. Don't despair. You've done nothing that can't be undone."

With those reassurances in mind, I'd push myself up from the table to watch him repair my mistake. Because he was not just a paper tailor. He was also a paper surgeon.

He'd mend the wounds with precisely measured bits of scotch tape bound to the backs of the dresses so the stitching would be invisible. When he was finished, they looked as good as new. He was a paper miracle worker.

My mother watched us from the stove, where she prepared food to satisfy both of their palates. For her, hot and sour soup, whose chili oil made my father's eyes water just from sharing the same room as its powerful essence, and for him, Olivier salad, a far blander mound of hard-boiled eggs, peas, and potatoes slathered in mayonnaise. Then there was always a third dish, one they could both sample: sautéed carrots and beets coated in soy paste. I still don't know if this is a traditional Chinese dish that happened to incorporate elements of my father's Russian heritage, or if my mother invented it after she listed herself in a catalog and agreed to marry a man she'd only seen in a photograph. She arrived in the United States two years before I was born, and was relieved and grateful to discover she could love the stranger who would be her husband. Grateful to be a wife in America, that her daring yielded positive results. Grateful enough to cook and eat beets.

"You spoil her. You fix her mistake over and over. She'll never learn. She'll never do well herself."

"You is right, my love, *lyubov moya,*" my father answered. "Of course you is right."

But he was my paper friend. He continued to fix my mistakes, over and over again. Until the day he died.

Uncle Nikita moved from his apartment into ours the day after my father's funeral. I was fourteen then. "Ivan would very not want you alone," he said. "I watch over you. Keep you safe. For my brother."

He slept on the couch that night, and the night after that. When he was still in our living room a week later, drinking Moskovskaya out of my mother's porcelain teacups, she said, "Nikita, you been so good to us. But you don't have to stay here no more. We're fine. I have Mei-Li and she have me.

28

We do okay."

His stare didn't waver from the television, where the American soccer team struggled against South Africa. Nikita loved to see Americans lose. His voice was gruff, almost threatening, when he said, "It isn't right to leave women on their own."

My mother gripped her hands at her waist and smiled in a way that scared me. "We be fine. Mei-Li is smart girl. And I am strong. We take care of each other. And you live close. If we need anything, we find you in no time. But you can go home. Don't be uncomfortable just for us."

His gaze slid toward her. The darkness in his eyes made me put my pencil down. "Listen, Fan, you do not sound so hospitable."

My mother chuckled and shook her head. "Oh no. You misunderstand."

Nikita shot to his feet and whacked my mother upside the head. It wasn't forceful, but the sudden cruelty of it still caused me to gasp. "Do not you talk back to me. If I say you is inhospitable, you is inhospitable," he said, and then he returned to the game as if nothing had happened.

Violence in our home was so strange, neither my mother nor I knew how to react. I couldn't see her face from where she was

29

standing, but her body was rigid. After a few frozen moments, she turned on her heels, walked down the hall, and closed her bedroom door behind her. The announcer's voice hummed in the background, but I couldn't focus on his words. I could hardly even breathe. Nikita didn't look back at me. He sloshed another helping of Moskovskaya into my mother's teacup, one of the few items she'd brought with her from China, and when the American team scored a goal, he screamed, *"Otva'li, mu'dak, b'lyad!"* and hurled the cup against the wall, where it smashed.

As I brushed my teeth that night, he walked down the hall and into my mother's room. The brush stilled in my hand. I caught a glimpse of her sitting on her bed, a photo album open in her lap. When he appeared, her eyes widened in surprise, and perhaps in fear, but she said nothing to stop him. He closed the door.

Instead of going to bed, I gathered the shards of my mother's teacup and laid them on the kitchen table. As Nikita's grunts and my mother's whimpers drifted through the walls, I hummed to myself and tried to glue her precious keepsake back together. But this time what was done could not be undone. It had been broken into too many pieces.

If I ever have a daughter, I will give her a male name. Something like Zhaolong, meaning "like a dragon." Boys get names like that in my mother's country. Jianjun: "building the army." Lei: "thunder." Huo-jin: "fire metal." Yingjie: "brave and heroic." Girls are too often defined by their grace, their docility. Baozhai: "dainty and loving." Luli: "dewy jasmine." Renxiang: "benevolent fragrance."

My name, Mei-Li, means "beautiful." What good did beauty ever do me?

It took a year from that first awful night for Uncle Nikita to come into my bedroom. Perhaps I should be grateful it took him that long.

My mother tugged on his arm. She asked him to come back to her room. But she knew she couldn't stop him. Her name is Fan, which means "orchid." A sudden change in weather will cause an orchid's petals to drop and will wither its stem. Although she was strong and courageous, having traveled to a country with a foreign tongue in order to marry a man she'd never met, my uncle was stronger. Nikita is a Russian name meaning "supreme, unbeatable."

My uncle wrapped his thick hands around her neck and squeezed until her eyes bulged. He wanted both of us to know he was capable of killing us. We only lived because he let us. He was the god of our universe.

Or maybe he wanted my mother and me to understand that, if one of us left, if one us so much as said a word against him, he could kill the other. That was his leverage.

My mother sputtered. Her fingers clawed at his unrelenting noose.

"Stop! Do whatever you want to me. Just stop," I cried.

And he did what he wanted. He was going to, anyway. He alternated between my mother and me for the next two years.

One day, when my mother was sick with the stomach flu and Nikita wanted beef stroganoff for dinner, I brought home the wrong cut of meat. He walked me down to the corner grocery store to show me exactly how stupid I'd been.

That's where I first met Sister Evelyn. She stole glances at Uncle Nikita and me, and I don't know how she understood but, when our eyes met, she recognized something in me. I felt it. She saw me in a way nobody else had — not my neighbors, not my teachers, not my Aunt Antonina. Or perhaps those people did see that thing in me, that broken thing, but they chose to look away because it was easier, safer. Sister Evelyn didn't look away. And neither did I. I saw something in her too.

As we approached the counter with a package of cube steak and a bottle of Nikita's Moskovskaya, she appeared with a cart full of bagged groceries, wearing an oversized Mets sweatshirt. "Excuse me," she said sweetly to Nikita. "I couldn't get my shopping cart over that step in front of the door, so I left it out on the sidewalk, and now I need to transfer all of these heavy bags. You're big and strong. Would you help a feeble old woman?"

As soon as Nikita was out the door, she grabbed my wrist and her voice dropped into a lower, throaty register. "Two eighty-four Chauncey Street."

I pulled my arm back. "What?"

"Two eighty-four Chauncey Street. Mercy House. We can help you."

Uncle Nikita had half of the bags in the outside cart now. Later that night he would describe his act of heroism to my mother as she shivered with fever. Because despite everything, sometimes it seemed he wanted her approval. Even beasts long to be loved.

"Help me with what?" I asked.

She meant business and didn't have much

time. She leveled her stare. "You don't deserve any of this. You need to get yourself out of this situation as soon as possible. Two eighty-four Chauncey Street. It's the one with the angel doorknocker. Arrive any time. Day or night. You can be safe." Then she turned to the Middle Eastern man behind the counter and nodded. "Sorry about the switch, Abdul. I'll bring your cart back tomorrow."

The next morning, before Uncle Nikita woke, I told my mother what the old woman had said, and that I wanted us to leave. She didn't look up from where she diced cooked beets for vinegret. She didn't make anything but Russian meals anymore. Not Chinese, and never her hybrid. She replied to me in Mandarin, "I have no work, no friends, and no family. How would I survive? Where would I go? Back to China?" Red juice pooled on the cutting board like fresh blood.

I asked her four more times. *Let's go to Mercy House. At least listen to what they have to say.* But her answer was always the same. And I couldn't imagine leaving her alone with him. If I stayed, at least we had each other.

I resigned myself to this fate until the day Nikita didn't like the tone I used to tell him dinner was ready and he put a knife to my throat. The steel was cool and sharp against my skin and his breath was warm and sour. His eyes were crazed; his pupils dilated the way they did when he thrust himself into me. He was getting pleasure from this moment. It pleased him to have his way with my body, to have his way with my life.

That's when I decided I would be more than just beautiful. I would be like the dragon.

I told my mother, when I left for work at the theater the next day, I wouldn't be returning. And I wanted her to come with me, to meet me at Mercy House at three o'clock, during Nikita's taxi shift.

I waited on the front steps of 284 Chauncey Street for two hours before I lifted the angel doorknocker.

Sister Evelyn answered. "I'm glad you decided to come," she said. And then she opened the door wider. "Welcome home."

Worry for my mother filled my stomach, my head, and my mouth. There wasn't room for anything else. It took a week to keep down a proper meal, and twice that before I spoke. I was afraid that if I parted my lips, my mother would spill out. So I kept her in. I stored up my worry and rage until I couldn't hold them in any more, and they bubbled out of me. No matter how badly I wanted to be like the dragon, it couldn't happen all at once. I'd have to learn.

Hope for my mother lives on. Here's the thing about orchids. Even after their last petal drops, they can always bloom again.

CHAPTER 3

Sister Maria wore a men's crew-neck sweater, but her cleavage line was still visible, running almost up to her clavicle, and her belly bulged beneath an electric-yellow apron that read "Hot Stuff Coming Through." While Evelyn assembled ingredients for a slow cooker dinner, Sister Maria removed muffins from the oven. She eyed the browned mounds in their tin and said, "Bran is nobody's favorite, but it won't kill us to be health conscious. Our bodies are temples, after all."

After she dusted her hands of flour and slipped the apron over her neck, Maria prepared for her daily Reiki ritual. She arranged her pad on top of the kitchen table and pressed play on her 1990s-era boom box, which emitted ethereal Eastern flute music, just in time for the first resident to descend the stairs for her treatment.

"Morning, Sisters," Esther said as she

shuffled in, rubbing sleep from an eye with the heel of a hand. At five foot nothing, Esther was a compact woman from Haiti. She immigrated as a girl, so her speech offered only a trace of her roots, revealed most clearly when her puckered lips made short *o*'s long, and when words beginning with *th,* like "think" or "thanks," sounded like they started with a soft, almost imperceptible *d.* Her skin was smooth chestnut, her chest ample, and her limbs solid — so solid Evelyn wondered why she had tolerated her ex-boyfriend's mistreatment for as long as she did. But Evelyn had been in this ugly business long enough to know victims weren't just at the mercy of their abusers' physical strength. Emotional control was often a more formidable force. Esther arrived on the sisters' doorstep two months earlier with a bloody nose, an overnight bag, and a positive pregnancy test. She wasn't pregnant anymore.

"Blessed morning, Esther," Maria said with a grin so broad and genuine Evelyn didn't know whether to roll her eyes or hug the woman. Inspired by *The Sound of Music* and *The Flying Nun,* Maria had joined their order forty years earlier, back in the late 1960s after the change to Vatican II, in the sweet spot when becoming a nun wasn't such an ordeal but the station was still respected by the general population. But it was not quite as fun as Maria had expected; she imagined living with a bunch of women would be like a sleepover that lasted a lifetime. She'd made the best of it though, sunbathing nude on the roof of the convent, curling women's hair with toilet paper rolls, organizing games of charades, and writing and directing plays and spoof songs that teased the older nuns.

Maria clasped her hands atop her belly. "How'd you sleep?"

"Can't complain," Esther said.

"Who says?" Evelyn asked. She swiped the steel of a butcher knife across her pant leg and positioned a carrot on her cutting board.

She chopped onions, garlic, carrots, and celery; rinsed dried navy beans and picked through them for stones; measured water for broth; and shook in thyme, paprika, rosemary, and salt. All the while, at her back, Maria circled the transformed kitchen table. She cupped Esther's ears, pressed her thumbs into her forehead, lay her hands on her stomach, clasped her hips, and squeezed her feet. When she was done with physical contact, she stepped back, raised both palms as if to beseech the immobile Esther to stop, and concentrated on casting positive energy in her direction. Finally, Maria approached the table once again and gestured over Esther in grand sweeping motions, cleansing her aura.

When they first launched Mercy House decades earlier, Evelyn wasn't just skeptical of Maria's Reiki practice — she disdained it. Maria might be gullible enough to buy into all that Japanese energy and aura bull cocky, but that didn't mean Evelyn had to. And why should hours of that nonsense excuse Maria from household chores? But the residents did seem to sit up from her table calmed, reassured, and more at peace. After months of begging (*Please, Evie. Rei means "God's wisdom." Let me share with you what little of God's wisdom I have to offer. It's my ministry, dammit!*), Evelyn relented and allowed Maria to perform her practice on her. And while Evelyn didn't think she gained anything from the energy-beaming or aura-cleansing portion of the routine, if nothing else, she did find great comfort in being touched. Without a lover, or even any close family members, when else in her life did she experience such prolonged human contact? The warmth of Maria's hands resting so assuredly on her breastbone stilled her pulsing anxiety. It caused Evelyn to recall a moment back at the convent when she was training to be a nun. Her friend Eloise had sensed Evelyn's loneliness, her distress, and had placed her hand on Evelyn's. It made all the difference. Physical communication had been a powerful thing when words were forbidden.

The residents of Mercy House, who had suffered so much violent interaction, deserved to feel a healing, nourishing, loving hand on their skin. Who was Evelyn to deny them that, and who knew — maybe there was something to the energy and aura bull cocky too.

"Morning," a small voice said from behind Evelyn.

Evelyn turned to find Lucia in the doorway, leaning against the wall as if hoping it might camouflage her. "Lucia. Good morning. How'd you sleep?"

"Okay, thanks," she said. Evelyn smiled, nodded curtly, and then focused her attention back to the counter. She placed the lid on the slow cooker, turned the switch to low, and began to replace the seasonings into their rack when Lucia said, "It was all right for a night."

Gripping the rosemary, Evelyn's hand stilled in midair, and she rotated slowly. She caught a deliberate look from Maria, a

41

warning to be gentle, to be less *Evelyn-like.* She nodded, inhaled through her nostrils, and faced Lucia. "Dear, this isn't a Super 8. Women don't normally stay here for only one night."

Lucia shifted in her stance. "Why the hell not?"

Maria coughed to tell Evelyn she wasn't being sweet enough, sensitive enough. Evelyn had to forcibly control her eye roll and put on a more nurturing voice than came naturally to her. No matter how long she did this, she struggled with patience, and with guiding girls into making their own decisions rather than telling them directly what was best. "Because healing takes time. And more often than not, violence comes from the home. It isn't usually easy to find a new home so quickly."

Lucia's jaw jutted to the side and she said, even more quietly, "Who said I wanted a new home? Who said I wanted a new anything?"

Evelyn placed the rosemary shaker back onto the counter. A voice in her head screamed, *He hurt you. He hurt you over and over again. You deserve to love and to be loved.* But instead of saying any of that, she gripped her hands at her waist and dug a thumbnail into the skin of her index finger.

"Might you be able to stay here at least one more night, just so you can think things through? That way we have the chance to talk about your options."

Lucia stared down at the floor and gently kicked her foot against the kitchen tile. "I guess."

Evelyn clapped her hands together. " 'I guess' is good enough for me," she said, although it certainly wasn't. "Well, I have to run, but if you need anything, place your order with Sister Maria here." She set a few of Maria's bran muffins aside, tipped the tin so that the remaining ones tumbled into a basket, and then hooked her wrist beneath the basket's handle. After a nod to Maria, which she hoped communicated *Are you happy?* she walked past Lucia and down the hallway, toward the front door. But at the coatrack, a thought occurred to her, and she paused to lift her Mets cap off its hook. "Don't wait up," she said.

The homes on Chauncey Street were as diverse as the women who arrived at Mercy House. One side was lined with eggshell-brick, four-story tenements dulled by years of dirt and dust. Some fronts were ornamented by fire escapes, like conspicuous facial piercings. Some had decorative red-

and-green moulding like bold makeup. Some walkways were gated to add an extra layer of security, or at least the illusion of security, since many gates weren't locked. Some exteriors were made inviting with potted plants while others had bars installed over their windows.

Opposite the apartments, on Mercy House's side of Chauncey Street, were red-brick row houses. Mercy House shared one wall with the Sahas, a quiet Indian family of eight, including parents, grandparents, and four children under the age of ten. Naveen, the father, was an anesthesiologist back in his home country, but was currently working in a restaurant on Atlantic Avenue while he took the United States Medical Licensing Examination. Evelyn felt sorry for him — how unfair to be told you might not be qualified for the very job to which you've dedicated your life — but she did appreciate the periodic containers of tomato-coconut soup he left on their front step. Mercy House shared its other wall with a group of recent college graduates of the New School. She didn't know much about them except that they liked to blast indie rock music after midnight and, based on the withered skeleton of a pine tossed on their sidewalk that morning, they were late throwing out their Christmas tree.

Evelyn liked the look and feel of the connected dwellings on Chauncey Street. It was almost like they were all holding hands down the block, from Ralph to Howard Avenue. A community forced by architecture. Although there was a lot of turnover, especially as the culture of the neighborhood evolved, there were also some longtime residents. People who were there that terrible morning a few years earlier when Evelyn woke to find the word "whores" spray-painted across the outside of their home in thick black letters. Maybe the hateful artist would have preferred the scarlet ink of Hester Prynne, but it would have blended too well with his redbrick canvas. Several of Chauncey Street's habitants came outside that day, toting buckets of soapy water and sponges. Evelyn had to buy graffiti remover and rent a pressure washer to erase that ugly word, but the offers of help were still appreciated.

Evelyn had recently enjoyed her favorite part about the block. During the holiday season, she distributed battery-operated candles equipped with a timer to each home and, every night at 5 P.M., all the windows lit at once. It was important that the women of Mercy House could look out the window, see all the flames glowing around them, and be comforted. Especially at Christmastime, when they were away from everything they knew. And Evelyn wanted potential residents of Mercy House to turn onto Chauncey and know it was a place for shelter, a sanctuary street.

"How you doin' this morning, Sister?"

Evelyn gripped the icy iron railing with her free hand and steadied her feet on the steps before she looked up. Across the street, Joylette, a single mother of three teenage boys, was hanging laundry on her second-floor fire escape. Evelyn risked releasing her hold in order to wave. "Just fine, thanks. You finally have a day off?"

"Has hell frozen over?"

"Not that I've been told."

"Then I guess my shift starts in twenty-five minutes."

"Do those handsome boys of yours appreciate how hard you work for them?"

"Has hell frozen over?"

Evelyn laughed and ventured another step. "Maybe it should."

She allowed herself one more glimpse up at Joylette; she wished she could offer to help — no, insist on it — to relieve that woman who took it upon herself to run her family's world so she could have the time, the luxury, to stop for a coffee and sit before work. But Evelyn had her own world to run.

"The Mets suck," Nigel barked as Evelyn approached. He sat against the steel grate of a closed storefront on Ralph Avenue, around the corner from Mercy House. A navy knit cap was pulled over straggly straw-colored hair, and a bushy gray beard tickled his chest. He was dressed in appropriate layers for the cold, and Evelyn was pleased to see he was still wearing the bubble coat and work boots she'd given to him for Christmas the previous month — that he hadn't pawned them for something less noble.

"I like an underdog," she said.

"*Underdog.* Now there's TV worth watching." He lifted his chin to snoop the contents of her basket. "Blueberry?" he asked, hopeful.

"Not so fast," she said and pulled the basket back against her body. "What do you have for me?"

Nigel settled back into his spot. "A girl came by in the middle of the night. Maybe two or three o'clock."

"That much I know. I opened the door for her, as you may have noticed."

He glared up at Evelyn and sighed. "Was

47

I finished? Not sure of her people. Spics, probably."

Evelyn swallowed her urge to address his hateful language. Curses were one thing. Prejudice was another. But she had more pressing matters. "Was she followed?"

"No, she was by herself. Pretty little thing in the dark all alone. Not too bright."

"Did you recognize her?" she asked. Nigel sucked his bottom lip into his mouth until his top teeth scraped the hairs of his beard. She raised her eyebrows. "Well?"

"Four muffins."

"You aren't my only stop, you know," she said. He shrugged and turned his head away to show his indifference. This was their dance. "Three muffins."

Nigel faced her again. "She hangs around with Juan or Jorge or whatever his fucking name is. The thug with the cross on his face."

"Shit," Evelyn said. She knew just who he was describing. Angel Perez had a Gothic cross tattooed on his cheek. The tip was a dagger, and it dripped inky blood down his neck. He was also a ranking member of Los Soldados, one of the most violent gangs in Brooklyn. To be initiated, you had to murder a stranger. "Shit."

"Yeah, shit. It hits the fan. The world goes

to it. You can sprinkle glitter on it but it still stinks. Hey, you may not like the info, but that don't mean it's free." He extended his hands, and she plucked three muffins from the basket and deposited them into his open palms. He smiled smugly, as if he were getting away with something, and then took a bite. Evelyn walked past him toward her next destination. "This ain't blueberry!" Nigel cried after her. "It's bullshit. That's what it is, Sister. Bullshit."

Before Evelyn panicked, she wanted to determine the exact gravity of the situation. She needed more information.

As she walked north on Ralph Avenue, a sharp wind cut through the fabric of her coat and chilled her skin. *This is what you get for buying winter wear at a flea market. Wool, my ass,* she thought, and pinched her collar closed with a bare hand. She cursed herself for remembering her Mets cap but forgetting gloves. But the cap was an icebreaker. Gloves weren't nearly as valuable.

The clouds were heavy with snow, and their slate was a dull contrast to the three-story brickface buildings on either side of the avenue. The store awnings were in desperate need of repair: the yellow of the halal shop was streaked with dirt and the green of the African market was faded and torn across the first letter, making it appear to read "frican Grocery Store."

Lights were beginning to flash on in the adjacent retailers: Goodwill, Family Dollar, and Bargain Hunters. A McDonald's bag skittered across the sidewalk; Evelyn stepped forward as if to pick it up, but then she spotted a crushed Styrofoam coffee cup just beyond it. It would be impossible to clean the entire street, so what was the point in disposing of a single bag?

"Morning, Sister," a childish voice said from outside her peripheral vision. Evelyn rotated stiffly to find Alfred, a ten-year-old boy from her parish, zipping around the corner on Heelys, sneakers whose back end housed a wheel. Alfred's mother didn't get off from work until noon on Sunday, after all the English services, so they were one of the few African American families who attended the Spanish Mass.

"Morning, Alfred. Don't break your neck," Evelyn said and hurried onward.

St. Joseph of Mercy Church took up the entire next corner, sharing the intersection with a Popeyes, a Western Union, and a deli grocer run largely on food stamps. The church's Gothic Revival architecture included a main house and a tower capped by four spindly pinnacles. A rose window at the center and three white marble arcades at the entrance accented the facade. It was a beautiful piece of history made even more stunning in contrast: the church was sandwiched between rundown row houses to the east, and Hong Kong City Chinese Restaurant to the north. This wasn't an unusual sight in Bedford-Stuyvesant, where over eight thousand buildings were constructed in the nineteenth century.

Miss Linda sat hunched on the bus stop bench in front of the church. The hem of her pink leopard-print skirt fell at her shins, revealing bare, ashy ankles. Her once-white sneakers were now sooty with filth and peeling at the toes.

"Miss Linda, please, go sit inside," Evelyn said, gesturing to the church. Her words came out more impatient than she intended.

"I don't want to bother no one."

"Who is there to bother? We can hardly get people there on Sunday, never mind at eight o'clock on a Tuesday morning. The place is empty."

Miss Linda's gaze drifted up to Evelyn's and lingered for a moment before dropping back to the sidewalk. Her jaw shifted from side to side. "I abuse your generosity. I shouldn't make a habit of that."

"Why the hell not?"

"I'm fine just where I am."

"Oh for cripes' sake. I have things to do, Miss Linda. But you know I can't leave you sitting out here in the cold. Please just go inside so I can be on my way. If you insist on being a knucklehead, you can come back out as soon as you defrost."

She nodded slowly. "Maybe just for a minute."

"Good. And take a couple of these." She handed Miss Linda three muffins, one at a time, which the woman slipped into the black plastic bags at her side.

Miss Linda placed her hands on the bench and heaved herself to her feet. "I hope you accept as much kindness as you give, Sister. It ain't right to be the one always dishing it out. It just ain't right," she said, and ambled toward the church entrance.

Evelyn continued north on Ralph Avenue for another quarter mile, pausing once more to provide a homeless man a bit of breakfast. Then she turned right onto Gates Avenue.

Bedford-Stuyvesant, or, as the natives called it, Bed-Stuy, was undergoing a transformation. Like many other Brooklyn neighborhoods, it was once so dangerous Evelyn hesitated to stop at red lights, but now, for better or worse, it was gentrifying. Starbucks was creeping onto the borders near Park Slope and Clinton Hill. Fringe bakeries began to peddle overpriced donuts or cupcakes or whatever the hell was the current trend. Mothers pushed baby strollers down the sidewalks on their way to vegan smoothie shops. Joggers appeared as if from nowhere. Rents skyrocketed. There was even a Whole Foods. Where once a drunken stranger had groped Evelyn without any passerby intervening, it was now becoming an area you could walk around with complete confidence. At least during daylight hours.

North of Gates Avenue trailed a bit behind the rest of Bed-Stuy's evolution cycle and, at night, crime trickled down from that zone. Evelyn still wasn't surprised to read about local robberies, stabbings, or shootings in the morning paper.

Several housing projects also happened to be located north of Gates Avenue; in fact, some Mercy House residents came from the Sumner Houses or the Tompkins Projects. The latter was also home to several known gang members — including Angel Perez.

Evelyn found James in an empty parking lot, leaning against a brick wall painted with a mural of Bed-Stuy born and bred rap artists: Fabolous, Mos Def, Biggie Smalls, and

Lil' Kim. The previous graffiti on that wall had been phallic and uninspired; Evelyn thought it was a shame this muralist wasn't paid for his or her contribution to the community.

"Morning, James," Evelyn called from a distance to afford him enough time to tuck away his liquor.

"Mister Sister," James said, returning her greeting with a nickname he invented after watching her fend off a mugger; he'd never met a nun with such a set of balls.

"I need some information." Evelyn was out of breath from the mile-long walk, and her knees and ankles ached beneath the weight of her body. Moisture pooled beneath her breasts, which had rounded to a size that would have made her younger self envious, but had, in the last couple decades, fallen to rest on her belly, as if they were defeated by the knowledge of their ultimate futility. She leaned her rump against the hood of a rusted sedan.

"It's yours if I got it." A woolen hat embroidered with a single snowflake peeked out from beneath a gray sweatshirt hood. Evelyn found the design incredibly endearing.

"How much do you know about Angel Perez?" She rooted around in her basket.

Four muffins remained. She handed one to James and took a bite from another.

"I know he's a mean-ass son of a bitch." James lifted the muffin as if to toast Evelyn and then took a bite.

"How often do you see him around here?"

"Often enough."

"Do you recognize who he's with? Friends, girlfriends?"

James eyed Evelyn while he chewed. "If you're asking something, go ahead and ask it."

Evelyn struggled to swallow the bran; the walk had parched her. She could use a long pull from a water bottle — or better yet, a beer — and her mind ran through a list of the nearest convenience stores. "Is he the type who rotates girls in and out, or does he put his claws into one at a time?"

James chewed and stared at her dully. The whites of his eyes were cloudy, perhaps yellowed. It reminded Evelyn of her father's in his last years, and she wondered if James suffered from liver disease, if he sought medical attention for it, if he was even aware of the possibility. "I don't spend time in the boy's bedroom, but I'd wager a bit of both."

"What do you mean?"

"I only ever see him out with one girl, but that don't mean he don't spread his love around when she ain't looking."

Evelyn closed her eyes and nodded. That's the answer she was afraid of. That one girl — Angel's one girl — was sitting at her kitchen table. And he'd want her back.

James intuited her concern. "Let me guess. You got a new girl last night, and Angel got trouble in paradise?"

"That bruise on her eye didn't look like paradise to me."

James's lips parted into a smile, revealing a tooth gap. "Hey, love hurts."

Only a person who wouldn't be on the receiving end of domestic abuse could say such an asinine thing. She shook her head. "If you really loved someone, you wouldn't hurt them."

James's eyelids lowered and he extended his hand for another baked good. "Maybe you ain't never really loved nobody."

Her final stop was a necessary evil.

At the end of Gates she turned to head north on Broadway, an avenue that ran under the J train. The steel beams of the track overhead created the illusion of being inside a tunnel, and when the train thundered above, her whole world rattled and screeched; it almost felt like the locomotive roared right through her.

She was now in the section of Bed-Stuy where bananas sold for nineteen cents a pound, people took buses to work rather than the subway, and liquor store owners had to sit behind bulletproof glass.

A few vacant storefronts with roll-down security doors were marred by illegible graffiti. The acrid scent of piss stung Evelyn's nostrils and she walked a little faster.

She was early for her next appointment, so she stopped in a bodega for a bottle of water and a bag of potato chips for Lucia. While she waited to be rung up, her eyes scanned the *New York Post,* their neighborhood's periodical of choice. She still remembered the front-page story about Umar Farouk Abdulmutallab, the infamous underwear bomber, who had hidden explosives in his pants and attempted to detonate them while onboard a Northwest Airlines flight on Christmas Day. The headline had read "Great Balls of Fire!" in all caps. That paper couldn't take anything seriously. Evelyn passed the G Spot, a clothing store where mannequins posed in the display window wearing Lycra dresses with holes cut in odd places and fake leather pants with corset ties up the legs. Evelyn imagined trying to shimmy her way into one of those outfits. "Lord help us all," she said.

The door of Avenue Pharmacy dinged as Evelyn pushed it open. Steve was doing his morning count at the open register. He thumbed the bills faster than a bank teller. Evelyn found the swishing sound almost soothing.

Her small cardboard box was already waiting on the counter. She pulled it against her hip and nodded at Steve, not wanting to interrupt. He nodded back, his lips working through the numbers. His white coat was stiff with starch and impeccably clean. But his features were tired and almost hung from his face, and his eyes, positioned just too close together, were dull; perhaps the light had extinguished back when necrotizing fasciitis poisoned his son's blood and killed him. Surely that was the reason Steve agreed to this arrangement. Evelyn felt guilty leaving him looking so downcast, but she had an appointment to make. Besides, she'd be back in thirty minutes. She'd minister to him then.

Sharpie was already waiting on the sidewalk outside Miss Bubbles Laundromat, his hands shoved into the front pockets of his jeans. When he saw Evelyn coming, he nodded and dipped inside without waiting for her.

The place smelled of sitting water and

detergent. Sharpie lounged on a folding chair in the shadows of the back corner.

Evelyn didn't know where Sharpie got his nickname, but she'd guess it was the dark eyebrows that looked like they'd been drawn in. But it could just as easily have been his frame; he was tall enough to be mistaken for a basketball player, and thin enough to be named for a permanent marker.

"Hey, Sharpie. Want a muffin? I have one left. Just for you."

His ebony eyebrows pulled together as if her suggestion was ridiculous. But they quickly relaxed. "Yeah, okay."

The Laundromat owner, an older Asian woman, slipped into the back room, out of sight. Evelyn hated the idea that she was involved in a transaction this woman didn't want to witness. And she wondered what debt Sharpie held over the woman's head that obliged her business to host his seedy operations.

"Let's trade, then," Evelyn said and placed her last remaining muffin on top of the cardboard box. Sharpie took both. Then he stuck his free hand inside his Timberland winter coat and pulled out a sterile sampling bag filled with used syringes that she'd bring back to Steve.

This wasn't Evelyn's preferred strategy for

addressing the drug problem in her area. In fact, she'd tried several more palatable methods. She'd found dealers alternate jobs — at soup kitchens, restaurants, grocery stores — but they all eventually quit and went back to the streets, where they made more money on their own schedules. She'd posted flyers about Narcotics Anonymous meetings, and when they were inevitably torn down, she'd posted more. She'd even tipped the cops off to when and where drugs were sold, but she soon discovered that when dealers were arrested, others simply rose up to take their place. After years of fighting and failing to purge the area of drugs, she resigned herself to at least making users safer, to reduce the incidents of hepatitis, HIV, tetanus, and other bacterial infections. An opportunity presented itself when a lapsed Catholic she knew from his boyhood became the head honcho of the local drug circuit. She approached him on the street one day and appealed to the guilt and fear her religion tended to imbed in its faithful, promising to pray for his deceased father's soul if he agreed not to sell to kids younger than eighteen, and if he provided sterile needles to his users along with their junk. Sharpie reluctantly agreed — his father had been convicted of two counts of murder in the first degree; his soul would need her prayers. Talking Steve into the needle exchange program was easy; he was a good person, and the cause made him feel connected to his deceased son. But Sharpie refused to pick up or drop off the needles himself. That was fine; Evelyn wouldn't have trusted him to anyway. Like it or not, she had to stay involved.

"I score food and you walk with some filthy ass needles? Sister, you got the shit end of this deal," Sharpie said and bit into the muffin.

She held the sterile sampling bag by its corner. The skinny syringes inside probably contained blood and residue of the brown heroin that obliterated the mental anguish plaguing so many, the same anguish that had plagued Evelyn in a previous life, and sometimes snuck its way back into her current one. She'd never gone so far as opioids. In her darkest days, she'd turned to the Irish drug of choice, and had floated on alcohol's current for much of the 1960s. Even all those decades later, having drug paraphernalia in her possession awakened an old thirst, or at least a curiosity. How much better might she feel if she just gave in? She reminded herself such a feeling was only an illusion, a selfish escape from a place that still existed, even if you closed your eyes to it. A place that needed her.

She dropped the paraphernalia into her now-empty basket and nestled the bodega's plastic bag on top to make her stash discreet. Then she said to Sharpie, "Yeah, I'd say you're getting away with murder."

Back in the 1990s, after the AIDS crisis had roared through New York City but before needle exchange programs were established, Evelyn had cleaned syringes herself. She would sit in her little concrete backyard beside a bucket of water and a bucket of bleach, fill the syringes with one liquid, then the other, empty the blood residue into the storm drain, remove the plungers, soak the disassembled pieces in the Clorox and then rinse them, her hands red and stiff from the cold air despite her rubber gloves, whispering the Magnificat all the while. *He casts the mighty from their thrones and raises the lowly. He fills the starving with good things, sends the rich away empty.* And every morning, she woke and wondered if this was the day they'd finally make her sick.

At least this was better than that.

CHAPTER 4

Evelyn returned to Mercy House to find Maria performing Reiki on Katrina, a seventeen-year-old waiflike flower child with blond hair streaked with pink. She'd been a resident for about a month, and in that time Evelyn had spent hours counseling her, beginning with polite small talk and gradually, methodically, scraping away the defensive exterior to reach the root.

Katrina was rescued from abusive birth parents at eight years old, and then spent a decade being shuffled around foster homes. With her high-pitched and airy voice, fair skin, spattering of freckles across the bridge of her nose, bubble-gum lips, and slight frame, she was an easy target. She was assaulted most recently by her foster father, who convinced her she was too weak, sweet, and innocent to be safe in the house on her own, but that he would protect her. First he hugged her tight. Then he took her on er-

63

rands. Then he invited her to nap on his bed. Then he persuaded her to sleep there overnight while her foster mother was away. He took advantage of a girl who was starved for love.

Katrina often woke up sobbing.

Perhaps as a counterbalance to the ugliness of her foster home, she perpetually wore earbuds and carried an outdated CD player around with her, and spent her free time listening to music and crafting, knitting the sisters and residents scarves and lopsided winter hats, and constructing glittery cards to send to foster children she'd met along her route.

Evelyn propped the bag of potato chips on the counter where Lucia could see it.

The glass of the kitchen window rattled in its pane. Evelyn turned to find Sister Josephine standing in the entryway, her eyes rounded, as if she'd seen Beelzebub himself.

Maria addressed Katrina in her Reiki trance voice. "Imagine a babbling brook. A lovely babbling brook." Then she and Evelyn hurried down the hall.

Josephine wore attire typical of Vatican II nuns released from their habit: a long, loose cardigan over a button-down shirt and a floor-length skirt — all shapeless. Her purse rocked on her wrist. Permanent creases

64

radiated around the circumference of her lips, like millimeter marks on a ruler. A former resident called Josephine "Sister Gollum" because of her frail frame, but this nickname had one serious flaw — Josephine's impeccable pose. She always stood erect, with picture-perfect posture, as if she were made of wood.

Josephine had joined the Sisters of St. Joseph of Mercy before the shift to Vatican II, drawn to the vocation by its earnestness and its devotion to knowledge and work. Her passion was scholarly; she was entranced by the literature of the mystics and the history of nuns. Back when she was a teenager, nuns were the pioneers of feminism, and joining the sisterhood was one of the only ways for a girl to pursue higher education, so that's what she did. In her lifetime, she'd earned a doctorate in theology and two master's degrees, one in nursing and one in philosophy.

"It's what we've feared," Josephine said. "It's him."

"Him?" Evelyn asked, her hands clenching into fists at her side, her pulse rising.

"Him," Josephine confirmed with a single nod. "He knows, and he's coming."

Rumors had been circulating their order for months that Bishop Robert Hawkins —

whom they called the Hawk — was coming for an extended stay as part of the apostolic visitation, a nationwide Vatican-initiated scrutiny of religious sisters. A team of investigators was spending two years touring the United States, sticking their beaks into every order, examining them with microscopic eyes, hunting for deviations from doctrine. Hawkins was chosen by Cardinal Franc Rode, who initiated this great "nun-quisition," reproaching American nuns for their "secular mentality" and "feminist spirit."

Although nuns across the country took the same vows, the culture and beliefs of orders were as varied as the culture and beliefs of all Americans. On one end of the spectrum were the conservative orders. These nuns still wore habits and lived cloistered lives cut off from the rest of society, like medieval nuns. Some were so extreme they self-flagellated, and were so isolated they received Communion through a gate. On the other end were liberal nuns, sisters who didn't attend church regularly, who didn't consider themselves servants of the Vatican, who went so far as to refer to God as a She, and who wanted female ordination. One hundred and fifty such women had performed the Mass ceremony despite the papal edict that forbade it, and they were promptly ex-communicated.

The Sisters of St. Joseph of Mercy, Evelyn's order, fell somewhere in the middle, perhaps with a leaning more toward the "God as She" end of the spectrum. It was their type of order that many church leaders begrudged, calling them "radical feminists." It was their type of order the Catholic Church hoped to "repair" — and, if not repair, then to purge.

In addition to the sisters' beliefs, the Vatican — led by Pope Benedict XVI — took issue with their missions. They did not approve of much of the nuns' work in the United States. They alleged sisters spent too much time focusing on social justice — advocating for human rights — and not enough time advancing church doctrine — *No abortions! No contraception! No homosexuality! No divorce!* They wanted less emphasis on love, equality, and fairness, and more energy spent promoting rules and regulations. Spare the rod, spoil the American child.

A year earlier, in 2009, the Vatican had distributed a questionnaire to the fifty-thousand-some-odd remaining American nuns, a fraction of their maximum number of two hundred thousand in 1965. Evelyn did not take this survey seriously.

Question: How do you understand and express the vow and virtue of obedience?
Answer: Well, that depends. Did my superior say, "Simon says?"

Question: What are the procedures for dealing with matters of criminal activity?
Answer: We make the wrongdoer smoke the entire pack of criminal activity — all in one sitting.

Question: How does the manner of dress, as specified in the proper law of your religious institute, bear witness to your consecration, and to the dignity and simplicity of your vocation?
Answer: I try to keep body glitter to a minimum. But I'm only human!

Although she supposed it was technically true, Evelyn didn't consider herself a servant of the Vatican. She'd never been to Rome, she'd never met the current Pontiff, and she had virtually no desire to do so. Pope Benedict XVI wore red velvet capes with ermine fur trim. He commissioned his own cologne, which Evelyn called Pope-pourri. He was chauffeured around in a Mercedes. He had a personal library of more than twenty thousand books. It took two hundred architects and engineers to restore his Rome palace, and he resided in his other palace while the construction was underway. That lavish lifestyle bore little resemblance to her experience in Bedford-Stuyvesant, where gunfire rattled through the night, where she added more broth to stretch soup for dinner, where she applied for endless grants in order to afford heat and electricity, where girls cried themselves to sleep because they were hurt and scared and lonely. She and Pope Benedict may have shared the same God, the same Blessed Mother, but this community was her congregation. It was here she best served, and it was in the faces of her neighbors that she witnessed the love and compassion of Jesus Christ. She may have attended Mass once or twice a week, but Mercy House wasn't just her ministry — it was her true church.

The Vatican didn't quite see it that way.

Evelyn's priest, Father John, a childhood friend who had grown up down the block from her family and become an affable man — if a little spineless — explained the Vatican's intention in benign clichés: *They just want to touch base with you. They are taking the pulse of our parish. They want to get to know your work better and find better ways to support you. You all are great; you have nothing to be concerned about.*

But the sisters knew the truth. The Vatican had swept three thousand cases of priest pedophilia under the rug, protecting those criminals at the cost of their own morality and worldwide respect, but when it came to nuns, they wanted blood. This was an inquisition. A probing. And, if need be, a culling.

The sisters were rightfully concerned. Not just for the sake of Mercy House and their identities as nuns, but for their own survival. The church owned their house and provided them health insurance, cell phones, and a weekly stipend. They were senior citizens without belongings or bank accounts — who would support them if they were tossed from the order? Who would hire them? Where would they sleep? What would they eat? They might very well end up living in the kind of shelter they'd devoted their lives to operating.

To make matters worse, not only was Bishop Robert Hawkins a threat to the sisters' work and well-being, he and Evelyn had a history. In fact, he was one of the few people on God's good green earth whom Evelyn despised.

March 1962

Evie still wore the white veil of the novitiate when Father Robert Hawkins first touched her. She was twenty-one years old.

He began innocently enough. While she polished the sacred vessels for that morning's service, Father Hawkins grazed her hip with his fingertips as he skirted behind her to access his vestment. He wasn't even supposed to be there at the same time as Evie, but who was she to correct him? Anyway, she didn't mind the company; she'd spent nearly two years in isolation. Her family didn't bother to contact her anymore, and the vow of silence was secluding. She was lonely. Besides, Father Hawkins wasn't necessarily a handsome man, but he was a competent young priest, and that made him attractive in his own way. She may have taken a vow of celibacy, but she was still human and had occasional fancies she didn't immediately squelch. If nothing else, it was nice to feel acknowledged at a time when, as a nun, she was meant to be invisible. So, when he didn't leave, and in fact slipped the heavy emerald brocade chasuble over his head right then and there, she felt privileged that he was comfortable enough with her to dress in such close proximity. She savored the warmth that lingered from his touch.

He returned at the same time the next morning, and he slipped his hand into hers to commend her for her efforts. Then he recommended she use more starch when cleaning his collars and cassocks. This was 1962 and she was a nun in training — she wasn't used to being commended for anything, especially not by a priest. She didn't care that it was followed by criticism; she had to stop herself from squeezing him back too eagerly.

The day after that, his fingertips lingered over a strand of hair that had loosened from her veil. He rubbed it between his fingers. "I admit, sometimes I wonder what it all looks like under there. But I suppose there's a reason it must be left to the imagination," he said before tucking the piece back. Uneasiness flickered inside Evelyn then, like the hint of nausea before sickness hits, but she said nothing. She wasn't allowed to.

After a couple weeks of increasing intimacy — his hand lingering on her knee as he sat beside her in a pew; holding the small of her back as they walked down a deserted hall; the front of his body briefly pressing

against her backside as he passed by her —
Evelyn felt a strange mix of caution and
fondness about their budding friendship.
But he was a priest, and she trusted he knew
where the line of propriety fell better than
she did.

Then, one morning after a service, Father
Hawkins again appeared in the sacristy
when he wasn't supposed to. Evelyn was
washing a wine-stained altar linen in the pi-
scina, a basin whose drain emptied directly
into the ground to prevent holy liquid from
entering the septic system. He watched her
work over her shoulder, standing so close
she could feel his breath on her neck. He
smelled of incense and all the leftover
consecrated port he'd swallowed from the
chalice after Communion had been distributed.

"That's some spot. I can't believe I was so
sloppy," he said. His voice was hoarse, and
Evelyn thought he felt guilty for adding
more work to her load. She made a hand
gesture to indicate it was nothing he should
worry about. "I bet other priests are just as
bad, if not worse," he said, and Evelyn was
aware then that his breathing was irregular.
"But I don't want you to think of me as just
another priest." He swallowed, and she
could hear the thickness of his saliva as his

tongue slopped against the roof his mouth. "I certainly don't think of you as just another nun. Or nun in formation, I suppose." Then he stepped forward and moved his groin against her, digging himself into her backside. "We have a special bond, don't we?"

She froze. Although she'd never experienced such a thing before, she recognized his hardness immediately, and it made her insides feel rotten. She moved toward the door but he held her waist in an unforgiving grip and said, "Stay. There's work to be done. You have your chores. Your obediences. I admire you, Evelyn. When I'm with you, I can't, I just can't . . ." He trailed off and began rocking himself against her.

Heat flooded from her neck down her chest. She crushed her stomach against the basin, trying to create distance between them. But he only shifted forward after her.

This was the age of Vatican I; she was supposed to save all her words for the forty-five minutes following lunch and dinner. But one word, "Please," escaped her lips.

"Shhhhh." His fingers clumsily groped her cheek and then fell down to clasp her waist again for leverage. His lurching quickened, and soon became urgent, causing the basin to shake the wall behind it. The silver

Communion items on the adjacent counter — the chalice, ciborium, paten, and cruets — clattered against the marble top.

The many layers of their holy clothes were not thick enough to protect Evelyn. Her back was clammy with sweat. Her throat knotted. She struggled to breathe. She squeezed her eyes shut and silently prayed Psalm 46: "God is our refuge and strength, an ever-present help in trouble. Therefore we will not fear, though the earth give way and the mountains fall into the heart of the sea, though its waters roar and foam and the mountains quake with their surging." By the end of the verse, tears spilled down her face and dripped off her chin into the basin, joining the stream of sacred waters. *Where are you, Lord?* her mind screamed. *Where are you?*

Finally, Father Hawkins quaked behind her. He groaned with parted lips and shoved his crotch into her body with four deliberate and ever-slowing thrusts, soiling both of their robes. After, released from the throes of his lust, he cleared his throat, dropped his hands from her hips, and stepped backward.

"You tempted me, damn you," he said, his tone derisive. "These cassocks will need cleaning. Consider it part of your penance."

When he was gone, she bent over the basin reserved for consecrated liquid and vomited down the drain. Stomach acid burned her nose and throat. She remained stooped over the ceramic, alternatively spitting and gasping for breath. Her gasps became sobs. She knew, even then, that he'd fractured something inside her, something that would never fully heal. She could never be the same, and the truth of that nearly brought her to her knees.

When she'd caught her breath, she searched the sacristy for guidance, for answers. Should she run to her bedroom and hide there until someone came looking? Stay right here and scream for help? Go find somebody? But who? Another novitiate? A pronounced nun? The wicked Mother Superior? Some nuns revered Father Hawkins. What if it they believed she'd tempted him?

What if she had? What if she'd inherited the trait of her biblical namesake — what if she'd turned a good man evil?

Evie stayed quiet. She memorized Father Hawkins's schedule and avoided his routes as best she could. But he knew where to find her.

He joined her in the sacristy again the following week. In the passing years, what would terrify Evelyn the most would be the detached expression on his face as he cornered her. He appeared unmoved by her pleading. His jaw was set and his eyes were unseeing. He pressed her against the basin like a butcher slaughtering a lamb. This time he wanted more and gathered up handfuls of her robes until her backside was exposed. He wrenched her underwear aside and sliced into her like a hunting knife.

When he finished he said, "Serving your priest is akin to serving your God." Then he left her there hollowed out, her sacred virginity torn to shreds.

She'd entered the convent as she was meant to — as pure and clean as fresh linens. But the blood and semen dripping between her legs permanently stained that fabric. And if she gave herself over to God, He would see that imperfection. It was part of her. It could not be erased.

She continued to wear a white veil along with the other novitiates, although she felt her filth like sticky grime on her skin. She continued to pray, do chores, and keep her vow of silence. And he continued to rape her.

After several months of regularity, his visits grew further and further apart until they stopped altogether. Evie didn't know if he'd simply grown bored or if he'd found another target. And although she was relieved it was over, there was a small part of her tucked away in the darkest corner of her mind that felt rejected. He'd cast her aside, just as her family had. She was incidental. A throwaway. And she despised the part of her that seemed to want the abuse to continue. She tried to drown that part with sacramental wine, cough syrup, or Sister Mary Joseph's secret stash of whiskey. She was drunk for as much of the days as she could manage, slurring through morning prayer, tripping through her chores, vomiting before lunch. But she didn't care. That despicable part of her made her unworthy of not just the habit, but of life itself.

In the dead of night, she stole the scissors used to shear the hair of women about to take their first professions, and brought them to the common bathroom. She sobbed without constraint, her face cracked open and ugly in the small mirror above the sink. Her family had put her in the convent, had forgotten about her, and was too busy with their own lives to notice she'd been desecrated. Father Robert Hawkins acted like he was entitled to her, until he grew bored of her. Her soul had been sullied and she was alone. No family, no friends, no intact identity — no sign of God, even. Maybe He was disappointed in her for what she'd done, or for what she hadn't done — she was letting Father Hawkins move on to the next girl, letting another person feel that destitute. But she was disappointed in God too. He'd let this happen to her. She'd lived her entire life by the teachings and rituals of the Catholic Church. Now a supposedly sacred man did something so wicked, she didn't know what to believe. Evelyn pressed the sharp blade against her wrist so hard it cut through skin.

That's when Eloise found her.

Eloise stepped forward as if this was exactly what she had expected to find. She took the scissors from Evelyn with one hand, wrapped the fingers of her other hand around the open cut, and squeezed to stop the blood. Then she broke the Profound Silence. "Tell me," she said, looking directly into Evelyn's eyes. "Tell me what happened to you."

Evelyn's lips quivered around her opened mouth. She bent over and cried so hard the sounds were strangled in her throat until she heaved in the breath of the drowning.

"I'm a fake," she choked out. "I'm not good. I'm not holy."

"Of course you are."

Her knees buckled beneath her, but Eloise held her up. "How can I give myself to God when I'm so full of sin?"

"We're all sinners. You know that." Eloise struggled to hold Evelyn up any longer; she let the scissors clatter to the floor, braced Evelyn, and lowered them both to the tile.

Evelyn shook her head. "Not like me." She pressed her eyes closed and said, "I'm Eve. A temptress. 'For God will judge the sexually immoral and adulterous.' "

Recognition hardened behind Eloise's features. "Who was it?" she asked. "Father O'Reilly?" Evelyn twisted away from Eloise so she didn't have to look at her and rested her forehead against the cool wall. "Father Hawkins?"

Hearing his name flooded her insides with wretchedness like rising muddy water; Evelyn's face cracked open. "I don't deserve to become a nun . . ." Her shoulders shuddered with a new wave of sobs. "I'm ruined."

Eloise stroked her arm. "Something terrible happened to you. It's *him* who doesn't deserve to be a priest. *He* is the ruined one."

"I don't know what to do. Even if I told the church what he did, nothing would happen," Evelyn said between gasps. "They'd

80

protect him."

"The church might protect him. But when the time comes, God won't." Eloise slipped her fingers through Evelyn's. "And until then, I'll protect you, if you like."

And so Evelyn stayed in the Catholic Church and continued to find her way through the dark — because, it turned out, there was light too.

January 2010

"When is he coming?" Evelyn asked between clenched teeth. She was afraid if she opened her mouth too widely she'd be sick.

"In one week."

That fact precipitated a cold sweat on Evelyn's lower back.

"How long does he plan to stay?" Maria asked as a shrill whisper.

"As long as it takes. And that's a quote," Josephine answered. She patted the front of her body until she found what she was searching for in her front cardigan pocket — a pack of cigarettes. Winston Red, the same brand she'd smoked since Evelyn met her back in the late 1960s.

Maria's brow furrowed and she bit down on the knuckle of her index finger. "Goodness."

"It gets worse," Josephine continued, tap-

81

ping the bottom of the pack against the heel of her hand, without pausing to retrieve a stick. "He's staying here."

"Here?" Evelyn demanded.

Josephine nodded. "Here."

"But we're women. He's a man, and we're women," Maria said, gesturing clumsily to her female-specific body parts. Josephine shrugged.

Evelyn knew some men could just elbow their way into anyone's business, regardless of how uncomfortable it made them feel. To reassure Maria, she said, "I don't think we're his type," although she knew that wasn't true.

"Evelyn," Josephine scolded. "You have no reason to believe —"

"It doesn't matter," Evelyn interrupted. "I won't allow him to sleep on our sidewalk, never mind under our roof."

Josephine's head jutted forward. "I'm sure you realize sleeping arrangements are the least of our concerns. We can't allow this." She sighed, forced her shoulders to relax, lowered her voice, and said, "We can't allow him to see what we do here, what we've *done.*"

Evelyn pressed her eyelids closed. She thought of the five residents; they were all at varying levels of physical and emotional recovery, and none were ready yet to be on their own. And what of the other girls still on the streets, future residents yet to arrive? The sisters still had work to do. She'd have to swallow her odium as well as her pride and face the man she dreaded with courtesy and restraint.

But that wasn't all. Somehow, she'd also have to prevent the Hawk from investigating their operation. If he looked too closely, he'd find a reason to shut them down. And she couldn't allow that.

She would have thought it a terrible coincidence that the man who so violently attacked her also happened to be the man to investigate her. But because there was such a high incidence of sexual assault by priests, it wasn't unlikely that one of the holy men participating in the apostolic visitation would be guilty of such a crime. And since they were visiting all orders in the United States, *someone* would have to be the nun to face her rapist. Evelyn supposed it might as well be her. She couldn't bear to wonder how many other *hers* of Bishop Hawkins there were.

When she opened her eyes, she said, "He's coming. There's little we can do about that. So let him come. Let him see what he can find." Then Evelyn sighed, as if to exhale the stress of one issue from her body before addressing the next. "We have another problem. Our newest guest. Lucia."

"Lovely girl," Maria said. "We're both Libras."

"Yeah, well, she doesn't run in lovely circles. You might be familiar with her boyfriend."

Josephine's forehead wrinkled. "Does he belong to the parish?"

"I wish. It's Angel Perez, of Los Soldados. Needless to say, his first name is ironic."

"Crap baskets," Maria said.

"Yeah. Major crap baskets," Evelyn agreed.

Josephine shrugged. "Well, what can we do?"

Evelyn leaned forward and made a point to keep her voice hushed despite her rising anxiety. "You don't think this is an issue?"

"It's not ideal, of course. But what choice do we have? You aren't suggesting we kick her out?"

Evelyn sat back on her heels. Over the years her feet had lost their once angular shape, bloating and bowing into rounded hooves. They ached all day long. "No, of course not."

Maria's arms wrapped around the front of her body, as if she were embracing herself.

"But Evelyn has a right to be concerned. Angel probably isn't the type to simply let 'his woman' go," she said, using finger quotes and a macho voice for emphasis. "He and his boys are bound to look for her. We need to be cautious. Not just for her sake, but for the safety of the other girls."

The sisters knew the residents' abusers could pose a threat. Over the past couple decades, they'd had several men — boy-friends, husbands, stepfathers, fathers, uncles, acquaintances — yelling on their front porch, pounding on their door and windows, dropping nasty letters in their mailbox, calling their phone, and lurking around the corner, waiting for the chance to spot their victim.

Because of these hazardous interactions, the nuns activated a top-of-the-line security system at night and enforced a policy that the residents couldn't answer the door themselves.

But they'd never dealt with a gang leader before. Evelyn shuddered to think what Angel Perez was capable of. In his case, they'd need to take a further precaution.

Evelyn said, "So we're in agreement. Since she can't be seen outside, Lucia is on house arrest. She can't leave the premises for any reason whatsoever — at least until we can confirm Angel and his crew have moved on, or until we move her to another location, outside his jurisdiction, for lack of a better word."

Josephine shook her head. "This isn't a prison, Evelyn. And we aren't prison officers."

Evelyn stuffed her hands in her pockets. "True. But if a child was taken out to sea, would a mother not swim after her because she wasn't a lifeguard?"

CHAPTER 5

LUCIA

My mom acted like she was just one good fuck away from becoming a millionaire. Every Saturday night she squeezed into the same hoochie dress from the G Spot, her ass hanging out one end and her tits falling out the other, and she wiggled her middle-aged-lady feet, bunions and all, into magenta strappy stilettos she had to glue back together every morning because they were plastic pieces of shit.

While she clipped on her big hoop earrings, she saw my reflection in the hallway mirror and said, "Wish me luck, *nena*. I'm getting me some of that rich yucca tonight."

I was going out too, so I stood behind her, painting liquid liner onto my lids. I didn't need a mirror. I could make my eyes smoky riding a bus on the fucking BQE. "Good luck."

"*Mira,*" she said, and turned to face me.

Then she slid her hand down my tank top and scooped my tits up to the top of my bra. "Let those *chiches* out. They can't breathe stuffed down in there."

"Don't touch me like that. It's weird," I said, pushing her hand away.

She pushed me back and made a clicking sound with her mouth. "When did my daughter become such an uptight gringa?"

She said that because she knew it was the meanest thing she could say to me, and she's kind of a *bicha.*

"It isn't my fault I never been to Puerto Rico. But that don't make me any less of a *boricua.*"

She smiled like she felt bad for me. "Yeah, *querida.* It kind of does." Then she pinched the side of my tit to piss me off. "So, you seeing Angel tonight?"

"Yeah."

"Don't tense up like that. You'll get wrinkles." She pressed her thumb into the spot between my eyebrows. "He isn't perfect, but no one is. At least he makes that bank. With him as your man, you'll never have to stand in the welfare line. And believe me. That ain't nothing."

My mom knew Angel kept *putas* on the side. "It's just fucking," she said. "As long as you're still seeing that *plata,* that's all

88

that counts."

My mom was what happened when you grew up poor in La Perla, and your bedtime stories were about life in the mainland, where streets were paved with *oro*. That girl fell asleep, dreamed in currency, and woke up a gold digger in her forties.

But I grew up different. Watching my mom drool over any *chacho* with a fake Rolex taught me there were more important things than money. Like self-respect. Dignity. Strength. This wasn't Puerto Rico, and it wasn't the fucking 1940s. You didn't need a man anymore. Look at women who were so badass they only used one name: Selena, Oprah, Beyoncé. That could be me: Lucia.

I said that, but then I kicked it with a guy like Angel.

Maybe I liked him at the beginning because I knew it'd make my mom proud, and after years of banging one loser after another, searching for her ticket to a cushier life, she could use something good, I thought. And he was everything she ever wanted. Showy. His wallet was always fat. He wore bling, and sometimes clipped sparkles around my neck too. He smoked expensive cigars. He bought rounds for everyone at the club. But he also checked out asses right in front of me, even chatted up other sluts while I waited on the side-lines. And he didn't even bother to hide evidence of booty calls in his apartment. One night in bed, I got some other puta's thong caught in my toes. He didn't even say sorry. He just laughed.

I was so pissed, I jumped out of bed and threw the thong in his face. "Stop laughing, you piece of shit!"

He didn't like that. He crossed the bed and a shadow fell over his face. "Do you know who I am, *traga leche*? Do you know who I am?" He slapped my face. I'd never been hit by a man before. When I was a kid, my mom hit me all the time. But this felt different. While my mom hit me with every-thing she had, Angel was holding back. There was rumbling beneath that slap; it was warning of more to come, and that's what scared me. He hit me again and said, "Tell me who I am." I backed up against the wall and he slapped me again. "Say it," he said. Another hit. "Say it."

I was crying almost too hard to speak, but I said it anyway. "Angel Perez."

"That's right," he said, and then gentler, "That's right, *corazón.*" He swiped his thumb under my eye to wipe away my tears. "Don't you forget that."

When my friend Alondra saw my face the

next day, she said, *"Mierda,* Lucia. Look at you. That motherfucking *mamabicho."*

I touched my cheek. "It's just an allergic reaction. New face cream. I guess that's what I get for buying discount shit."

Her mouth bunched up and she rolled her eyes. "That ain't no face cream, and it ain't the last time that's gonna happen either. Trust me, my mother has been with her Angel Perez for ten years. I know. Do what you want, it's your life, but if you ever want to get away for a little while, I know a place."

"What do you mean, you know a place?"

Alondra stepped closer and lowered her voice. "Mira, this black chick from my block? She and her boyfriend were just chillin' on the corner, and this cop starts giving them a hard time. He was all like, 'This is why you people never amount to nothing, hanging around up to no good when you should be in school, bettering yourself' or whatever. And when my friend steps up to him, just to tell him there was no school that day, he shoves her back against the wall. Then this chubby old lady comes out of nowhere, yelling at the cop like, 'Get your hands off that girl! What's her crime? Existing in your world?' And she's waving her arms and squawking like a bird. Turns out she's a nun, not like in a habit or nothing, but still a holy woman, you know? And when the cop left, she told my friend if she ever had a hard time again, with the police or anybody else, there is a safe house for women in Brooklyn. Even if you don't want to stay over or nothing, they can just give you advice. I can get the address for you if you want."

I stuffed my fingers in the back pockets of my jeans. "Thanks, but I don't need a safe house. My place is fine."

As my mom and I were about to head out, one boricua in search of her rich chacho and one boricua americana returning to the one she had found, I felt like one of the cockroaches we caught on a glue trap on our kitchen counter. Stuck, its antennas reaching and twisting, probably looking for a way out, so blinded by its instinct to survive, it couldn't even see there was no use. It was fucked.

"Say hi to Angel for me," my mom said, and she tucked a loose curl behind my ear. "You're lucky, you know that, nena?"

I nodded, but I didn't feel lucky at all.

CHAPTER 6

Lucia twisted the front doorknob and triggered a bleep from the security system. The nuns flocked to her from separate corners of the house.

"Lucia, have you eaten breakfast? It's the most important meal of the day, you know," Maria chirped from the staircase.

"I don't really eat in the morning," Lucia said. Her wounded eye was beginning to purple, like a ripening plum. Bruises, like the abusive relationships that spawned them, worsened before they disappeared.

Maria stepped down onto the landing. "Well, have you met the other girls? Because we have a group talk session that starts in ten minutes. It's the daily GIA, which stands for the Great I Am." Maria accented each word by rocking her hips and pointing alternating index fingers like guns firing. "I came up with the name. It's a biblical reference. Get it? But it isn't necessarily a religious session. We focus on things we like about ourselves and about each other. It'd be a great opportunity for you to get to know your other housemates."

Lucia shifted in her stance. "I'm just going around the corner to get some smokes. Maybe I'll stop by after."

"I have cigarettes," Josephine said from the hallway behind Evelyn. Evelyn turned with a raised eyebrow. Josephine wasn't one to share her nicotine, her most treasured vice.

"Thanks, but I like my brand," Lucia said. She scanned the sisters' faces wanly. "Look, maybe I'll come back after. I'll probably be back for chitchat time or whatever."

After her long morning, Evelyn was too tired to beat around the bush. She stood in the living room doorway and huffed air out through her nostrils. "Lucia, I'm sorry but you just can't leave."

Lucia took a step back and grabbed the doorknob. "Why the hell not?" she asked, her lip curling.

"Because you came here for our help, and we have to give it our way."

"I never said I wanted to stay, or that I wanted your help. If I knew this place came with strings and shit, I never would have come."

Maria laid a gentle hand on Lucia's forearm. "We've been doing this a long time. Please, trust us."

Lucia shrugged her off. "I just met you. I don't trust you for shit. Fuck it. I'm out of here." She turned her back on the sisters, gripped the doorknob, and pulled — but the door didn't budge. She tried again, tugging with both hands this time, but the door just rattled in its place.

Evelyn had wedged her foot in front of the door.

Lucia shot the nuns a look over her shoulder. Her expression was warped by annoyance, but her eyes betrayed fear. Ashamed of herself, Evelyn retracted her foot.

"Oh for heaven's sake, Evie," Josephine scolded. "The poor girl is terrified and there you are behaving like a child." She shooed the other nuns back. "Listen, Lucia. We are so thankful you decided to join us here, and we are eager to help you. But we can't ignore the dangers you bring with you because of your associations. And while we understand your reluctance to trust us, especially after we attempted to barricade you in without explanation," she added with a snide glance back at Evie, "we are also reluctant to trust that your friends won't come looking for you. If they see you on the street and follow you here, things could take an ugly turn for everyone. So if you want to stay at Mercy House, you have to literally *stay* at Mercy House. For the safety of both you and the other girls." Josephine sighed deeply, revealing her exhaustion. "Stay or leave. Sadly, you cannot do both. Whichever you choose, however, is entirely up to you."

"We hope you'll stay," Maria added.

"You came to us," Evelyn said. "There must have been a reason."

Lucia eyed the women. For a split second, Evelyn was convinced Lucia would reach for the door and flee, return to Angel, her abuser — accept the mistreatment she'd grown accustomed to — and there would be nothing the sisters could do about it. It wouldn't be the first time they'd lost a resident back to a violent environment. But then Lucia's arm dropped down to her side. "I'm leaving as soon as I feel claustrophobic again. So don't crowd me."

Maria clapped her hands at her breast. "GIA meeting!" she squealed loud enough for the other girls to hear. "GIA meeting!"

Aside from her bedroom, which held the appeal of being strictly hers, the living room was Evelyn's favorite space in Mercy House. The fabric of the basil-colored armchairs was worn down to the webbing in places, but the chairs were overstuffed and easy to settle into. The gold and currant Oriental rug, salvaged from a flea market, was stained in spots where residents had spilled hot chocolate or coffee, but those marks were a reminder of the existence of human error and forgiveness — and God knew Evelyn had been the clumsy hand behind a spill or two. A large tapestry featuring Saint Joseph, a father who was not the father, wearing a crown of roses and holding baby Jesus hung over the mantel. It was a generous gift to the sisters from the parish's priest and Evelyn's friend, Father John. And best of all, the fireplace: a cherrywood mantel topped a slate hearth. With limited funds to afford oil for heat, the sisters kept the fire almost constantly ablaze throughout the winter months. Evelyn had become quite the Girl Scout.

They were blessed with an endless supply of wood, donated to them by Sal Faraldo, the Italian owner of a local salvage yard. Sal was a former parishioner; Evelyn had tutored him in Sunday school. Now he lived a life of luxury out on Long Island, which Evelyn suspected was not subsidized by his salvage yard business alone. While Evelyn didn't encourage Mafia culture, she also wasn't above accepting their donations. If they wanted to play at religion, who was she to judge?

"So, who would like to start us off?" Maria asked. She leaned back into a velvet armchair far from the crackling inferno. Perhaps because of her size, Maria overheated easily, and despite her strategic choice of seating, always left GIA meetings damper than when she arrived.

Although Maria coined the term "GIA meeting," the gatherings were actually Evelyn's idea, indirectly. Normally she wouldn't condone a daily meditation on one's own strengths — how vain could you get? — but the residents of Mercy House so often forgot their worth. They'd been emotionally and physically pummeled for so long, it was essential to force them to inflate their egos, even if superficially. So when the sisters were wondering how to make the girls feel better about themselves, Evelyn said, "It's almost as if they should state, each and every day, at least one thing that makes them good." Maria's face had lit up at that. Perhaps with the acronym already in mind, she winked and answered, "How about what makes them *great*?"

"I'll go," Desiree said, raising a hand. Hair coiled into a dark cloud around her face, and she slumped across a majority of the two-seater couch, despite the fact that Katrina, whose hands were busy knitting, and Mei-Li, who had generously looped one of Katrina's lumpier masterpieces around her neck, were relegated to the floor. Desiree's knees were spread in a manner Evelyn's mother would have called unseemly. "Great I am, great I am," Desiree said, stretching each word like taffy to emphasize her contemplation. "Great I am at . . . blow jobs," she finished with a declarative flourish. Lucia snorted from across the room.

Maria sighed. "You can't use the same affirmation as yesterday, Desiree," she said. "You know that."

Desiree grinned. "Why not? It's as true today as it was yesterday." She nodded toward Lucia. "And just for your information, I'm as skilled at blow jobs as I am at speaking in tongues. Some people call me the twat whisperer."

Evelyn rolled her eyes. This bodacious behavior was Desiree's shtick, especially with newcomers, an exaggeration of her true self, or at least a singular perception of it. She was in your face so you wouldn't bother getting close enough to examine her vulnerability. She pretended she didn't take anything seriously so you wouldn't detect what really mattered to her. She showcased her sexuality so you'd assume it was exactly where she wanted it — on display. But Evelyn had seen her stripped of pretenses, tired and withdrawn, persona unmasked, wrapped in the cocoon of a wool blanket, sipping tea and reading *To Kill A Mockingbird* by the fire, tearing up for Boo and Tom. Still, Evelyn never outed her performance.

There, in the living room, Evelyn played along, saying, "Lucia's new to these meetings. Don't scare her off."

Desiree lifted her hands, feigning bewilderment. "Hey, I'm just marketing myself and my business. Isn't that what those career counselor bitches you brought in last week told us to do?"

Josephine uncrossed her legs and then recrossed them. "We won't even mention your crudity, but no repeats, Des. Rules are rules. You'll have to be more inventive. Maybe you can share something you did in the last couple days? Something you are proud of?"

Desiree leaned forward and gripped her knees. "I just did." She smacked her hands together, fell back on the couch, and wrapped her arms around her middle as she howled with laughter. The tight ringlets of her twist out vibrated.

By now, the other residents were unaffected by such histrionics. Esther's nostrils flared and she shook her head. Mei-Li smiled vacantly. One of Katrina's hands departed her knitting to finger the earbud wires hanging from her neck — when she felt anxious, she'd slip the buds into her ears and complete her escape.

"Hilarious, Des. Really. But we all know that's bull. If there's one thing we can agree on, it's that Mercy House isn't an aphrodisiac. No one here has gotten any in months," Evelyn said, taking back control of the room. "But that's good. It's part of the healing process."

"Since Desiree is having some trouble, maybe we can help her out. Can someone offer a positive affirmation about Des on her behalf?" Josephine asked. She clasped her hands in her lap as she surveyed the room with eyebrows raised, prompting contributions.

Mei-Li's gaze drifted out the window, a stale smile still lingering around her lips. Esther examined her cuticles. Lucia's forehead furrowed, as if disgusted by this process, or at least skeptical about it. Finally Katrina reluctantly lifted a hand from her knitting.

"She did a really nice job cleaning the

bathroom," she said as a soft offering. Desiree huffed her dissatisfaction with the comment. Katrina's fingers grazed an earbud on her shoulder. "She also has really strong energy. It fills the room. I admire that. I'm so — you know — like, small." She glanced in Desiree's direction and smiled. Des's head bobbed slightly as she glared back.

Evelyn could sense Katrina's growing discomfort and was about to change the subject when Desiree's expression cracked. "Thanks, Trina. And listen, girl: You're small, but so what? Shakespeare said something like, 'Even though she's small, she's fierce,' or some shit like that."

Katrina allowed her smile to grow, and then her needles clicked back together.

"There you go," Evelyn said. Gratitude for that interaction expanded in her chest and she raised her fist as if lifting a glass for a toast. "To fierce shit."

Some laughter scattered around the room before the other girls echoed half-heartedly, "To fierce shit."

The meeting proceeded without event, as the residents, as well as the sisters, took an hour to build up themselves and one another. Mei-Li relented that she had pretty hair. Katrina offered a watercolor she'd painted that week. Esther said she made the best chicken and cashews in Bed-Stuy, and the others made her promise to prove it that weekend. Lucia, after some prodding, shrugged and suggested it was pretty cool to be bilingual. Maria mentioned her singing voice — in her warbly croon that sounded like a dove cooing in protest. Josephine noted that she was proficient at mental math. And Evelyn, who enjoyed listening to everybody else's affirmations but begrudged fabricating her own, said, "Someone once told me I have nice eyes. So maybe that's true."

After everyone shared a favorite quality, Maria clapped her hands together. "All right. Before we disperse, are there any final comments or questions?"

Desiree's hand shot into the air, and although Evelyn knew the resident was bound to say something inappropriate, she couldn't help but look forward to it. A benefit of Desiree's plucky approach was her ability to establish intimacy with a person from the start, to break through someone's protective armor by refusing to acknowledge it — to touch them without ever really touching them. She began her question before she was called upon. "I'm still trying to figure ya'll out. Your rules are hella random. You don't wear habits. But you still can't fuck. And when Sister Maria's hippie skirt bunched up yesterday, I saw her legs were mad hairy. So I was wondering, are ya'll not allowed to shave because you're nuns?"

Maria's face reddened and she tugged on the hem of her pants. For a moment, Evelyn wondered what it would have been like to want to make her legs smooth for someone else's caress, to think of her body as a shared entity, a gift. But Maria's embarrassment was more pressing than such wistful ponderings. She cleared her throat and addressed Desiree. "Dear, it has nothing to do with being nuns. We don't shave our legs because we're old."

CHAPTER 7

DESIREE

I was fourteen when Daryl circled me like some Discovery Channel great white. He was twenty. My momma was cracked out — still is — and I never met the sperm half of my gene pool, so I must have looked like an orphaned seal pup to Daryl, just floating out there in the open waters of the projects, all by herself. And he was smooth. He walked me home from school. Asked me about my day. He even bought me the Phat Farm kicks I wanted and a daily McDonald's Big N' Tasty. A Big N' Tasty was as good as a diamond ring to a hungry girl with my kind of booty. He was my hero. And yeah, if you want to get all Freudian about it, maybe I thought of him like a father too. The boy didn't have to work too hard. I was in love with his onion ass in no time. It didn't hurt that he was fine as hell.

And yeah, he banged me when I was a

minor. But what girl from my block made it to sixteen without getting her hymen pounded to shit, whether she wanted it or not? That wasn't the worst thing he did. Not even close.

One day after school, we was lying around naked at his crib, smoking a blunt in bed when, out of nowhere, he started to cry. I'd never seen a grown-ass man cry before, especially not Daryl. He was hardcore hood. He hardly ever laughed, never mind cried.

I begged him to tell me what was wrong. He was quiet at first, but eventually he admitted he was in deep with some thugs. He said they was gonna kill him. And I believed it. After all, they didn't call it Do or Die Bed-Stuy for nothing.

"How much?" I asked.

He couldn't even look at me. "A G. By tomorrow." I didn't even know what that kind of paper looked like. "And there ain't nothing I can do. They won't let me deal."

I pushed myself to my knees and let the bedsheet drop so my little-girl breasts was showing. That always cheered him up. "What about me? Maybe I can start selling to pay back your money."

His eyes were red and watery. "You'd do that? For real?"

The sight of him so weak and grateful

nearly broke me in two. I nodded.

He ran his fingers down the side of my cheek and looked at me like I was the most beautiful thing he'd ever seen. And the most important. " 'Cause, if you ain't frontin', there is one thing you could do."

"What?"

"They won't let you sell. Sharpie made some deal and they don't let youngins on the street no more. But he did say there was one way you could wipe my debt clean."

I grabbed his wrist. "I'll do it."

"He wants you to blow him."

I sat back and pulled the sheet up to cover my chest. "Nuh-uh."

"You know I wouldn't ask unless I had to. You're my girl, Des. But I told him you're mad good at it, and now he wants to see for himself."

"I ain't no hood rat."

"It ain't like that. It's just one time. If you don't do it, I'm dead. Is that what you want?"

I thought about coming home from school every day to my momma sprawled out on the couch, her eyes rolled back in her head, her face scabby as hell. Who knew who she sucked off that day for dope. There, in Daryl's crib, he held me. He looked at me like I was something. Without him, I was nothing. Nobody. Was I really not gonna do one bad thing, a bad thing my momma did every day of the week, to save his life? To save us?

So I did it, just like he knew I would, probably from the moment he first laid eyes on me walking down Myrtle Avenue, a kid who was so lonely she talked loud and often, just so someone would look her way.

Maybe he was never in deep with Sharpie to begin with.

It wasn't long after the first favor that Daryl asked for another. And if I did it once, why wouldn't I do it again? So I gave head to one guy after the other. Then I let them fuck me. Pretty soon it was just an easy way for me and Daryl to make bank.

He had me workin' for a few months before he started to ghost. First he wasn't home at his usual times. Then he didn't answer the phone. Then he didn't return my calls at all. Turns out he was circling some other tween in the projects. Because Daryl is a hustler. He never loved me. He was just stackin' chips, like any good player. And I wasn't his only hand.

By the time I figured him out, I'd become a hustler too. What was I gonna do? Join the army? The nunnery? Hell no. I dropped out of school. I kept working. I was a hood rat for real now.

It was around then that Sister Evelyn found me. I was chillin' at the bottom of the slide in the Marcy Projects playground, waiting for my ten o'clock to show, when this fat-ass white lady came up on me. There's no good reason for a Casper to be on Myrtle Avenue that time of night, so I came to the only conclusion there was. "If you came for some pootie tang, I'm busy, but I'll get to you in a minute."

"That's a very kind offer," she said. "But you can't afford me."

I made a snapping sound with my gum. "I don't pay for that shit. And definitely not with someone whose pussy spits dust."

And the bitch actually laughed. "Yes, I'm sure I've outgrown the market. I'm just here to tell you, if you ever want to look into other professions, we can help you at Mercy House. You're clever. God gave you a brain — you should use it."

"Mercy House? You ain't from around here, are you? You mean Marcy Houses."

"No, I mean Mercy House. It isn't a project. It's a house on Chauncey Street. You've been handed some disadvantages. We aren't a cure-all; just a safe place, if you need one. And maybe we can provide a few resources to help you level the playing field.

When you're ready, look for the angel doorknocker. You deserve to love and to be loved."

"Thanks, but I'm good," I said. "I'm good just where I am."

And I was. Sure, it wasn't a girl's dream come true, but it wasn't so bad either.

Then Daryl, the father-figure, love-of-my-life-turned-dirty-ass pimp, started showing up at my door, demanding more and more of my earnings. First twenty percent, then fifty, then ninety. And if I shorted him, he beat me. Punched me in the ribs, grabbed a fistful of hair and rammed my face into the wall, choked me until I made these ugly gagging sounds. All while my momma was passed out on the couch in the next room. Sometimes she'd moan or tell him to quit it, but most of the time it was all she could do just to keep breathing.

With each pounding I felt like an organ would burst, or that my skull would crack open.

The last time I saw him, he knocked my head so hard I blacked out. When I came to, my left eye was swollen shut and my right eye was stuck closed with dried blood. I forced it open and found a head-shaped hole in the drywall.

He almost killed me for doing what I

started doing to save his life. People who read thick books call that shit irony.

Well, I wasn't about to fuck for damn near free, and Daryl wasn't about to stop collecting whatever the hell he wanted to collect. I needed a quiet place to think about how to get out of that mess.

When I came up on Chauncey Street, my whole body hurting something fierce, the block was lit up like a damn Christmas movie. It looked like the view of Manhattan at night, with all those twinkling buildings. I'm not one to get emotional, but you never would have known it from the tears I cried as I walked up that sparkling street to the house with the angel doorknocker.

A stranger I'd later know as Sister Maria answered and gathered me in her arms. I couldn't remember the last time I'd been held by someone who wasn't paying me. She smelled like sugar cookies, like a grandma from a storybook. "Oh you poor thing," she said. "Come here. You're safe now."

I appreciated Sister Maria's love. It was like being welcomed into a foreign country. But I wanted to talk to Sister Evelyn. Even then I knew she'd been through something. Something that had taught us the same language.

CHAPTER 8

After the GIA meeting concluded, Evelyn finally had time to consider what the sisters should do about the Hawk's imminent landing. It would take time to prepare the house — to cleanse the house, more like. They had to revise their past, rehearse their show. She needed to get to work.

Evelyn ascended the stairs to the second floor. Down the hall, she flicked on the light, lifted onto her tiptoes, and reached for the string attached to the attic door. God must have run out of Fanning family height genes by the time Evie's angry red baby face made its way into the world, because she felt almost as wide as she was tall. The underused muscles hiding inside her thick calves quivered. She clamped the string knot between her index and middle finger and heaved it down, inciting a hot sear through her wrist and elbow, but the hatch relented. The wooden ladder unfolded easily, and

Evelyn guided her foot onto the first rung. It creaked. She was too old and too fat to be climbing rickety ladders, but there were worse ways to die, if it came to that.

When Evelyn was waist-deep into the storage space, she let her belly drop forward onto the plywood floor. Her feet, which had hardened into talons in an attempt to curl around the rungs, relaxed, and she sighed.

The attic was dim, dank, and smelled of mothballed sweaters. It was largely uncluttered, as the women didn't own much. There were two boxes labeled "CHRISTmas Decorations," bursting with ornaments, an olivewood nativity scene, candles for the neighborhood windows, and colored lights, all of which the obsessive-compulsive Josephine had promptly dismantled, packed up, and stored on New Year's Day. There was an air mattress for extending their capacity, which Evelyn only then remembered the existence of. There were three boxes labeled with each of the sisters' names, reserved for storing photo albums and other keepsakes that would take up too much space, or be too distracting, in their bedrooms, which were reserved for rest and prayer. There was a cardboard wardrobe box Maria had labeled "Bad Habits," which contained the full-length and modified woolen robes they hadn't worn in forty years, the uniforms that at times swathed Evelyn in security and at other times suffocated her. Evelyn thought it was a sadder version of brides preserving and storing their gowns, and yet she was tempted to open that box, to revisit the uniforms. But she wasn't in the attic for casual remembrances; she was there to sift through storage file box after storage file box of former residents' records.

Mercy House was founded in 1984, back when Evelyn was still working as a nurse, after she'd treated the same patient five times for various injuries of domestic violence. She felt like she was constantly wiping blood away without ever bothering to clot the wound. Her efforts were futile, a waste of time and resources. After listening to another one of Evelyn's many rants on the subject in the common room of their convent, Josephine finally threw up her arms and said, "Well, why don't you do something about it?"

Evelyn had paused, her mouth still open, full of unspoken words of outrage. Then she closed it, swallowed those words, and smiled. "Why don't *we* do something?"

Maria, who had also been on the receiving end of Evelyn's venting more than once, jumped up from her seat on the couch and cried, "Me too, me too!"

They all contributed their strengths to the project. As a true academic and philosopher, Josephine was invaluable in the initial research, writing proposals and mission statements, and applying for grants. Evelyn served as their boots on the ground. She was relentless in scouting facilities, interviewing the operators of similar services, and following up with grant organizations that failed to get in touch promptly. Maria was an excellent cheerleader, providing pep talks when the outcome seemed bleak and infectious enthusiasm when presenting their case to Mother Superior. When Mother Superior finally decided every detail of their vision was clear and feasible, she met with Father John and didn't leave his office until he approved.

Sister Evelyn, Sister Maria, and Sister Josephine went from friends to partners, although the latter wasn't grand enough a word to encapsulate the relationship of love and support that had cultivated since the initial founding. They'd become more like family than Evelyn's own siblings, who had long since drifted from her life.

Twenty-five years later and here they were, still seeking to bridge the gap between what their population of women deserved and all the ways in which society had failed them through inequitable education; unaffordable housing; mass incarceration; low wages and unemployment; and a cycle of poverty, addiction, and abuse. It was the longest Evelyn had spent doing any one thing, perhaps because it was the most satisfying — more satisfying than prayer, more satisfying than religious education, and even more satisfying than nursing. Although, she still used her nursing on occasion. There had been times — periods of extreme need — when she put her skills to work. Most recently, nine years prior, when she volunteered at a local hospital treating victims and emergency workers on 9/11, and fielding phone calls from frantic family members so they could hear a human voice rather than a recording. And before that, when Mercy House initially opened, she juggled two full-time jobs: working with AIDS patients by day and sheltering abused women by night. But, all in all, the last two and a half decades of her life had been devoted to this Bed-Stuy shelter and its residents, all of whose cases had been carefully cataloged in the ten or so boxes before her.

Evelyn stared at the collection with her fists on her hips. Sifting through all this material in a mere week would be a task of biblical proportions — not to mention the not-insignificant censoring that would be required.

Where to begin? she wondered. *Undoubtedly, as God did. In the beginning.*

May 1994

Evelyn dry heaved in the waiting room bathroom during the first abortion. She gripped the porcelain rim of the toilet and whispered the Prayer of Saint Francis into the bowl as a strand of discolored drool stretched down from her bottom lip. "Lord, make me an instrument of your peace. Where there is hatred, let me sow love. Where there is injury, pardon. Where there is doubt, faith . . ."

The patient that day was a soft-spoken woman named Vanessa. She had coarse brown curls and skin the rich color and gloss of an espresso bean. She'd been pulled over for a blown taillight, and when she admitted having marijuana in her possession, the police officer dragged her from her vehicle, handcuffed her, and shoved her in the back of his squad car. He directed his partner to go get a cup of coffee. Then he asked Vanessa what she was willing to do to avoid jail time; he didn't wait for an answer before he unbuckled his pants.

Vanessa was at Mercy House for several days before she shared her story. When Evelyn begged her to report it, Vanessa said, "What's the sense in reporting a crime to the very people who committed it?" Weeks later, she discovered she was pregnant, and pounded her still-flat belly with her fists.

In the days that followed Vanessa's discovery, there was a vacant quality in her eyes that unsettled Evelyn. Finally, over a bowl of oatmeal that was cooling into a congealed crust, Vanessa said with resolve, "I need to have an abortion." In the moment, Evelyn only cleared her dish, scraping its contents into the garbage. But after many periods of prayer, she came to a decision. She wouldn't have guessed she'd come to such a progressive revelation at fifty-four years of age, but a voice inside Evelyn told her it was the right thing to do. She would claim it was God's voice, but nobody would have believed her. She would also claim it was her conscience, because she was starting to believe they were one in the same.

Vanessa emerged from the procedure with a stony expression, her suffering only apparent through trembling hands and red-rimmed eyes that were once again suggesting signs of life. Evelyn suppressed her doubts about what they'd done — she would wrestle them on her own time. She took Vanessa by the elbow and guided her onto city streets that roared with activity — honking horns, rushing commuters, dog walkers, strolling lovers — where everybody else carried on as if an unborn child had not just been terminated.

In their living room that night, after the girls had gone to sleep, Evelyn told Maria and Josephine what she had condoned, and even facilitated. Maria covered her face with her hands. Every muscle in Josephine's body tightened; she stood as hard and unmoving as an obelisk.

"How dare you," Josephine seethed between gritted teeth. "What you did was not only ungodly, it was selfish. How could you fail to consult us over something that could impact us in such a powerful way?"

"What does this have to do with you?" Evelyn asked, as an accusation.

Josephine looked as if she might burst from her skin. "If the church finds out, if they even suspect something, we will be excommunicated. Kicked to the curb. What will we do then? How will we survive without support, at our age?"

"A woman was raped. By a policeman. A woman extinguished a life growing inside her, and that's what concerns you at this moment? What will happen to *us*?"

Something violent flashed in Josephine's eyes. "Oh, Evelyn. You are so right. It is the least of the issue, but it is the only speck I have the courage to confront at this moment. I don't wish to imagine the life you stole from that fetus: who she might have become, what she might have done, how she might have glorified the Lord. I don't want to ask you how you will live with yourself. I don't want to reproach you for daring to play God. Because I fear the anger inside me right now, Evelyn. And I fear the sadness too."

Evelyn's heart hurt from guilt, anger toward Josephine, and the knowledge that she was probably right. "Your sorrow? Your sorrow?" she demanded. Her voice escalated, until rage cracked open into weeping. Maria hurried across the room and took Evelyn into her arms.

Through their vow of obedience, they'd committed themselves as servants of the Catholic Church, an institution that had been very clear about its stance on abortion. Exodus 21:23 stated a strike against a pregnant woman that resulted in injury to the child should be punished with eye for an eye, or "life for life." And the church's acceptance of abortion hadn't evolved much in the thousands of years since the biblical ages. Pope John Paul II said the church's teaching on the subject was "unchanged and unchangeable. . . . No circumstance, no purpose, no law whatsoever can ever make licit an act which is intrinsically illicit, since it is contrary to the Law of God which is written in every human heart, knowable by reason itself, and proclaimed by the Church." Pope John Paul II was, in many ways — and especially when it came to female reproductive rights — a holy but wholly pigheaded man; he wasn't Evelyn's favorite leader, but he wasn't her least favorite either.

According to the pope, Evelyn had committed a crime against the church, no matter her reasons. And according to Exodus, she should pay for that crime with her life. She prayed both sources were wrong, but worry still itched the back of her skull and crawled around her belly like a pile of worms.

The next instance arrived almost a year later. A man murdered his wife, and then raped his fourteen-year-old daughter in the same room. That time, as Evelyn was leaving the house, prepared to escort the pregnant girl to a clinic, Josephine placed her hand on Evelyn's shoulder. Her face was drawn when she whispered, "Let me help you."

January 2010
Evelyn holed up in the attic for days, descending only for GIA meetings, meals, neighborhood walks, and sleep. She relied on the other sisters to run the house: cleaning, cooking, administrative duties, counseling, and rehabilitating the girls. When Evelyn retreated upstairs, she was sent off with a grateful smile from Josephine or a hand squeeze from Maria. Though they didn't often discuss the labors being conducted in the attic — morally questionable acts in their deceit and fraudulence — they all agreed about the necessity, and appreciated her efforts and willingness to conduct the dirty work. Occasionally Mei-Li surfaced with a sandwich, a genuine smile, and a tender touch of Evelyn's hand that quieted the rough waters of her soul, if only for a moment.

After hours of concentration, her mind was weary and needed rest. She allowed her gaze to wander the attic, and when it landed on her keepsake box, she indulged in a small break.

She lifted the lid with some trepidation,

knowing not all memories were fond. Some were haunting. This was where she stored her ghosts.

Draped along the top of the pile was the rosary her father had given her when she joined the nunnery. His mother had given them to him when she sent him to the United States at fourteen years old because she couldn't afford to keep him and his siblings in Ireland. They were made of plastic ivory-colored beads that appeared yellow with age, but Evelyn knew they looked that way from the beginning. When her father had laced them around her fingers in the car outside the convent, he'd said, "I hope I haven't given you too much." And she resented him for those words. What her father should have said was that he had no right to make such a vow to God in the first place. Their relationship in those years had become strained already. He was charismatic with children, but distant with adults; she, his youngest, had just entered womanhood, and he was finding more and more comfort in his bottle of Jameson. That send-off sentiment severed what little connection remained. A young Evelyn gripped the rosary in her hand and replied flatly, "You haven't." And then she got out of the car and began the process of becoming

Sister Mary Michael.

In the attic, Evelyn placed the rosary on the scarred wood floor beside her and lifted out a curling black-and-white photo of her parents and four older siblings standing in front of their brownstone apartment in Park Slope. The back was labeled with faded pen: *All of us. 1962.* She'd received this rare correspondence from her family in the period when Father Hawkins was assaulting her, back when she felt like a worthless shell of a human. The phrasing written on the back — *all* of us — had been like a kick to the ribs while she was already moaning on the floor. She'd thought, *What about me?*

In the photo, Sean, her oldest brother, was standing on the edge of the group, a gap between him and their mother. It would be only a few years until he'd no longer be part of "all of us" either.

The next layer was a wide-toothed wooden comb that had belonged to Eloise. She used to misplace it on a regular basis in the convent, and Evelyn always knew where it was. When Eloise left, Evelyn found it on one of the sinks in the bathroom and suspected, this time, it was forgotten purposefully. She kept it as a reminder of the person who had lifted her up from the fragmented heap Father Hawkins had left behind.

Beneath the comb was a black-and-white photo of Evelyn and Eloise from the day they took their vows and became Sister Mary Michael and Sister Incarnata. They wore their full habits and stood shoulder to shoulder on the stone steps of the convent chapel. Eloise beamed at the camera with that open grin that showed the love she had for the world. And while young Evelyn faced front, she was looking at her friend in a way that still embarrassed old Evelyn.

She reached in for the next item: a tarnished silver flask. Vatican II ended nun prohibition, and so, when Eloise left, Evelyn didn't need to turn to cough syrup to dull her grief. They kept a supply of whiskey in the common room. Evelyn filled and emptied that flask more often than she prayed.

April 4, 1968

Evelyn was drunk the night Martin Luther King Jr. was assassinated.

It had been almost a year since Eloise had signed the indult of secularization, was given a small sum called a charity by the church — so that she wouldn't turn to prostitution to support herself, like another deserted nun had — and left the order.

Evelyn had rolled out of bed at eight in the morning and gone straight to work at

125

the hospital without speaking to anybody, and, when she returned, she retreated to her room to listen to Buddy Holly records. Those days, she acted more like a stranger with too many roommates than like a nun living in a community.

On the night of April 4, Evelyn staggered into the recreation room, singing the Buddy Holly song she'd been listening to on repeat under her breath. When she saw a crowd gathered around the television, watching Walter Cronkite at his news desk, she said, "Guess I missed the invitation to the party."

Josephine said, "Didn't you hear? Dr. King was shot."

Evelyn blinked, trying to fight her way out of her haze. After a moment, she gave up, staggered toward the liquor cabinet, and retrieved a fresh bottle. She cradled it in the crook of her elbow and teetered back to her room.

The next morning, Evelyn shuffled into the kitchen wearing her modified nursing habit and found Josephine fixing herself a cup of coffee. Josephine smiled sadly and said, "I woke up this morning with such a heavy heart."

Evelyn pulled open the refrigerator door. "Why's that?"

"Because of Dr. King, of course."

Evelyn grabbed the pitcher of orange juice and placed it on the counter. Then she opened a cabinet to retrieve a glass. "What about Dr. King?"

When seconds passed without a response, Evelyn abandoned her hunt for a clean glass and turned to Josephine, whose eyes were wide. Evelyn rolled her shoulders back defensively.

"Oh, Evelyn," Josephine said as an entreaty. "It's time."

Just as Eloise had a few years before, over the next couple months, Josephine nursed Evelyn back to sobriety, through the shaking, insomnia, and vomiting, through the hopelessness and anger. And, in a way, she and Maria never stepped down from that post.

January 2010

In the attic, Evelyn's knees throbbed, so she shifted onto her backside and stretched out her legs. Her body wasn't used to these contortions and would punish her all night.

The next item she handled with care — a stiffened letter Eloise had penned after she moved to Washington, D.C., to promote the Poor People's Campaign. It was just one of many letters and phone calls she'd received from Eloise over the course of the year that went unanswered.

March 1, 1968

Dear Evelyn,
Things are going well in this neck of
the woods as we fight to improve the
economic disparity in this country. The
more noise we make, the more likely
we'll be heard, and I do believe people
— important people — are beginning to
listen. What we are demanding isn't radical. It's basic human decency, an opportunity for people of all creeds and
colors to earn a living wage. To give the
possibility of prosperity to all. To right
what has for so long been wrong.

It's true what you see on television.
Dr. King is an inspiration, and a disciple
of God. Any honest Christian knows he
is a 20th-century model of Jesus's teachings, with a love for God as well as a
love for his fellow man. Of course he is
fallible — susceptible to temptation like
anyone else — but he is a powerful
symbol, a visionary, and an engine of
change. I thank the Lord for his influence.

If you feel called to join the movement,
there is always room for you here. We

would benefit from your wry humor, work ethic, and intelligence. But if you feel you'd be of more use at the hospital and in the convent, I respect that. Either way, please get in touch with me. It saddens me that I haven't heard from you in eight months. I wish you'd send a note, even if just to say you are okay. You are important to me. We were such friends. The kind that, even in silence, can make each other laugh so hard someone pees a little. (Remember trying to wash the urine out of my big old habit in that tiny sink! To this day, whenever I picture your impression of Sister James Marie sleeping in Mass, I have to look for the nearest bathroom.) We were the kind of friends you're lucky to make once in a lifetime. I don't expect to find another.

I miss you. Let's forget about what happened in Newark.

Your friend,
Eloise

"Watcha reading?" Maria's bright voice chirped, startling Evelyn. Her head popped up through the hatch like an alert prairie dog's. Evelyn wiped her eyes and Maria's facial expression dropped. "Took a trip down memory lane?"

"You could say that."

"Is that a letter from Eloise?" she asked, craning her neck to see for herself.

Evelyn dropped the letter back into her box, stuffed the other items on top, and closed the lid. "I should get back to our records."

"If you say so. Who's up to bat?"

It was day three of Evelyn's sorting, and she'd managed to arrive at the year 2000. She might have worked her way through the records more quickly, but it was impossible not to reminisce. Her mind often wandered, reflecting back on each of their residents — on the many ways Mercy House had helped them, and the ways in which it hadn't.

She pulled out the next record. "A beauty, this one. Marina Esposito. Remember her?"

Maria snorted, surely recalling Marina's frequent display of personality fireworks. She often screamed at other residents over minor infractions, and one time even threw a coffee mug at another girl for daring to comment that Marina wasn't much of a morning person. When Josephine insisted Marina apologize and take responsibility for her actions, Marina slapped Josephine across the face. Picturing Josephine's fast blinking and sputtering expression of shock still made Evelyn snicker, albeit guiltily.

"Which pile does our dear Mrs. Esposito belong to?" Maria asked, nodding to the two stacks before Evelyn.

"Oh, she's a keeper," Evelyn said and slipped the file into one of the many boxes on her right. Evelyn wasn't particularly proud of that case — Marina had stayed at Mercy House for only three nights before returning to her husband and children; Evelyn suspected the retreat was more of a statement to her family in an effort to be appreciated than a needed safe haven. But, in that case, the sisters had done everything by the book. There was nothing to hide. And so the record would stay.

The box to the left — the files to . . . modify — currently held forty folders, which wasn't so shocking considering the number that could stand untouched, but Evelyn knew the nuns had become even more progressive at the turn of the century, so the percentage needing modification was bound to increase.

So far, their forty crimes included helping women secure birth control; encouraging divorce, and then guiding victims through the process; supporting lesbians without any attempt to make them repent their sexuality; releasing women into the houses of their

131

unmarried lovers without encouraging marriage in the Catholic Church; confirming a woman's autistic son in a private ceremony after a local priest reported the boy was incapable of such a mental commitment; Sister Maria's practice of Eastern medicine; and providing marijuana to treat anxiety. What they didn't contain, what Evelyn couldn't bear to put in writing despite her years of training in compulsive record-keeping as a nurse, despite the house's need for meticulous records in obtaining grants or using them as evidence in the women's future court cases, was the most significant, the most blatant and shameful crime against the Catholic Church: arranging and accompanying women as they obtained abortions.

Most women didn't have the finances to pay for the procedures themselves, so the sisters often funded them too. They resorted to money outside church subsidies and grants — which sometimes meant participating in clinical trials and donating their blood plasma to pharmaceutical companies. "Well, Sisters," Evelyn had once said, lying on a gurney beside Josephine and Maria. "We are quite literally selling our bodies for cash. Wouldn't Mother Superior be proud?"

Because Evelyn's conflicted feeling about

this practice prevented her from putting it in writing, at least she wouldn't have to destroy the abortion files. But, sitting in the attic, she'd have to cook up new files to replace the other incriminating cases. It would have been wise if they'd behaved like corrupt accountants all along, keeping two sets of books for Mercy House — one for their own records, and one for Big Brother, or should she say Big Father. But Evelyn never would have guessed they'd have to undergo such scrutiny, that they'd have to defend the service to which they'd committed their lives. Especially when her male counterparts, the Catholic priests, had been and continued to be so fiercely defended, although many were guilty of the indefensible.

"Evelyn, have we done the right thing?" Maria asked. There was something about the raw sincerity in her voice, the cartoon emotion in her eyes, and the way her head tilted to the side, that reminded Evelyn of the velveteen rabbit — the character from the children's book her older brother Sean sometimes read to her — neglected by its owner, desperate for love.

Evelyn wasn't sure if Maria was referring to their past deeds — or misdeeds, depending on their judges — or if she was referring to the handling of these records.

"Of course we have," Evelyn said. Her certainty, no matter how artificial, made Maria smile.

"Sister Evelyn, Sister Maria . . ." Josephine's voice carried up from the first floor. There was something strained in her intonation. Suggestive. Maybe even foreboding. "Good news. Bishop Hawkins has arrived early. Won't you come down and say hello?"

CHAPTER 9

"Shit!" Evelyn spat into the dusty air. "Shit, shit, shit." Maria's rounded eyes searched the attic frantically, as if the solution was hiding behind the clutter. "How do we . . . what should we . . ."

"I don't know. I haven't finished yet. Not nearly." Evelyn's fingers stroked the forty files in the box to her left, and her eyes scanned the three boxes behind them — the ones she had yet to sort through. She was so concerned about the records over the past couple days, she hadn't even allowed herself the time to worry about the Hawk himself. "Go, Maria. Go downstairs and say hello. Chat the prick up."

"And what are you going to do?" Maria whispered, as if the Hawk could hear them from two flights down.

"Nothing good," Evelyn answered without lifting her gaze from their twenty-five years of records, memories, accomplishments, and failures.

Maria lingered for a moment longer. Then she reached across the plywood floor to pat Evelyn's hand. "Bless you, Sister," she said, and then she disappeared.

Evelyn sat back on her heels and said, "Forgive me, Father, for I will sin." Then she leaned forward, shimmied the top back onto the box to her right, gripped its handles, and heaved it onto another box of acceptable files. There were six boxes in all to show the bishop. Just over half their work, ending in the year 2000. It would have to be enough. She slid the six boxes aside, and then faced the remaining four — one of incriminating records and three of unsorted records — four boxes that would need to be destroyed. But how to camouflage them in case the Hawk flew upstairs? She patted her pockets, searching for a pen. None. Her eyes scanned the room, as if she might spot a box of markers stowed away — hey, stranger miracles had happened. Although apparently not to her, as all she spotted were mousetraps, dust motes, and the sisters' keepsake boxes. Her eyebrow lifted.

She crawled over to Josephine's box, peeled off the top, and sorted through the items: a wooden Jerusalem cross pendant on a leather strap; yellowed copies of *The*

Book of Margery Kempe and *The Confessions of Saint Augustine;* a suede bookmark, worn on the edges; a thin stack of lace handkerchiefs; the veil and starched guimpe from Josephine's habit; a red-satin-covered photo album; a nickel-alloy pocket watch; assorted letters; and a stack of holy cards similar to Evelyn's own collection — as a girl she'd collected saints the way boys collected baseball players. Nothing of use.

Evelyn closed Josephine's box and turned to Maria's. She found a cream silk slip, so small Evelyn had trouble believing it had ever fit; an empty bottle of Gilbey's London Dry Gin; a pink feather boa; a framed black-and-white family photo; several diaries locked with keyhole covers; a plastic bag of keys; some loose sepia photos of teenage girls sunbathing on the beach; a silver jewelry box; and a gold cylinder of Maybelline lipstick, sinfully red.

Bingo.

As strange as it was for somebody to save makeup for decades, Evelyn didn't question it. This was her miracle. She uncapped the tube, crawled back over to the four inculpating boxes, and scrawled a red lipstick label on the side of each: "Evelyn," "Maria," "Josephine," and "CHRISTmas Decorations." Then she shoved each box toward the one with the label it duplicated. She pressed the cap on the lipstick tube until she heard it click, dropped it back into Maria's collection, and closed the box's lid. When she pushed herself to her feet and surveyed the room, she was out of breath, but surprisingly satisfied by the feigned organization of the attic. Everything seemed to have its place: records, memories, and decorations. It was hardly noticeable that the labels of four boxes burned with scarlet letters.

Time had not been generous; Bishop Robert Hawkins looked like a mole man. He was stooped in stature, with puffy cheeks and whiskers that traveled farther up his face than one would expect. His eyes were squinted, but not from smiling — it was more like he was constantly trying to make his way around in the dark. His lips were purplish and fleshy. He wore a black cassock, a white collar, and a gold amethyst ring, and an intricately designed cross rested on his potbelly. The sight of him in the entryway of Mercy House — in *her* entryway — made Evelyn's ears fill with a deafening hiss.

"Did we interrupt your nap, Sister?" the bishop asked as Evelyn descended the stairs. She wondered how many others he'd abused since he'd forced himself on her. How many lives he'd shattered. "Nice to see you, Bishop Hawkins. I hope you are well."

The bishop nodded his appreciation. "I see my reputation precedes me. I'm afraid I don't know your name."

She wanted to dropkick the lying bastard and watch him gasp for breath. She stuck out her hand. "Helen Hywater," she said.

His lips puckered as if he tasted something bitter.

Josephine forced a laugh, laced an arm around Evelyn's shoulder, and pinched her bicep. "Sister Evelyn is kidding, of course. She serves the Lord with joy and gladness of heart, and we are all blessed for it."

"We are blessed, we are blessed!" Maria said with the varied cadence of a black preacher. Josephine shot her a look and Maria shrugged, as if that lilt had been just as surprising to her.

"Yes, well, thank you for joining us, Sister Evelyn," Bishop Hawkins said.

Mercy House was theirs. They obtained grants to run the facility. They rescued and rehabilitated the girls. They committed all their days to this one single cause. Thank you for joining *us*? *He* was the guest. "My pleasure," she muttered.

"Well, I see this house is holding itself together," he said, surveying the cracked plaster ceiling. "Barely."

"It's not much, but it's home," Maria said with a content smile, not detecting his patronization.

The bishop clasped his hands at his crotch and rocked back onto his heels. "I'll be staying upstairs, I presume. Hopefully it's cleaner up there. My bags are in the car."

The nuns exchanged meaningful stares and Josephine said, "Bishop, we are so happy to have you here. It truly is an honor, and we welcome you. But I'm sure you can appreciate how uncomfortable our residents might feel with a strange male presence in the house."

"I want to fully immerse myself in the workings of this center. You can assure them I am not a threat."

Screw you, screw you, screw you! Evelyn thought. Her hands grabbed the loose fabric of the legs of her jeans and clutched it at her sides. "That'll put their minds at ease." The flippancy in her voice earned her a second pinch from Josephine. Little did Josephine know how much Evelyn was already filtering.

"What Evelyn means is recovery is a lot more complicated than simple reassurances.

It takes time for victims to trust again, to feel safe. Since the purpose of this house is to serve as a sanctuary, and these residents are our top priority, we wouldn't want to jeopardize their feelings of security. I'm sure, as someone who is dedicated to helping the poor, abused, and marginalized, that you understand."

The bishop ran his index finger across the chair rail, inspected the dusty results, flicked the filth away, and frowned. "Perhaps I'd be better rested if I stayed in a hotel, anyway. Sister Evelyn," he said, his gaze flickering up to hers, "you appreciate the importance of rest."

Evelyn wanted to lunge at the man, but didn't want to unravel Josephine's artful persuasion. He wouldn't be staying with them — that was what was important. She spread her lips into a smile so artificial it insulted her cheeks. "Even God rested on the seventh day. I, for one, am humble enough to admit I am not as mighty as God."

"Yes, well, I had hoped to tour the house today and dine with you and your guests this evening, but now I have to concern myself with finding a place to lay my head. So, if you'll excuse me." He unhooked his wool coat from the rack. "I'll return in the morning, Sisters," he said and left without waiting for their goodbyes.

Evelyn leaned out the door he had left ajar and called down the sidewalk, "There's a very accommodating motel two blocks down. They rent by the hour."

When she closed Mercy House's front door behind her rapist, the entryway blurred around her. Her fingers grazed the wall, anchoring her as she floated down the hall to the nearest bathroom. She turned on the faucet and then, so the other women wouldn't hear, quietly vomited into the toilet.

Father John didn't work in the grandest space in St. Joseph of Mercy Church. He had donated his office, with its oversized windows and wood paneling, to be used as a center for the youth group, support meetings, and various other church ministries, and had appropriated for himself a windowless corner of the building, which he decorated with secondhand furniture, statues of saints, and a black-and-white photo of his mother.

Father John, or little Johnny MacLeese, as the kids had called him, grew up down the block from the Fanning family. Ten years his senior, Evelyn spent many afternoons and evenings babysitting the little sweet-heart. Since she always knew she would become a nun, and therefore would never have a family, she treasured those times, and often persuaded Johnny to play house so that she could pretend she was his mother.

Evelyn was thrilled when Father John took over St. Joseph of Mercy Church in the late 1990s. So many priests strutted around church premises like proud cockatiels, as if they were in charge of so much more than an order of nuns and the restoration of a decaying sanctuary. They mistook imparting absolution on God's behalf as being God Himself. And although she hadn't spoken to Johnny MacLeese in many years at the time, she remembered him as a gentle boy, and hoped he hadn't outgrown that quality, as it was a characteristic to treasure in a priest. She wasn't disappointed. Since his arrival, he had led them with grace and humility.

Although it was almost eight o'clock at night, Evelyn knew she'd find him in his office in the almost-dark, pouring over budgets or drafting a sermon by lamplight, his fingers laced through a heap of silvered hair that could use a wash and a cut.

She switched on the overhead fluorescents

143

and he startled at the sudden brightness. But when his eyes adjusted and he found Evelyn in the doorway, his squinting eyes remained narrowed in a smile.

"Sister Evelyn! What a lovely surprise. To what do I owe the pleasure of a visit from one of my favorite nuns?"

She stepped in front of the chair that faced his desk but didn't sit. "We need to talk about Bishop Hawkins."

The priest's eyebrows rose on his forehead. "Already?"

"He's a dangerous man," Evelyn said and clasped her hands at her waist to emphasize her solemnity.

Father John flicked his hand as if to brush away her worry. "He's a little rough around the edges, sure, but 'dangerous' seems a bit dramatic, doesn't it?"

"That may be the go-to adjective for men to call women with whom they disagree, but have you ever known me to be dramatic, Father?"

"I have not. I apologize," he said, placing his hand over his heart to demonstrate his sincerity. "Forgive me for letting my maleness show so obtrusively. All I meant is that I find it hard to believe Bishop Hawkins is dangerous. He's a man of God, after all."

Evelyn scoffed. "That doesn't mean much

these days."

Father John reclined in his chair. "Now who is generalizing?" he asked with a wink. But when Evelyn didn't soften at his tease, he pushed himself to his feet, walked around his desk to be closer to her, and leaned his backside against the front edge. "I know he seems a bit . . . churlish. But you of all people should know outer appearances can be deceiving. And a gruff exterior isn't the only thing you two have in common. When he isn't touring the country checking up on our beloved nuns or running his diocese, he heads a summer camp for low-income kids. You should see the photos on his website, children hanging off him every which way. They love him. How bad a guy could he be?" Evelyn opened her mouth, first to eradicate any correlation between the Hawk's character and her own, and second to remind Father John that just because a person is evil doesn't mean they are evil in all things, but Father John pressed on. "We're on the same team," he said, gesturing between them, but she knew he meant more than just the two people in that room; he was referring to all holy men and women. "We just want what is best for the church, for one another, and for all of God's children."

Evelyn almost envied his relentless optimism. She sighed deeply. "I know that's true for you."

Father John folded his arms over his chest and looked down at Evelyn from above the frame of his glasses. "Do you have general concerns, or did something happen with Bishop Hawkins?"

Even if she told him about her history with the bishop, what could he do? Defrock him? Toss the man in jail? Father John was a subordinate too, with more influence and protection than Evelyn, but still subject to the church hierarchy. The truth would only burden him and purposelessly tarnish his idealism. Besides, she wasn't there to talk about what had happened with the bishop. She was there to get assurances for Mercy House. She shook her head. "No, nothing happened."

His expression lifted in relief. "Will you give the guy a chance? For me?"

It was then that Evelyn remembered how oblivious people with a sense of security could be. Father John had no idea what was at stake for the women at 284 Chauncey Street. He didn't know what it was to be at someone else's mercy. He couldn't help her. She nodded brusquely, turned, and walked out of his office, not even pausing when he called after her, "Sister?"

That night, after the girls had gone to sleep, Evelyn handed the four boxes marked by lipstick down the attic hatch to Josephine and Maria. She felt like a parent sneaking presents past the closed bedroom doors of their children on Christmas Eve, but without any of the magic.

They hauled the files downstairs to the living room and sat together on the rug before the blazing hearth. Evelyn exhaled a long breath, and then peeled off the lid of the box nearest her.

"I can't think of any other way," she said to the others as much as to herself.

"Just because they're gone doesn't mean they didn't happen," Maria said, clinging to a box of records as if it were a life raft.

Evelyn pulled out the first file in the row. Anna Walsh. An addict of Irish heritage. When working with her, Evelyn felt she was working with a version of her past self, which made it all the more satisfying when Anna — clean for three years — earned her associate degree. Evelyn rubbed the manila folder between her fingers. She whispered, "Hail, holy Queen, Mother of mercy, our life, our sweetness, and our hope. To thee do we cry, poor banished children of Eve. To thee do we send up our sighs, mourning and weeping in this valley of tears. Turn then, most gracious Advocate, thine eyes of mercy toward us, and after this, our exile, show unto us the blessed fruit of thy womb, Jesus. O clement, O loving, O sweet Virgin Mary. Amen." Then she tossed the folder onto the flames.

Inside these files were the stories of rape victims who now worked in crisis centers. Abused women who now enjoyed healthy marriages. Women who were once self-loathing but had learned to love themselves. Broken women, rebuilt. This was the nuns' life work, and they mourned each and every lost document. They gripped each record in their hands for a moment, with Maria sometimes pressing it to her chest, before ultimately feeding the file to the flames. Not a word was exchanged between them as the papers blackened and curled. Now the only proof of their accomplishments would lie in memories, in the same place that held their regrets.

But at least Bishop Hawkins could never find them there.

On her way out for a neighborhood walk the next morning, Evelyn slipped a sandwich bag of quarters into her pocket; she would distribute change to anyone who looked like they could use some generosity of spirit and fill parking meters on the verge of expiring. But just as she reached for the front doorknob, it turned all on its own, and opened to reveal Bishop Hawkins's face, flushed from the cold.

She should have pushed the door closed. She should have demanded he ask permission to be let inside. Instead, as was her way with him, she stepped back. "How'd you unlock the door?" she asked, and entered the security code before the alarm woke the entire house.

The bishop removed his leather gloves, handed them to Evelyn, and then walked past her to the kitchen. "Father John was kind enough to supply me with a spare key, as you overlooked such a courtesy."

Evelyn's toes curled in her shoes. Father John wouldn't recognize a wolf in sheep's clothing if one howled in his face.

He opened cabinets and clanged around the kitchen while she stood in the foyer, still shocked by his sudden appearance. By the time she got ahold of herself, she realized she was gripping gloves that were still warm from his filthy touch, like she was his damned butler. She dropped the gloves on the floor and crushed them beneath her work boot.

Bishop Hawkins was seated at the kitchen table, drinking coffee out of Evelyn's favorite mug, his coat draped neatly over the back of his chair. He looked comfortable. Although, in his clergy vestments, he'd never assimilate with civilians, not like Evelyn did, in her faded New York Jets sweatshirt and decade-old Levi's.

Evelyn cleared her throat. "I hope the bedbugs didn't bite."

"The Brooklyn Bridge Marriott suited me just fine," the bishop said. His long fingers stretched and curled around the base of the mug, fondling it almost lewdly.

She remembered those fingers around her waist, and then the next day around the Communion chalice, serving her the blood of Christ. She remembered his guttural moan. *You wanted this, you whore. You made me do this. This is your sin, not mine.* Her nostrils flared.

"I'm glad you're here, Elizabeth. I hoped to speak to you," he said and gestured to the seat beside him. Evelyn was sure his error was intentional, and a surge of animosity rushed from her heart to her fingertips. He continued, "Please, explain to me what it is you believe Mercy House accom-

150

plishes."

Evelyn squeezed her arms to her sides. "Surely you don't mean to imply the insight I will provide is merely my own perception, rather than a reality."

Bishop Hawkins chuckled and waved his hand. "You're reading too deeply into my words. Don't think so hard so early in the morning."

Evelyn gnawed on her bottom lip while she studied the rodent man, the criminal. Oh, how she longed to indict him then and there, to humiliate him. "I'm cranky before caffeine."

His expression cracked with false pretense. "No, I'm the rude one. I should have offered you some coffee."

Evelyn's eyelids closed and remained that way for a moment, perhaps reluctant to let herself reenter the room with this pompous prick, who was colonizing everything down to their Folgers. She forced herself toward the coffeepot and then sat beside the Hawk. "What would you like to know?"

"Why don't you tell me what you do here?"

Evelyn let herself find comfort in the spiel she so often pitched to grant committees. "More than anything, Mercy House provides a safe place. Many women in abusive situations remain there for lack of a better option. We're here as an option. They can arrive any time of day and stay as long as they need. We take in victims of violence, emotional abuse, and rape —" At that word, her stare averted and she pushed forward quickly, although he deserved for her to linger, to let it fester between them, to meet her stare. "And we provide shelter, food, medical assistance, counseling, and rehabilitation support services like helping them study for their GEDs, and providing career training, legal advice, and housing relocation."

"Thank you, Sister. But what I meant was, what do *you* do here?"

Evelyn spoke slowly. "I just told you."

"And you're qualified for this type of work? Didn't your convent have you trained as a nurse?"

She imagined splashing her hot coffee in his face. She wondered if his cry would be throaty or high pitched. "They did, and I worked as one for twenty years."

"Don't you think you are squandering your nursing education while you play at being a social worker who serves, at the most, what, six individuals at a time? Don't you find that to be a waste of the church's resources and, in that sense, a form of stealing from the church?" Evelyn opened her mouth to respond but the bishop leaned back in his chair and continued, "I find it curious that your list of aids did not include prayer. And what better way to help these women than to save their souls?"

A lump hardened in Evelyn's throat. The bishop wasn't looking for confirmation that the nuns prayed with the women — which they did, when they thought it would be received as restorative rather than irritating, or worse, distancing. He was looking for confirmation that they didn't, or wouldn't. And no matter the truth, he would find what he was looking for. Evelyn gripped her thighs.

"Sister, sister!" Desiree sang the title theme song to the 1990s ABC sitcom as she bounded down the stairs. And, not for the first time, Evelyn thought, *Thank you, Lord, for Desiree.*

"To be continued," the bishop muttered and lifted the coffee cup to his prune-like lips.

As Desiree sauntered into the room, still humming her tune, Evelyn realized what Katrina had observed in GIA earlier that week was true. While Evelyn's body was still stiff from her conversation with the bishop, Desiree's boundless energy was already defusing the tension in the room. "Morning, Sister," Desiree said. Then her stare fell on the bishop. "Morning . . . creepy-as-fuck cracker."

Evelyn stifled a snicker. "Desiree, this is Bishop Hawkins. He's visiting for a couple days. Bishop Hawkins, this is Desiree, one of our current residents."

Bishop Hawkins held out his hand in greeting. "Pleasure to meet you."

Desiree studied him, her mouth twisted with skepticism. When she concluded the man wasn't worth her courtesy, she murmured, "Mm-hmm," and turned her attention back to Evelyn. "Where's Sister Maria at?" she asked. "I'm tired of being last in line for Reiki. She's all out of the good energy by the time she gets to me. I woke up at the crack ass of dawn to get a primo spot, and she ain't even here?"

Evelyn sensed the bishop sit taller in his seat, but she refused to look at him. *Damn it, Desiree.* "She didn't sleep well last night. She's still in bed," Evelyn said. Her mind frantically searched for a topic changer. "Hey, how about we surprise the other girls with donuts this morning? Wouldn't that be nice? Maybe you can help me place the order."

The bishop held up his hand to halt the

conversation. "One moment, Sister," he said and shifted his body toward Desiree. "I'm sorry, can you remind me of your name, miss?"

Desiree took a step back and leaned up against the doorway. "Maybe you should have listened the first time."

His smile strained. "Please."

"It's Desiree."

"Desiree. Very pretty," he said. "Now, tell me, what did you say Sister Maria provides you with in the morning?" He shifted forward and clasped his hands on the table.

Desiree's tongue bulged beneath her lips. She eyed the bishop, clever enough to identify him as a threat, which was more than Evelyn could say for her younger self. "What are you, my probation officer? I ain't on trial."

This time the bishop held up both hands, offering feigned surrender. "Of course you aren't. You misunderstand me. I'm just curious. I simply didn't recognize the terminology you used."

Desiree transferred her weight to her other leg and placed her hands on her hips. "You ain't never heard of Reiki? It's Japanese or Chinese or one of them *ese*s. Healing through touch and energy and all that Eastern shit."

The bishop nodded thoughtfully. "Reiki. That's what I thought you said, Desiree, I just couldn't believe it." He faced Evelyn. His voice was eerily pleasant considering his context as he said, "Since Reiki is a practice based on either hooey or sorcery, since it is a corruption of our Christian principles, to promote it in a Catholic-operated facility would be so clearly incompatible with our doctrine, I simply couldn't believe what I was hearing. Thank you so very much for repeating it. Now, I believe it."

Desiree's arms dropped and her hands furled and unfurled at her side. She'd been used, a pawn in a man's game — again. Evelyn wanted to reach out to her, to touch her shoulder, offer comfort, but she felt anchored to her seat. She ran Mercy House to save women, and there she was, allowing a man to manipulate and degrade one of her charges, right before her eyes. Because she was afraid what this man might do to Mercy House? No, more than that. She was afraid of him, plain and simple, even after all these years.

Desiree's mouth twitched, and then a shadow crossed over her face and seemed to still her, hardening her from the inside out. When she spoke to the bishop, it was

with deliberate composure. "You may have more degrees than a thermometer, but you're ugly as hell." Her hands traced her figure. "These curves say God loved me best, you arrogant motherfucker." Then she sauntered out of the room.

The bishop's cheeks reddened and he gripped the handle of his mug until his knuckles paled. He turned to Evelyn and said, "Wake the other sisters. I wish to speak to you all at once."

CHAPTER 10

Upstairs, Evelyn's heart pounded, and not just from her brisk climb. The bishop hadn't spent more than an hour inside Mercy House, and already he'd stumbled over their skeletons and was acting as if Mercy House was a dishonor to the church. A disservice rather than a service. It didn't bode well.

She paused in the doorway of Desiree's room, where she found the resident shaking a dresser by its lip and groaning her outrage.

"Des," Evelyn said gently, peeking her head inside. "I feel exactly the same way. But you've done nothing wrong. We've done nothing wrong."

Mei-Li sat up in her bed; her sweatshirt hood was pulled over her head and tied taut enough that only the very center of her face was exposed. She slept in this cotton cocoon every night. Mei-Li blinked through her grogginess, trying to make sense of Desiree's alarming behavior.

To her, Evelyn said, "If the bishop asks to speak with you, say as little as possible."

She issued the same drive-by warning in the next room, where Lucia, Katrina, and Esther stirred from their sleep. Then she continued down the hall to Maria's and Josephine's rooms, which were opposite each other. In her whirlwind, she felt like Paul Revere cautioning the colonists about the impending arrival of the Brits. Except, in this case, the threat wasn't coming; it had already landed and was downstairs drinking the sisters' coffee.

From the hallway, Evelyn addressed both nuns, whose doors were open. "In our haste to ready the house for the bishop, we didn't ready the girls. We didn't tell them not to mention Reiki," she managed to say between heaving breaths.

"Good point," Josephine said dazedly, squinting against the light. "We should mention that this morning."

"Too late."

Josephine pushed herself up onto her elbows. "How so?"

"Because he's here, and Desiree was with him, and it's too late."

"He's here?" Maria tugged her sleep mask onto her forehead. "Who let him in so early?"

Evelyn shrugged. "He obtained his own entrance."

"Weasel," Maria said.

"Yes, yes. He doesn't deserve the nickname the Hawk. Hawks are majestic. He's a weasel, a mole man, a snake. He's a lot of things, including displeased. He wants to speak to us downstairs. We need to prepare ourselves, Sisters. The nun-quisition? It has begun."

The three women found the bishop lounging in a living room armchair, his feet crossed at the ankle and swinging gently. Since nobody wanted to choose the seat directly beside him, the nuns crammed together onto the couch opposite the mantel. Evelyn couldn't bear to make eye contact with the man, so she focused on the fireplace, or rather, on the wrought iron draft guard that covered the fireplace. The black square blocked the mouth of the hearth and made it look as if the sisters were silencing its once-vibrant flames — censoring it. And perhaps they were, because behind the screen lay their heap of charred files, which were too hot to dispose of the previous night. The draft guard was an iron curtain over their secrets, and sitting directly beside it was their investigator.

"It has come to my attention that at least one of your approaches to service here is not in alignment with the doctrine of the Catholic Church. It is very troubling, and although I'm confident the offense I heard about this morning is a singular departure from our principles rather than a symptom of a more invasive malignancy," he said, his lofty tone implying he was confident of the exact opposite, "it would be irresponsible of me not to take a closer look at your conduct. For the sake of thoroughness, I have no choice but to review the ins and outs of Mercy House, and perhaps the easiest way for me to do this would be to peruse your records. But before we begin down that path, allow me to address the infraction I've observed thus far. Your heretical use of Reiki will be discontinued immediately," he said as a decree.

Maria stiffened beside Evelyn. "Bishop, please. If I can just try to explain the benefits," she began.

He held up his hand. "I'm sure one could fabricate benefits to fashioning voodoo dolls of the women's aggressors and letting the victims stab the figures with pins, but that wouldn't make it a proper practice, would it?"

That was the first decent idea Evelyn had

heard from the bishop. She could certainly see the therapeutic merit in such an exercise; she wouldn't mind skewering a doll version of him, as a matter of fact. But the bishop held everything they cared about in his draconian hands; she didn't dare utter a word that might inspire him to squash it. Instead, she rested her palm on Maria's knee — a gesture to both quiet her and offer communion. The bishop's nostrils flared with distaste. Evelyn retracted her arm instinctively, although she wasn't sure why.

"You seem to spend more time preaching hocus-pocus than the word of God. That will be remedied, in the interest of the church as well as your residents. In addition to ceasing your Reiki rituals, you will devote more time to Christian ministry. This shall include daily prayer and biblical readings as well as weekly confession and Communion. Administered by Father John, of course," he added, as if to remind the nuns of what they already knew: the church considered them unqualified to perform the last two sacraments.

This time, Josephine intervened. "Of course we are happy to provide religious mediation if requested, and often times it is. We pray with our residents quite frequently. But we must also respect their individual ideologies. What if they are Jewish? Should we ignore their wounds and instead tell them Jesus is the only way? What of Buddhists? Muslims? Atheists? If you are suggesting we help only those who share our faith, forgive me, but limiting our care to Catholic victims alone is not in the spirit of Christianity. Psalm 82:4 says, 'Rescue the weak and the needy; deliver them from the hand of the wicked.' It does not qualify that we should attend to only the Catholic needy."

Bishop Hawkins sat taller in his chair so that he could look down his nose at Josephine. " 'He said to them, "Go into all the world and preach the gospel to all creation." ' Mark 16:15. Do not challenge me with verse, Sister. You will not win."

Evelyn had another verse for him on her tongue, this one Matthew 23:28. "In the same way, on the outside you appear to people as righteous, but on the inside you are full of hypocrisy and wickedness." But she knew its delivery would do no good, so instead she steadied her voice to sound as calm and rational as possible, despite the trembling in her bones. "I fully believe it is more effective to spread the word leading by example. We represent our beliefs in the way we live and through the loving support we provide. If we force Catholic doctrine down the throats of our residents, we risk driving them away. Because as soon as they feel uncomfortable, they will leave, rendering this place useless."

The bishop's mouth quivered. "Your words, not mine."

"What I mean is, while conversion has its place, it is not the purpose of this facility. Rescue and rehabilitation —"

His jaw hardened and he folded his hands in his lap. "This is not a debate, Sister. Have you forgotten your vow of obedience?" She heard his voice from those dark days in the sacristy: *Serving your priest is akin to serving your God.* Evelyn dug her thumbnail into her index finger. Her mind screamed, *My vow of obedience is to God. Not to the Vatican, and not to you, you pig, you ogre, you devil!* but she fought to keep her expression blank. The bishop allowed a beat of silence to fester before a taut smile pulled across his face. "I'm sure you'll find these amendments will improve the results of your work here. Now then. Let's be done with this unpleasantness. Please direct me to where I might find your records."

But Evelyn knew the unpleasantness was only just beginning.

■ ■ ■ ■

The sisters directed Bishop Hawkins up the attic ladder. Once he disappeared into the rafters, Evelyn was tempted to close the hatch and lock him in. The bishop shuffled around above them like a scavenging rat in the ceiling, and they returned to the first floor to await the inevitable repercussions of their transgressions.

"So, what's the plan?" Maria asked in a hushed tone, sounding like a true conspirator.

"I'm not the mastermind behind this," Josephine said when she found the other two looking to her. She plucked her cigarette pack from her pocket, shook one out, and stuck it between her lips. Then she thrummed her thumb against her lighter until it ignited and she leaned into the flame to make the end of her cigarette glow. She puffed twice and her cigarette-wielding hand fell back at the wrist, as if straining under its weight. Whereas once the habit of smoking lent her an elegance, now she looked dependent, desperate. She exhaled a stream of smoke between pursed lips and shifted the attention to her left. "Evelyn?" she asked.

"This is just a temporary plug to buy us time. I say we call the girls down here and do what we should have done weeks ago — prep them for what is to come. What to say to the Hawk, but more importantly, what not to say."

"Do we have time for that sort of . . . debriefing?" Maria asked.

Evelyn wasn't sure how soon the bishop would realize the last decade of files was missing, but she figured he'd at least comb through the existing records before discovering the collection ran short, buying them at least an hour or two.

"We have time," she said.

But they were barely through a cup of coffee when he thundered down the stairs. They exchanged knowing looks. Evelyn held her breath.

"Where do you keep the rest?" he asked, standing in the kitchen doorway.

"Whatever do you mean?" Maria began, affecting innocence.

Evelyn didn't lower the cup from her lips. "Ice dam," she said. She already had to visit the confession booth that week, she might as well add lying to her list of sins.

"What was that?" the bishop asked, annoyed.

She sighed and placed the mug onto the

tabletop. "I said, ice dam. New York was smacked with a snowstorm last month. You didn't hear about it out in sunny California? Well, we were slammed, and then the next week, Christmas Eve and Christmas Day, brought a forty-eight-hour stretch of a springlike sixty degrees. Unbeknownst to us, an ice dam had formed on the roof during the storm, and when the snow melted, it leaked into the attic. Unfortunately, the water ruined a couple boxes of records, the ones that spanned the last nine years. We were very disheartened, you can be sure, but that's Mother Nature for you. It was what you might call an act of God." She was impressed by her own cool tone, given that the big storm she boasted about was actually a mere four inches of accumulation.

"Really?" His question was soaked in skepticism, and he folded his arms over his chest. "I didn't notice any water damage on the ceiling or on the floorboards."

"A kind parishioner came to our rescue, along with his construction crew," Evelyn explained. "Blessed be His name."

"And the damage just happened to destroy your most recent records?"

"That's what I told you. I'm not sure how I could have been clearer," Evelyn said.

"I wonder if there is another possibility," the bishop said between clenched teeth.

"What other possibility could there be?" Josephine asked with a convincingly benign laugh. She touched the end of her cigarette against the rim of her coffee cup, and ashes fell into the black liquid and whirled, as if pirouetting.

Redness spread from the bishop's throat to his face and, when he spoke, his voice was choked. "Some people might suspect you are lying in order to protect yourselves. Some people might suggest the church operated better back when nuns lived in convents under strict supervision, with a life devoted to prayer rather than to propagating their liberal agenda. Some people might say a lot of things, but I'm not saying anything, other than this: I came here to review your records, and it seems awfully coincidental that those records happened to disappear in a natural disaster just last month." He jabbed his finger toward the women sitting at the table, causing Maria to flinch. "I want a list of names of all the women who resided here in the last decade, as well as a means of contacting each — phone number, address, whatever you have. What I lost in records I will discover through interviews."

"Surely you realize that is impossible," Josephine protested. "There have been so many. You can't expect us to know where they all are."

"Don't you tell me what I can or can't expect," he shouted. He then appeared to become cognizant of his simmering temper; he inhaled a calming breath through his nose, lowered his accusing index finger, and finished with wrath that was a bit more curbed, as if his interior monologue was consoling him: *You have them. You still have them.* "I'll begin my interviews with the women upstairs. Private interviews."

Despite the way in which he intimidated Evelyn, she couldn't allow that. "Are you out of your mind?" she demanded, heaving herself to her feet. "These are victims of abuse."

"And?" he asked, crossing his arms over his chest.

"And," Evelyn said, assigning the word two syllables, "they shouldn't be made to undergo questioning alone with a strange man."

The bishop upturned his hands so that his palms faced the ceiling in a mock shrug. " 'Questioning,' Sister? Try to restrain your emotions. It'd make this process a lot easier for everyone involved. I'm merely going to ask them a few questions."

Evelyn imagined her heels digging through the floorboards and mumbled, "Isn't that the very definition of 'questioning,' Bishop?"

His mouth moved to speak, but this time Josephine raised her hand to interrupt him. "Bishop, with all due respect, this is a matter of the welfare of our charges, and we won't budge on the issue. Sister Evelyn has the closest relationship with the residents and should be the one to sit with them. I swear she will not interfere with your interviews, not in words nor in body language, but I insist she remain present. If you find this arrangement problematic, I'd like to bring Father John into this discussion, or perhaps the Bishop of Brooklyn. Maybe we can all pray on it together."

Evelyn marveled at Josephine's cunning. Of course that was the only way — fight power with higher power.

The bishop scoffed. "I'm sure such a discussion will be unnecessary, as long as Sister Evelyn can manage to be seen and not heard."

For better or worse, Evelyn had spent many years developing just that skill.

There were three facts Evelyn worried her residents might disclose. Two were about Desiree: she was a proud bisexual and an

170

even prouder prostitute who gladly serviced both genders. The last significant and significantly damning truth was about Esther.

CHAPTER 11

ESTHER

My mother said I was always a serious child. I was the youngest, but while my brother and sisters played outside, chasing one another through the trees or drawing pictures on the ground with sticks, I preferred to help with the chores. I followed my mother down to the spring and brought back water in buckets we carried on our heads. I picked vegetables from the garden and washed them for dinner. I swept our dirt floor with a leafy branch I selected with care. My mother called me *lonbraj mwen,* "my shadow." And I called her the Haitian Creole word for mother, *Manman,* which I would later appreciate for its English implication, because it was true: my mother had the strength of two men.

When she got the opportunity to join her cousin in the United States, she did so without hesitation, even though it meant leaving us under the care of my eldest sister until Manman earned enough money to send for us. We were poor. Water dripped through the slats of our roof whenever it rained. We relieved ourselves in the woods and buried our excrement so it wouldn't stink or run into our water supply. We were illiterate. We didn't stand a chance in Haiti. And so she left us, so she could save us.

When we arrived in the United States two years later, I was afraid to see my mother. I thought maybe I wouldn't recognize her. Or worse: she wouldn't recognize me. And there were so many people in the airport. More people than I'd ever seen in one place. I held onto my sisters' wrists like they were branches beside a mighty river whose current wished to sweep me away. Although I fought them, tears pricked my eyes. But then she was there. Manman. And though she was fifteen hundred miles from home, she still smelled of Haitian soil.

My mother told us to forget about Haiti. She wanted us to become Americans. And so she allowed us to speak only English in the apartment. She no longer practiced vodou. Instead of fried goat and plantains, we ate chicken fingers and fries. But some things couldn't be changed; they were ingrained in us. We still walked like we were

balancing something on our heads, something important we didn't want to spill,
something as essential as water.

There were several good years living with
my mother and her cousin's family in
Brownsville. But then my grandmother
became ill back home, and my mother
returned to the island to care for her. When
her mother passed away months later, my
mother wasn't allowed to return to the
United States. She'd overstayed her visa
once before. Immigration wouldn't make
the same mistake twice.

There was an ocean between her and her
children once again, but this time closing
the distance would mean damning us to a
life of need. And she wouldn't do that. We'd
have to remain a world apart.

Without my mother anchoring us, my
brother and sisters drifted in different directions. My eldest sister married and moved
with her husband to South Carolina. When
she sent pictures of palm trees, my other
sister followed her, hoping for a taste of
home. And my brother moved to the Bronx
and currently earns money in ways that
would make my mother weep.

I was the only member of my family to
stay in Brownsville. I finished high school
and began taking classes at Kingsborough

Community College. I would get a degree, a good job, and a green card so I could visit my mother. See her again. That was the plan. As an undocumented teen, I was what the United States called a Dreamer.

In the meantime, I sent my mother letters, and once every two months she walked miles and miles to the nearest bus stop and rode into Port-au-Prince so we could video chat over Skype. Often I'd sit in the bedroom I shared with my second cousins, staring at the screen, waiting for her icon to appear, not knowing her bus had broken down or that the internet café decided to close early.

I met Emmanuel at the Caribbean restaurant where I worked, a place called Some 'Ting Nice. He'd recently emigrated from Haiti, and I ignored his wolfish smile, the way his eyes glinted like a steel blade, because he'd been to the village where my family lived, where my mother still was, and the cadence in his voice sounded to me like love.

I remained blind even when I learned his father was in a Haitian prison for murder. As my mother would say, the son of a tiger is a tiger. It took far too long for me to see his stripes.

He didn't like to watch me study. Perhaps

because education is power, and he couldn't allow me that. At first he lured me from my textbooks with sweetness. "Come, sit with me. I miss you." Or "There's a party at the Haitian Community Center. We should go." Or "Let's make griyo together. It would make your mother proud." But once he made himself the most important part of my life, once I loved him, he didn't have to add honey to his persuasion. Instead he said, "If you don't have time for me, I'll find a woman who does." Or "What kind of wife do you think you'll make with your nose in your book and nothing on the stove?" Or "What is the point of all of this? Do you think you'll become a doctor some day? How many Haitian women do you know who are doctors? Don't be foolish."

So I didn't study, and when I failed an important exam, I snapped and said, "See what happens when I listen to you?"

He crossed his arm over his body and backhanded my face. "How can you say such a thing to someone who loves you as much as I do?"

In vodou, there is no heaven or hell. There is only this world. And from my experience, that is heaven and hell enough.

I wish I could say I walked out on him that day, but I stayed with Emmanuel for one more year. Perhaps it's part of my ancestry. Haitian women have suffered by the hands of cruel men ever since Christopher Columbus landed on our shores. Or perhaps it's part of my nationality. My country became a wife brutalized by her husband when the United States occupied it over a century ago, exploiting its people as laborers, destroying their temples and the drums that kept its heartbeat. Or perhaps it's just me.

One afternoon, Emmanuel accused me of looking at his friend Junior with eyes of lust. And so he punished my eyes, purpling them. I had a Skype appointment with my mother that evening, but I couldn't let her see me so battered and swollen. So I skipped it. And when four o'clock came around, I pictured her sitting in the internet café, having walked seven miles in flip-flops, paying for an hour-long bus ride and the use of a computer, so excited to see my face and hear about my classes. She'd wait fifteen minutes. Maybe twenty. Maybe even thirty. And when my icon failed to appear, she would think I had finally forgotten about her, stranded across the sea, a mother without her children, in a place that was beginning to feel to me like a fading photograph.

I heaved gulping sobs of shame and sorrow. They cleansed me of all the cowardice I'd been harboring, and I came to the conclusion I should have come to long ago. If I stayed with Emmanuel, I would be accepting a lesser fate, and insulting my mother's sacrifice in getting us to this country. I was a Dreamer, and Emmanuel was poison to my dreams.

I went to his apartment and told him we were finished. His jaw tensed and his eyes burned with a tiger's fury. He held me down, tore off my pants, and proved I didn't have the power to end our relationship. He would have me for as long as he wanted me. He would draw blood.

In Haiti, one punishment for rape is marriage. I don't know whether this is meant to chastise the victim or the criminal. But I wasn't in Haiti anymore.

When I returned to my apartment, my second cousin intuited what had happened. She saw the loss of humanity in my posture. I could no longer balance something of great importance on the crown of my head. She told me about Mercy House. And for fear that Emmanuel would come for me, I went.

On my first night, Sister Evelyn served me a sandwich and tea and told me I shared a name with one of the great biblical heroines. Esther was an orphan who became queen, and through her beauty and intelligence she saved her people. But I was not like that biblical queen; I had not saved my people. I had betrayed them. I'd squandered the education that could bring me back to my mother. And the worst was to come. When I learned I was pregnant, I terminated my people. Anyway, I doubt how much meaning there is in a name. Emmanuel is also biblical. It means "God with us," but I did not feel God near in those dark moments with Emmanuel.

I knew I would pay for what I did to that life in my belly. In vodou, we learn you can't ignore the spirits, and my ancestors would not be pleased. There are always consequences to your actions, or as my mother would say, after the dance, the drum is heavy. And my drum was about to become too heavy to hold.

The earthquake was my reckoning.

I hadn't been back to Haiti in fifteen years, and yet I felt that earthquake in my bones. It ripped through my heart. It echoed in my hollow womb.

They are still sifting through the rubble, turning over rocks and finding bodies beneath, even weeks later. The dead fill mass graves. The living fill tent cities and become violent over rice. Peacekeepers fire rubber bullets.

I still haven't heard from my mother.

The evangelical minister Pat Robertson said Haitians are paying for their sins with that 7.0 magnitude quake. I am terrified that he is right.

Sister Evelyn came downstairs in the middle of the night and found me in the living room rewatching clips of Pat Robertson, my diary open in my lap to the date of my procedure. My heart raced. I couldn't breath. My body trembled uncontrollably, as if reliving the quake, but this time it originated from within me.

"Don't you listen to that giant-eared moron. He's equal parts hate and insanity," she said. But when she saw my panicked state, her face softened and she lowered to her knees before me. Her voice was gentle but assertive — a nurse's voice. "Look at me, Esther. Look into my eyes and follow my breathing. Deep inhale in, slow exhale out. That's it. That's right. Again. Deep inhale in, slow exhale out."

"If I'd just kept it," I managed to say.

"You can blame the earthquake on a fault, but the fault isn't yours. It's the one that runs through the Caribbean and North

American Plates. That's a little earth science wordplay. You can laugh at that later. Now, I don't mean to say you can't feel regret over what happened. That'd be perfectly normal, and if you wish we hadn't gone through with it, you can tell me. I'd understand. We can talk about it. Pray about it, if you wish. So, earthquake aside . . . do you wish we hadn't gone through with it?"

Sister Evelyn's expression was built in layers, like those of the Earth. On the surface, she was compassionate, focused on me. Open to whatever I was feeling. But beneath that layer there was harder stuff. A defensive wall. And she needed that wall to protect what was at her core. I didn't know what her bottom layer was made of, but I had a feeling it looked a lot like what was inside me.

If I regretted the abortion, her justifications would shake and topple over. It would crush her.

If I'd carried Emmanuel's baby, I'd never be free from him. His claim that I couldn't end the relationship would prove to be true. I'd no longer be a Dreamer. I'd be his. He'd hold power over me forever. So I took that evil seed he planted in me and ripped it out like a weed before it had the chance to rise up into my throat and strangle me.

There is much I regret in this life. But, earthquake aside, I don't believe the abortion is one of them.

CHAPTER 12

Katrina brought her knitting to her interview and ticked her needles together like a court stenographer at her keyboard. She wore a single earbud and let the other dangle down her chest. Evelyn heard the faraway drone of music from across the room, a miniature world whose entirety existed only for Katrina.

"What are you working on?" the bishop asked, trying to sound amiable.

Evelyn knew the answer: it was an extra-wide scarf for Joylette, who lived across the street. Katrina spent many mornings listening to her music and gazing out the front window, perhaps relishing the quiet of dawn in Brooklyn, or maybe searching for any sign of danger. At her station, she'd observed Joylette on the corner waiting for the B47, pulling her collar up to her chin and bobbing to keep warm; Katrina went to work.

"A bathing suit," she answered in such a deadpan, the bishop couldn't discern if she was serious or not.

Although Evelyn had seen Mei-Li rattle swears like a vulgar racetrack announcer, with the Hawk, she played the part of a perfect lady. She sat primly, legs crossed at the knee, her expression fixed into amiable engagement. The interview went smoothly, and he appeared encouraged by a pleasant conversation with at least one woman in the house.

As Evelyn walked Mei-Li out, the resident paused in the doorway, turned, and said, "Bishop Hawkins?"

"Yes?" he asked with the good nature of their newly established rapport.

"Cào nǐ zǔ zōng shí bā dài," she said.

His eyebrows twitched with incomprehension, but then he bent his head to receive the farewell.

When they were out of his earshot, Evelyn touched Mei-Li's arm. "What did that mean?" she asked.

Mei-Li beamed. "Fuck your ancestors to the eighteenth generation."

Esther entered the room, and Evelyn swallowed down only a speck of trepidation. She was confident Esther wouldn't volunteer information about her procedure — it preoccupied the young woman in the weeks following their visit to the medical facility and even now she often seemed distant. Still, Evelyn's muscles tensed as Esther took her seat, and she paled when the bishop asked a question he hadn't asked the other girls, a question that was startlingly relevant.

"The Catholic Church values Sister Evelyn's education as a nurse. Have you required any sort of medical attention since arriving at Mercy House?" he asked. His hands were clasped over a knee, and one thumb caressed the other.

"Yes," Esther said. She sat erect on the couch without using the back for support.

"What sort, if you don't mind me asking?"

"I've suffered panic attacks, which Sister has helped me through."

"That's all?"

"When I arrived, she treated some body aches. I believe my ribs were broken, but I didn't let on to that."

"Why not?"

"Because I knew they would make me go to the hospital and I didn't want to go to the hospital."

"And why was that?"

Esther shifted in her seat and swallowed before answering. "Because the doctors would have to call the police, and I wasn't ready for that. I was too afraid."

"Since your admittance, though, you have filed claims against your offender?" the bishop asked. And just like that, the conversation shifted from a medical discussion to a legal one. Evelyn studied Esther, perched so seriously on the couch cushion, and wondered at the workings behind her still features, because Evelyn knew Esther had no broken ribs. That would have been impossible to hide from Evelyn's trained eye. Why lie about that detail, if not to artfully redirect the bishop's interest? Her admiration for Esther inflated inside her chest.

It was Desiree's interview that concerned Evelyn most of all — the resident who sang her profession from the rafters, who introduced herself and issued that information all in the same breath. *Desiree: courtesan, trollop, harlot, whore, butt broker.* So, when she entered the room, Evelyn prayed: *Hail Mary, full of grace, the Lord is with thee. Blessed art thou amongst women and blessed is the fruit of thy womb, Jesus.* But she found she was not in the presence of the loud-mouthed, spirited young woman she had come to know. The individual who walked into the living room and sat on the side of the couch farthest from the Hawk was only a whisper of Desiree. That morning's humiliation at the hand of the bishop had tarnished her vibrancy, and Evelyn hated him for it.

"Hello, Desiree," the bishop said. Desiree focused her stare on the top left corner of the ceiling and didn't respond. "Thank you for coming downstairs. I have just a few things to ask you, and I thank you in advance for your honest answers. Where were you before arriving at Mercy House?"

Evelyn knew the answer to this question. She was living in her mother's apartment in the Jefferson House Projects. Many of Desiree's clients lived in the same complex as she did, and the rest she picked up after dark in a variety of nearby playgrounds. Evelyn could still picture the first time she saw Desiree, sitting on the bottom of the slide, humming to herself, rocking gently back and forth. She looked like a little girl waiting to be picked up by her mother.

Desiree's current johns were low-income, most surviving on government subsidies. She aspired to move up the ranks and become a high-class call girl, a corporate lady of the night, from streetwalker to Wall Street. You couldn't claim Desiree wasn't ambitious.

"Jefferson Projects," she answered truthfully.

"And what did you do?"

Evelyn held her breath. Desiree had told the truth before. If she told the truth now, it was only a matter of time before the bishop received confirmation that the nuns had done little in the way of saving her Mary Magdalene soul. Six excruciating seconds passed before Desiree responded. "Lots of stuff."

"I mean, what did you do for a living?"

"I was a street entertainer."

"Is that right? And what is your talent?"

Desiree's jaw slid to the left. When she righted it, she said, "I have many talents."

"I have no doubt. What I'm asking is how you earned money in the field of street entertainment."

Desiree flashed him a stare so sharp it could have pierced skin. "I have a lovely singing voice. Wanna hear it?"

"That's quite all right," he said. Her biting remark had made him uncomfortable — he wasn't used to being on that end of confrontation — and his hand retreated farther back on the armrest. Evelyn worked to keep her mouth neutral.

By the time Lucia took the hot seat, Evelyn had relaxed. If they could survive Desiree's loose lips, they could survive anything. After all, Lucia had just arrived. What sort of threat could she be after only two nights?

"I hear you are new here, so, welcome. What do you think of Mercy House so far?" the bishop asked.

"It's fine, I guess."

"The sisters are treating you well?"

"They're okay. A little creepy and controlling, but fine, I guess."

"And the other girls? Are you all getting on?"

Lucia's brow furrowed in disgust — too much disgust for the context of the question. A chill ran up Evelyn's spine. "Fuck no," she said, and her gaze swiveled from the bishop to Evelyn and back. "What kind of sick house is this? And what kind of pervert are you?"

"Excuse me?" the bishop demanded. He wouldn't tolerate reverse questioning.

The conversation was unraveling quickly. Evelyn's mind fumbled to take hold of it but she wasn't nimble enough and it slipped through.

"I mean, I know the fat chick is a dyke and a hooker and shit, but that don't mean I'm down to eat pussy or nothing like that. Jesus."

The bishop closed his eyes and flapped

189

his hand in front of his body, perhaps trying to dissipate the potent image in the air. "There's been a misunderstanding."

"You asked if we're getting it on. You said it in plain English."

The bishop shook his head emphatically. "No, no. Not getting *it* on. Getting on. Do you get along with one another? Platonically."

Lucia sat back against the couch. "Oh."

"But what you said is important. A resident here is a homosexual and a . . . and a prostitute? Surely this is news to Sister Evelyn, who has made it clear time and time again that she is only concerned with the welfare of those who stay here. Certainly she wouldn't put an innocent resident in peril by placing her in the same room as a sex fiend and a homosexual."

Lucia's stare flashed to Evelyn. "She knows," she said, simply. "They all do. They talk about it all the time."

"Then she has made it abundantly clear that the Sisters of St. Joseph of Mercy do not condone such sinful behavior, and are actively working to save Desiree through the grace of God?"

"How the hell should I know?"

"Yes, I'm not so sure myself," the bishop said, the words oozing off his tongue. Evelyn could feel his stare; it forced down her head like hands on the back of her skull. She focused on the floor between her feet, at the wine stain and strands of hair stuck in the rug fibers, because she knew this was it. The situation had spun wildly out of her control, and she couldn't bear to look into his face as he ended everything good in her life. "That'll be all, Lucy," he said.

"Lucia," she corrected.

"Hmm?"

"My name is Lucia."

"Yes. Fine."

When Lucia left the room, Evelyn finally lifted her gaze. Her voice trembled, like violin strings vibrating on their neck. "We do not discriminate based on race, creed, or sexual orientation. All victims are God's children, deserving of protection."

"I continue to be troubled by the principles of Mercy House. Because of what I've just heard, I will now be taking a look around the residents' bedrooms."

Evelyn's heart raced. "But Bishop —"

He clapped his hands and Evelyn flinched. "I do not want to hear your tired tale of protecting these victims of abuse. By neglecting to teach them the word of God, and by allowing them to share a home with a sexual predator" — Evelyn's cheeks burned with fury at his wildly hypocritical choice of words — "you have proven you have no concern for their fates in this life or the next. For these reasons, you have lost the privilege of restricting my movements here. I've given you far more provisos than you've deserved. You may call the girls down to this floor if you wish or let them stay where they are upstairs. Either way, I will be inspecting their rooms presently."

Before she could protest further, the bishop was on his feet and heading toward the stairs.

Evelyn shot up and rattled off the names of her residents. "Mei-Li, Katrina, Esther, Desiree, Lucia," she yelled toward the ceiling. "Lock your doors."

The bishop halted in the doorway but didn't bother to turn around. "Sister," he said, as a threat.

Evelyn stepped backward toward the kitchen, where the other nuns waited. With the bishop near, she no longer recognized herself. Where was the woman who fought back against an armed mugger? Who approached drug dealers on the street to negotiate their business practices? Who'd faced down thugs loitering on the sidewalk? Though the bishop wasn't an especially tall man, his presence towered over her; she had to resist the urge to shrink. Her hands shook, and she gripped them into fists at her sides. "I may not have much proviso power, or much power at all, but I have enough to insist you not barge into their rooms without consent, when they might be in any state of undress. You may inspect their rooms, Bishop, but only once they've invited you to do so."

The bishop breathed heavily. "You may request they vacate their rooms from here. I will not have you going upstairs to whisper warnings in their ears, or to try and sweep your wrongdoings under the rug. It's too late to clean up your mess. Don't fight what is inevitable."

"And what is it that's so inevitable?" she asked.

The bishop shot her a look over his shoulder. "Oh, Sister. It's not really a question if we all know the answer."

CHAPTER 13

Silent tears dripped off Maria's chin as they listened to the thuds and scrapes of the bishop rummaging around the girls' rooms upstairs. The five residents and three nuns huddled in the kitchen, some sipping tea and some clinging to their steaming mugs without drinking.

Evelyn recounted all of the events in the last twenty-four hours, trying to identify an injustice perpetrated by the bishop that the church might sympathize with; one not so vile they'd have to suppress it (like sexual assault), but serious enough to make them doubt any of his recommendations. But she knew clergymen were like prized children of wealthy parents — there would have to be an indisputable and public offense to ever get the church authorities to admit misconduct.

She reflected on the sexual abuse scandal in the Catholic Church. Over three thousand priests in the United States alone had been accused of sexual misconduct, for abusing girls and boys from as old as fifteen years of age to as young as three. Thousands of young victims trusted and admired their priests, never suspecting, never understanding that there was evil inside those men.

The idea that Evelyn was associated with these individuals, that she often served under them and was forced to acquiesce to them, sickened her. It was a disgrace to Catholicism, and an expensive one: the church paid literally billions of dollars in civil lawsuit settlements to protect clergymen who belonged in jail. The guilty parties were sent to treatment facilities, but more often than not they returned to circulation as priests, their new congregation oblivious to the dangerous perpetrator in their midst. And when the priests committed new crimes, ruined more lives, they were again relocated — not excommunicated.

So Evelyn knew even when delinquency was public, indisputable, and despicable — some of the worst acts a religious figure could commit — even then, or perhaps especially then, the church found a way to mute the truth.

She and the other nuns were up the proverbial shit creek.

"I don't get it. This is your house. Don't he need a warrant?" Desiree asked. When the nuns just looked at one another without answering, she continued, "How can you just let him go through our shit? It's *our* shit. What is he looking for, anyway? And what if he finds it? What happens then? You tell us to be strong, to protect ourselves, to speak up like fucking Scout Finch when somebody wrongs us. So, what about you? Why aren't you saying nothing?"

Josephine answered evenly, "Whatever he finds, and whatever happens after he finds it, none of it will be your fault." She laid her hand on Desiree's shoulder.

Desiree scowled and shrugged her off. "I know that. I ain't done nothing wrong."

"Did you do something wrong?" Katrina asked the nuns. She sat hunched over at the table. She'd spread glitter over a part in her hair, and it sparkled under the kitchen lights. Her voice was a light squeak through the bewildered fog. She tucked one of the earbuds into her ear and added, "Everyone makes mistakes."

"No," Evelyn said, uttering her first words in the kitchen. She stood a little taller — whether sincerely or for effect, she didn't know. "I don't believe we did."

A door slammed upstairs, and many in

the kitchen jumped at the sound. They concentrated on the Hawk's footsteps as he pounded down the upstairs hallway, and then beat each stair on his descent. The women responded to his approach in their own ways. Evelyn pressed further into the wall, Maria and Josephine straightened, Desiree rolled her shoulders back, Esther's gaze drifted toward the doorway, Lucia tucked her hair behind her ear, Mei-Li mouthed curses to herself almost imperceptibly, and Katrina stared at her feet.

When he emerged in the kitchen doorway, his figure appeared much grander than his humble height should express. In his arms, he cradled a pile of contraband. Based on the swell in his posture and the rise of his features, he was pleased — proud, even — about his discoveries: a box of Durex extra-sensitive condoms, a bottle of CVS-brand lubricant, a magenta rubber dildo, a lilac compact of birth control pills, and a small black spiral notebook.

"Your radical feminist mission is even more extreme than we feared. Contraception? Sex toys?" the bishop asked in disgust. Although, for all his contempt, he embraced the wickedness — including a presumably used vibrator — against himself rather tightly.

Esther stiffened at the table and thrust her arm toward the bishop's loot. "That is my journal. You have no right to that."

Evelyn's stomach contracted and her gaze darted to Josephine, who looked equally panicked. They both knew what could be in the journal. The bishop could have all he needed to shut down their operation — to close the Mercy House doors forever. Perhaps even to excommunicate them. The room wavered around Evelyn.

The bishop tightened his grip. "That's where you're mistaken. I, in fact, do have every right to this journal. It may be your diary, but it's also a log of the happenings in this house over the last several months, and since the sisters' files were destroyed, it's the only record we have."

Esther shot to her feet and her chair clattered to the tile floor. She was normally much more reserved, levelheaded. It was as if she knew what was at stake. "It is my personal property. You cannot take it."

"This house belongs to the Catholic Church, and this book was found inside this house. Therefore, this book belongs to the Catholic Church."

"*I* am inside this house. Do *I* also belong to the Catholic Church?" Esther asked and pounded a fist against her chest.

"It will be returned to you. I can't say the same for these accessories of fornication. They will be destroyed. You all should be ashamed. 'Repent, then, and turn to God, so that your sins may be wiped out.' " Since his arms were full of scandalous items, he then addressed the nuns with a nod of his head. "As for you, I advise you to consider these words: 'For this people's heart has become calloused; they hardly hear with their ears, and they have closed their eyes.' I have a meeting with Vatican leaders in three days. You can be sure I will report my findings to Cardinal Rode during that meeting." He uttered the name like a curse, and perhaps it was: Cardinal Rode was the Vatican instigator of the nun investigation. For his aggression, he was nicknamed the "Enforcer of Truth" and "God's Rottweiler." He was also rumored to have absolved a reverend who had molested his seminarians.

"Bishop, please —" Maria begged, reaching her hand out in supplication.

He rolled his shoulders back. "You are defiant daughters in desperate need of discipline. You have created an unsafe environment. I am shutting Mercy House down."

Fury rose to the surface of Evelyn's skin.

She lunged forward. The bishop's eyes widened as she flung herself on him; that flash of fear, that quiver of uncertainty in his mouth, ignited a dark satisfaction in Evelyn's core for, in that moment, he wasn't in control — he saw what it was to be defenseless. She beat his biceps with the sides of her wrists until he dropped the contents in his arms. Then she dove to the floor, grabbed the journal, and tossed it across the room to Maria, who caught it, dropped it into the sink, and turned the faucet on full force.

"Animals," the bishop cried. He shoved Evelyn and Josephine aside. As he moved for the sink, Mei-Li stuck out her foot; his shoe caught on hers and he crashed to his knees. He cried out in pain, and then in anger.

"Woops," Mei-Li said with a shrug and a smile.

He pushed himself back to his feet, slammed the water off, and lifted the soggy journal by the corner, letting excess water drip off. Then he wrapped it in a dishtowel. Evelyn feared the damage wasn't enough.

"This is why the Bible tells us, 'Women should remain silent in the churches. They are not allowed to speak, but must be in submission, as the law says.' You think we should let you become priests? Hell, we never should have released you from your habits."

The bishop clutched the journal to his side and bent over to retrieve his lost items. When he arrived at the front door, he had to lean backward and balance the dildo and condoms on his chest in order to grab the doorknob.

The women didn't speak until the door smacked closed behind him. Then Desiree slapped her hand against the table. "None of this would have happened if the new cunt didn't blab my business to Bishop Needle Dick."

"What did you say?" Lucia demanded, taking a step closer to Desiree.

Desiree pressed her hands on the table and pushed herself to her feet. "What, you don't *habla inglés*? I said none of this would have happened if you didn't blab my business."

"Ladies, please," Josephine said and moved between them.

Lucia rose onto her tiptoes to peer over Josephine's shoulder. "Maybe none of this would have happened if you weren't such a dirty ho. Ever think of that, puta?"

Maria grasped Desiree's meaty bicep just as Desiree sprang forward and reached

201

around Josephine toward Lucia, her fingers flexing as if grasping the air. "Get this bitch out of my face. I'm gonna kill you, skank. I'd rather be a ho than a snitch. Look what you did, skank rat. Look what you did!"

Lucia stumbled backward. Her eyes watered and she scraped her teeth against her scabbed, full bottom lip. "You know what? Fuck this place. I was safer before coming here. I'm getting the hell out of this house. You all are crazy bitches." She turned on the ball of her foot and stormed down the hall.

"Lucia, wait," Evelyn said. They might not have Mercy House for much longer, but she was determined to protect these women while they did. And Lucia wasn't ready to return to the world yet. She was bound to go back to Angel Perez and would most likely be punished for having left him in the first place. Evelyn followed Lucia out the front door. But Lucia was young and agile and Evelyn was old and plodding; Lucia was already down on the sidewalk, lacing her arms through the sleeves of her coat, when Evelyn's bare feet hit the chilled cement of the stoop. The cold sunk its teeth into her toes and wrapped itself around her ankles like a vine. "Lucia, we can help you!" Evelyn yelled. She started down, but as her foot landed on the third step, the cold had eaten its way through her skin to her bones and her ankle joint froze. She buckled. Her knee drove into the next step. Her hands shot out in front of her, and her palms skidded and scraped the rough surface. She turned her head to the side, bracing for the impact on her face, but her chest absorbed the brunt of the fall as it collided with the concrete.

As she lay in a pile, drooped between the sidewalk and her stoop, bleeding, aching, and moaning, Evelyn lifted her head and found Lucia bent at the knees, reaching down toward her, her mouth agape.

Then the front door of Mercy House creaked open from above. "Heavens, Evelyn," Maria said, and then shouted, "Josephine, come quick!"

Evelyn hadn't broken eye contact with Lucia, but as Maria descended the stairs behind Evelyn, Lucia's gaze lifted up to her. Then she straightened, looked back down to Evelyn, whispered, "I'm sorry," and hurried down the sidewalk, into the heart of Brooklyn.

The other sisters pleaded with Evelyn to let them take her to a hospital, but Evelyn refused. She was certain she'd been spared any broken bones, and for that she thanked the Lord. She wouldn't take up space in a busy emergency room; she wouldn't waste the precious time of doctors and nurses when there were plenty of patients more in need of care. The seriously ill, victims of violence — as Desiree said, this was Do or Die Bed-Stuy, after all.

What she wanted was a heavy pour of whiskey, but since those days were behind her, she'd have to settle for a handful of Tylenol and a hot bath.

For perhaps the first time, she appreciated the shower grab bar a parishioner had insisted on installing for the nuns. At the time, she'd scoffed at the addition. They may have been old, but they weren't elderly. And they weren't disabled, for God's sake. But now she gripped it with a prayer of thanks as she eased into the steaming water.

Normally she preferred showers; baths forced her to look down at herself and witness the degradation of her body. But she didn't trust she could stand after such a brutal fall, so she prepared herself for a full viewing of her aged form. Her physical self that had done so much, and yet, comparatively, so little. It would never realize some of its most basic purposes — making love to another person, growing a child in her womb, birthing that child and feeding it at her breast. Some said that was what God intended for women, why He created Eve in the first place. If that was true, what did it mean, then, that she, a woman of God, failed to fulfill that destiny?

It didn't matter what some people said. Some people were morons.

She liked to think her residents were her children, individuals she delivered into a new life and nurtured until they were strong enough to live on their own. And so she satisfied her purpose, just in a different way. If she'd had a husband and children, they would have distracted her from saving the hundreds of women who'd stayed under Mercy House's roof.

Although, she did often wonder what it would be like to feel the bare chest of the one you loved pressed against your own. But she didn't desire it as often as she used to.

What was once skin wrapped tautly around strong bones and firm muscles was now tissue paper draped around soft and brittle matter. Her thighs were lumpy and her skin hung loose, rippling around her knees like water coiling around a dropped stone. Varicose veins, swollen and raised, snaked down her calves, looking like ripe

Chinese eggplants ready to burst.

But she caught a glimpse of her reflection in the chrome bathtub faucet and remembered Eloise's words. "You have such true eyes. Look at them. Such beauty." There was a clarity about them that had withstood the years, so maybe her old friend had a point.

She held her breath as she lowered herself into the tub. The water lapped at her body in licks that began painful in their heat, but quickly turned soothing. When her rump hit the hard ceramic, she relaxed her entire body into the sides of the tub. The countless miniscule cuts on her palms stung as she lowered her hands into the water.

As her wrists immersed, she thought of the last time Hawkins destroyed her spirit, driving her to press scissors to her wrists. Thank God for Eloise, who appeared like the Angel of the Lord, took the scissors, held Evelyn until her sobs exhausted her, and then cooled her face with water from the sink, a kind of baptism. From that grim night, an alliance solidified. They made faces at each other during chores in a competition to see who would laugh first. They hid notes inside their billowy sleeves and passed them when no one was looking. They created code names for the other sisters. They developed hand gestures with secret meanings. And in moments of distress, they met in the garden to chat when speaking was prohibited. For the next ten years, through the first profession of their vows and beyond, Eloise was the most important person to Evelyn. Up until the day she left the convent, and Evelyn never saw her again.

Every now and then, Evelyn granted herself time to reflect on that friendship, which was still one of the most meaningful relationships of her life. Where was Eloise now? What was she doing? Was it possible she was in some other bathtub at that very moment, thinking of Evelyn? When she couldn't bear to remember Eloise any longer, she turned her wrists over.

The back of Evelyn's hands were speckled with liver spots the color of mud. There were about a dozen on each, half of them the size of pencil dots and half larger, like floating islands. The smaller ones were perfect circles, but the more significant spots were oblong, one even resembling a curvy cross. Evelyn was rather fond of that blemish, a natural tattoo of her mission and identity that her body had cunningly produced. She was generally, however, troubled by the marks, and by the shriveling of the skin around her knuckles, the yellowing of her fingernails. She was uncomfortable with how her body continued to change, to decay. If a younger Evelyn saw her hands now, she wouldn't recognize them as her own. If a younger Evelyn saw her now, she might decide to have sex while she still had the chance. Or perhaps, if a younger Evelyn saw her now, she wouldn't be thinking about appearances at all. She'd be too consumed by the disappointment that not enough about her had changed.

How had she allowed herself to be bulldozed again? From the time she was four years old she had let men bully her into corners. Sure, her father's maneuvering was far more benign than the bishop's technique, perhaps more luring than bullying, seducing with charm and paternal love, but the result was the same. She was intimidated by their grandeur, tempted by a possible connection, and time and time again, the men got their way.

She was nearly seventy years old, and though she was crusty, a tough lady by all appearances, she'd yet to stand up for herself when it really counted.

Her left knee bulged from the fall, protruding from her leg like an angry face. Her chest was scraped and puffy. Her hips were purpled. She resembled a Mercy House resident, a victim, but of course more wrinkled and doughy.

She didn't know what her future held. Would the bishop really shut Mercy House down? Would he push to expel the sisters from their order? She felt as if she was driving without headlights, and the road was windy — perhaps even a dead end.

"Everything okay in there, popo?" Mei-Li asked from the other side of the door.

"Fine," she answered. "Just fine."

As the last traces of heat dissipated from the bathwater, Evelyn heard the front door open and close, followed by the sound of animated voices downstairs.

"What's that? What's going on?" She clasped the grab bar and hoisted her heavy body up. Water rushed down her limbs. Her injured knee cried out and her back twinged.

"It's . . . it's Lucia. She came back," Mei-Li said.

Lukewarm water sloshed at Evelyn's shins and trickled down the surface of her skin and off the tips of her hair. As she stood in the tub, naked and rejoicing, she smiled, closed her eyes, and whispered, "Thank you, Lord."

Evelyn's tired feet sank into the plush bath mat, made from the kind of shag that could have suffocated Elvis, certainly a Sister Maria purchase. She yanked her ratty robe off the door hook, eager to make her way downstairs to welcome Lucia and possibly assuage Desiree. She was tying the belt closed when she heard a thump on the front door.

"Lucia! I know you're in there. I saw you. Come out," an accented male voice called from outside. On the surface, he sounded angry and unwavering. But there was a current beneath it that vibrated.

Evelyn's eyes widened. Angel Perez.

Shit.

CHAPTER 14

Evelyn threw open the bathroom door. "Go to your room and close the door," she said to Mei-Li and then hurried down the stairs. Her body protested every move, her robe flapped at her sides, and she nearly slipped on the excess water dripping off her feet, but she never slowed.

Josephine and Maria crowded in the landing at the front door, and several of the girls strained their necks to watch from the kitchen. Evelyn waved them toward her. "Esther, Katrina, and Lucia. Upstairs immediately. Lock yourselves in your rooms, call the police, and don't come out for anything." They stared at her, stupefied, until Evelyn clapped her hands together and shouted, "Now!"

Once the girls scrambled past Evelyn and up the stairs, and she heard the sound of the door locks clicking into place, she closed one eye and squinted out the peephole.

Angel Perez. One of the formidable leaders of Los Soldados. He wasn't especially tall — several inches short of six feet — but Evelyn could tell he was muscular, even under his puffy winter coat. His shaved head was bare, revealing a scar that sliced from his hairline down his cheek. Stubble shadowed his mustache and his chin. And there was that barbarous face tattoo, in which a cross, an icon of forgiveness and new life, was made into a weapon, wet with ink blood. His eyes darted up and down the block, as if he was afraid he had been followed.

Evelyn prayed the neighbors would stay inside.

He appeared to be alone. That was something, a salvation, even. Perhaps he was embarrassed to have to be there at all, ashamed his woman had left him, that he was forced to hunt her down. If that was the case, he would be reluctant to make a scene.

"The cops are already on their way," Evelyn said through the door.

Angel's mouth tightened. Then he reached into his coat and pulled out a pistol. Its black polymer was sinister, like tar glinting in the moonlight. Evelyn gasped as he widened his stance and leveled the Glock at the door. "Then we better make this quick. Send Lucia out."

"Gun, gun," Evelyn said in a panic and pushed Josephine and Maria into the living room. They stumbled back, but when Evelyn returned to the front door, they followed.

"It's hard to concentrate with that thing out. Can you put the gun away and then we'll talk?" Maria asked, too friendly for the circumstances. Evelyn pressed her face up against the peephole. The gun remained steady.

"Send out Lucia, or I'll shoot this door down and take her myself."

"You wouldn't shoot a bunch of old nuns," Evelyn said, hoping to appeal to the religious roots he had tattooed on his cheek.

Angel closed his eyes and pulled his lips back to expose clenched teeth. He shifted in his stance, opened his eyes, and gripped his gun harder. "I don't want to kill you, but the nice thing about being Catholic is, after you sin, all you gotta do is ask for forgiveness and bam!" he said, making the nuns jump. "Fresh slate." Evelyn opened her mouth to explain the other requirements for true forgiveness, but Angel jerked his hands to the side and shot a bullet through their living room window. The blast erupted inside their eardrums and was followed by glass shattering. The girls screamed upstairs, and Katrina continued to shriek, as if sounding an alarm. Evelyn's heart pounded at the base of her throat. Angel's impatience simmered to a boil. He yelled, "Open the fucking door, or the next bullet goes through your fucking heads."

Evelyn wasn't a stranger to the sound of gunshots; at night, they occasionally echoed in the distance. But she'd never heard one so close or so threatening. She sent another silent prayer to the heavens that the Sahas, the New School graduates, Joylette and her boys, and the rest of Chauncey Street would stay indoors. Then she took a deep breath to try to settle her terror and began speaking out loud. "Hail Mary, full of grace, the Lord is with thee." Evelyn signaled the other women to join in. Although perplexed, they conceded, and prayed together in the entryway. "Blessed art thou amongst women, and blessed is the fruit of thy womb, Jesus."

"Shut the fuck up," Angel shouted, but they barreled on.

"Holy Mary, Mother of God, pray for us sinners, now and at the hour of our death. Amen."

Another shot cracked against the house, just a couple feet from where Maria stood.

The sisters jumped and the screaming upstairs doubled. Evelyn reached out for Josephine and Maria, and they reciprocated, embracing one another just beyond the front door. Tears welled in Maria's eyes, and they began from the top. "Hail Mary, full of grace, the Lord is with thee." After this second round, a bullet exploded through the base of the front door and lodged itself in the floorboards beside their feet.

The idea of hurting prayerful religious sisters wasn't deterring Angel as effectively as Evelyn had hoped. Apparently this wasn't like in the movies, when sacred chanting would pierce the heart of a demon. As she gawked at the gouged floorboard just inches from her bare foot, she knew he had postponed a direct attack against the nuns as long as he was willing. The next shot would hit one of them.

"All right!" Evelyn called through the front door. "All right. You've made your point. I'm going to get Lucia. Just, please, don't hurt anybody else in the house."

Maria's eyes rounded and Josephine shook her head vehemently. "No, no, no," she whispered. How could Evelyn sacrifice one of their lambs?

Evelyn didn't have time to explain. She needed to move. But instead of heading upstairs, she ran down the hall and into the kitchen.

She threw open the cabinet beneath the sink and grabbed a can of Lysol disinfectant spray. She didn't bother closing the cabinet before moving to the drawer beside the oven. There she snapped up a multipurpose lighter. With those two items in hand, she sped back down the hall to where the other sisters waited, bewildered. "Back away," she insisted. When they retreated into the living room, she prayed under her breath. "The Lord is my rock, my fortress, and my deliverer," she said.

Then she flung open the front door.

For a moment that lingered for eternity, Evelyn stared into the cavern of the gun's muzzle, a pitch-black tunnel that ended at a bullet, just waiting to be released into her flesh.

But then she flicked on the lighter — a wavering ember alight in the darkness — and depressed the top of the aerosol can.

The flame flared as if from a dragon's mouth. And though it didn't have much reach, it was enough to startle Angel. Alarmed, his weapon-yielding arm retracted into his body. Then he fired.

The bullet ripped through Evelyn's side, tearing open the skin at her hip like a griz-

zly bear slicing into a carcass. A bellow born in her gut tore out her throat; the sound she produced was not recognizably her own. It was primal, like an animal mourning her young. She dropped to her knees on the stoop landing. Angel, thrown off balance by the shock of the flamethrower and by the recoil of the gunshot, tumbled backward down the stairs. He dropped the gun. Upon impact, another shot fired. The sound filled Evelyn's ears, followed by Angel's own howl.

The sisters were beside her. Maria gathered Evelyn's head into her lap and her tears dropped down onto Evelyn's face. "You're okay," she said, her voice steady. "You're okay."

"Not my head," Evelyn grunted. "My ass."

"Right, right," Maria said. She lowered Evelyn's head to the frozen cement and pressed her palms against Evelyn's side, igniting a searing agony. Evelyn clamped her teeth against a wail. Her blood spread down the small of her back, warm and sticky.

Josephine darted down the steps to where Angel's gun had skidded a couple feet from his writhing figure. She bent over to retrieve it, pointed the Glock away from Angel, and ejected the magazine. Her membership at the shooting range was finally being put into practice. She tucked the pistol into the waist of her skirt and turned her attention to Angel. "Help is on the way," she said, and clamped her hand over his bleeding abdomen.

"You did good. So, so good," Maria said.

Evelyn had protected them. She had stood up to their attackers — one of them, anyway. Her eyes fluttered closed.

"Sister, are you all right? What has happened?" She heard the voice of Dr. Saha above her, and then seconds later he said, "Take this. Apply pressure. An ambulance is on the way."

Sirens screeched in the distance and, as they grew closer, blue and red lights flashed in the darkness.

"Just a few more seconds, Evie. They're coming," Maria said.

Evelyn's mind drifted to that place between consciousness and sleep. From its perch floating above the scene, she heard the screech of tires. Vehicle doors slamming. Male voices. Cold fingers pressed against her throat. The pain was present but dulled. Hands gripped and lifted her body, and the pain roared loud enough to yank her back to reality. She opened her eyes to see specks of white swirling around the night sky; it was snowing. She quietly sang the words to

one of her favorite Buddy Holly songs —
words of stars and shadows, and hearts.
Then she was inside the ambulance, looking up at a smile forced across Maria's red,
tear-stained face.

"Almost convincing," Evelyn croaked. A
plastic bubble cupped her mouth and nose.
Her arm was pinched, and then felt icy.

Maria's brow furrowed and her smile
strained even further. "What is?"

But then Evelyn sunk back into the haze,
where the pain was quieter.

The bullet hit nothing but adipose tissue,
avoiding all organs, muscles, and bone. For
once in her life, Evelyn was happy to be fat;
a nice plump roll acted as a buffer to
everything vital. Although, if she wanted to
be a pessimist about it, the bullet might
have missed her entirely had she not been
overweight. But this was no time for pes-
simism. As far as gunshot wounds went, this
was the best-case scenario; all she required
was saline to flush out the wound, a blood
transfusion, and antibiotics. She was very
fortunate.

Angel died on the operating table.

Evelyn wasn't envious of the sisters who
would have to inform Lucia. She knew from
experience that a complicated loss didn't

219

make the grief any more bearable.

The next morning, Evelyn waited for the nurse wearing the copper bracelet and the Saint Juliana Falconieri religious medal to check her vitals and asked the apparent Catholic if she could visit Angel's body. The woman's lips compressed and wrinkled; Evelyn was sure she was about to say no, but then she turned to the collapsed wheelchair leaning against the wall and opened it with one decisive movement.

Open doors provided glimpses into the suffering of strangers: a leg lifted in traction; a pained moan; a face masked with oxygen; intravenous bags dripping antibiotics, saline, or morphine into peripheral lines. Through their discomfort, patients slept, talked with visitors, watched television on their laptops, stared up at the ceiling, wept. She felt a piece of each of them mirrored in her own heart. Her mouth moved but her prayer was silent. "Tend your sick ones, O Lord. Rest Your weary ones. Bless Your dying ones."

At the end of the hall, the nurse pressed the down arrow for the elevator and crossed her arms over her chest. Her hands quavered. She flexed her fingers but, when the tremors continued, she hid them beneath her biceps. A realization shifted into place in Evelyn's mind. The trembling. The Juliana Falconieri medal, patron saint of chronic illness. The copper bracelet. The nurse was too young for Parkinson's disease. Huntington, then? Multiple sclerosis? Either way, there were treatments but no cures. Only kindness.

"What's your name, dear?" Evelyn asked.

The nurse tucked a limp strand of cinnamon-brown hair behind her ear. She looked wearied, like she was coming to the end of a long shift. "Patty."

"Thanks for doing this, Patty. I won't forget it."

The elevator descended to the bottom floor and opened into a sterile world of stainless steel and fluorescent lighting.

The left side of the room was lined with cabinets, inside which Evelyn knew cadavers lay cold, their souls having already departed on their journey to meet God. On the right were industrial sinks. And at the center was an aisle of tables, three of which were occupied by shapes encased in plastic body bags.

Patty emerged from behind Evelyn, bent over each of the bags, and maneuvered Evelyn to the one at the center. "This is Angel Perez," she said, her voice reverent. "But if you wouldn't mind saying a few words for the one at the end, I'd appreciate it. She was a patient of mine. A real nice lady."

Evelyn wanted to tell her that she'd pray for them all, the three bodies still waiting to be examined, the ones who'd already been sliced open and sewn back up, the people with hearts still beating floors above them. Instead, she just squeezed her nurse's wrist.

Then she extended her hand toward Angel. If she hadn't been playing the hero, he never would have shot her, never would have fallen back, never would have discharged the bullet that ended his life. If she'd come out unarmed, perhaps they could have talked one-on-one, and he'd still be living, breathing, walking. He could have been forgiven, grown, loved, and been loved. He could have reached his full potential.

She'd wanted to lay her hand on him and pray. To pass some warmth onto the limbs that were stiff at least in part because of her. Her hand rested on the frigid table beside him instead.

She wondered who would come for Angel, if it'd be a funeral director or if it would be his own mother. Evelyn imagined the woman who had carried Angel in her womb, who had delivered him into this world and lived too long, long enough to see him enter the next, reaching out for him the way the Blessed Mother had reached for her son as he was taken, lifeless, off the cross.

Evelyn's eyes stung. She lowered her head and whispered, "In Your mercy and love, blot out the sins Angel has committed through human weakness. In this world he has died: let him live with You forever."

Later that afternoon, Evelyn woke to Sister Maria at her bedside, head bent over a fraying Danielle Steel novel.

"You don't have to be here," Evelyn said. Her lips were parched enough to crack. She winced as she reached for a nearby cup of water — her hip seared as if it'd been bayoneted — and Maria tapped her hand and waved it back.

"Don't you dare," she said. She carried the cup to Evelyn's face and directed the straw between her lips. "And, yes, I do have to be here."

Evelyn sucked the liquid into her mouth and relished its cool relief. "I have an entire hospital looking after me. You should be with the girls. They need you." Maria replaced the cup on the table and settled back in her chair. Her gaze drifted to the left of Evelyn, toward the hospital room door. She looked guilty. "Tell me," Evelyn said.

Maria shifted in her seat. "Well, I wouldn't leave you alone, except there is someone out in the hall who wants to visit."

"Who?"

"And I really think you ought to let her come in."

"Who?"

"Even though you wouldn't want to see her, under normal circumstances."

"For God's sake, Maria. Out with it."

Maria's stare settled back onto Evelyn, as if assessing whether or not she was ready for the information that would follow. She sighed. "Maureen."

The name was familiar, but just out of reach. "Who?"

"Maureen," Maria said, impatiently. "Your sister. Your *blood* sister."

Against all odds, Evelyn's five siblings, all between the ripe old ages of seventy-nine and eighty-five, were still alive and kicking. They'd avoided the typical culprits of death: heart disease, stroke, car accident, cancer, and stupidity. Certainly this was good luck, a blessing. Although that might be true, had any of them croaked, Evelyn would have been forced to attend the funerals, and it wouldn't have been since her mother's death thirty years earlier that she'd gotten together with her family. If it were true, she wouldn't have gone several decades only visiting, and even only speaking to, one of her siblings — her oldest brother, Sean.

Luke, Patricia, Maureen, and Fay sent the occasional Christmas card, or maybe a child's wedding invitation every so often, but even those stopped arriving after enough years.

Evelyn thought she had spotted her brother Luke on the subway once, but after she'd gathered up the nerve to approach him, and even touched his elbow, he turned out to be a Polish tourist. She was both relieved and disappointed.

Evelyn didn't know exactly why she was so averse to reconnecting with her siblings. It could be because they never expressed remorse for the enormous pressure they'd placed on her entry into the convent. Or because they hadn't cared to notice when she was drowning in the depths of alcoholism and despair.

But it could also be because Evelyn wasn't the only sibling those Irish assholes had abandoned.

May 1963
Evelyn's feet stilled on her bicycle pedals

and she sat back in her seat to enjoy the downhill ride. She and Eloise — now Sister Incarnata — were on their way back from the hospital where they were nurses practicing everything except obstetrics, because exposing nuns to infants could infect them with baby-fever, thereby threatening their vow of chastity. Both women gathered the excess fabric of their habits into their laps so it wouldn't get caught in the wheel spokes. Evelyn snuck a peak at Eloise's calves: it had been years since the sun had kissed them. They were pure, unsullied, like bridal satin.

When they reached the bottom of the hill, they slowed and slid off their bikes. Eloise let the wool fall to her ankles, a stage's dropped curtain.

They pushed their bikes through the gravel, leaving wheel-sized tracks in their wake. As they rounded the bend, Evelyn eyed something that made her fists tighten around the handlebars. Eloise noticed her tense and touched her shoulder to inquire. Evelyn pointed ahead at the two-tone Nash Metropolitan parked in the circle drive: her family's car.

Her mother, Bridget Fanning, sat on a bench in the foyer, hugging her purse to her belly, rocking back and forth and moaning under her breath. Seated beside their mother was Evelyn's sister Fay, her copper hair frizzed, her nylons sagged, and her legs crossed at her ham-shank ankles.

Mother Superior stood beside them. Her hands gripped each other at her navel, and the long sleeves of her habit met one another like the mouths on two sucking fish. She said to Evelyn, "Visitation isn't until tomorrow."

"Just let us speak to Evelyn," Fay demanded.

"It's Sister Mary Michael now."

"Please," Evie's mother said. She spoke from the back of her throat, where sobs originate. "It was an awful drive, and it's an awful occasion. You're a Sister of St. Joseph of *Mercy*, aren't you?"

Mother Superior's lips tightened. They looked about ready to disappear into her face. She gestured to the dark visitor's room and then glided away in the opposite direction.

Fay pushed herself to her feet and waddled across the hall, followed by their mother, but Evelyn's feet rooted her in place. They never visited. Why were they here now? She tried to swallow but the muscles in her throat had hardened.

"Do not be dismayed," Eloise whispered,

"for I am your God. I will strengthen you and help you."

Neither her sister nor her mother acknowledged Evelyn as she sat across from them at the table beneath the painting of Saint Joseph and baby Jesus. Her mother's breathing was labored, and her fingers whitened as they gripped the edge of the table. Fay gnawed her bottom lip.

Evelyn itched to speak, to demand to know what had happened, but she reminded herself of the value of silence, and waited.

"It's Sean," Fay finally said. Her mother whimpered.

Evelyn pictured her oldest brother, tall and wiry, with hair the color of yams. His had been the loudest voice at gatherings. He filled the doorway, and his stories carried above all others. He called her Spud, and the way he looped his arm around her shoulders and dropped all his weight onto her made her feel important.

She still remembered when he'd returned from war. Their house exploded with whoops and cries. He beamed in his uniform. Their sisters threw their arms around him and their brother pounded his back.

Evelyn hadn't seen him since she entered the convent. She wondered if his temples were beginning to silver, the way their

228

father's had. She wondered if he had died, like their father had.

"He killed his neighbor," Fay said, flatly.

Evelyn's arms fell to her sides and she bent forward. "What?" she asked, a little too loudly. The memory of the sound rang in the quiet.

Fay's stare traveled up to meet hers for the first time that day; perhaps Evelyn's outburst was finally a behavior her sister could recognize. The words flew from her mouth, then. "Beth was cheating, or at least Sean thought she was. He found his neighbor's sunglasses on her bedside table. He recognized them because they were Ray-Ban Wayfarers, and his neighbor Jerry always flaunted them like they were the greatest thing since sliced bread. Turns out, Jerry had only lent Beth the sunglasses because she was gardening and complaining about the light in her eyes. She forgot to return them before she went inside to shower and left them on her nightstand. So she wasn't sleeping with Jerry," Fay finished with a shrug. "She was sleeping with some other guy."

Evelyn's tongue felt thick and heavy as she formed the words, "So Sean . . . killed him?"

Fay sat back in her chair and her stare

dropped to her lap. "He stabbed him thirteen times. And he stuffed those Ray-Bans down his throat. Sean is in police custody until his trial, and the guy Beth was actually sleeping with moved into his house."

Evelyn imagined her charismatic brother plunging a blade through another man's flesh. When had he become so violent, so savage, someone she didn't recognize, someone she feared? Now he'd be treated like the animal he'd shown himself to be, sitting alone in a cold, dank jail cell and, eventually, burning in hell. She had to forcibly exhale and inhale. Her breathing roared in her ears, like waves crashing on a shore. It was all she could hear until her mother cried, "I wish he never came home from that war. I wish he died over there."

"Don't worry, Ma. He's dead to us now," Fay said, and crossed her arms over her chest.

Evelyn dug her nails into her palms and concentrated on a pill on the sleeve hem of her habit, the symbol of her sacrifice that supposedly delivered Sean home safely. She zeroed her focus in on that imperfection and blocked out the surrounding smooth area. She couldn't look at her mother or sister. All she wanted to see was that piece of black.

■ ■ ■ ■

January 2010

The last time Evelyn saw Maureen was at their mother's funeral; Maureen was a middle-aged woman then. She spent the afternoon admonishing her ornery teen-agers. Her expression had set into a scowl, as if the world had been unkind to her and she felt she didn't deserve it.

Now she would be an old woman.

Evelyn couldn't turn an eighty-year-old woman away, especially one who had jour-neyed out into the cold of winter to see her estranged sister. Could she?

"Tell her I'm sleeping," Evelyn said.

Maria swatted Evelyn's foot through the hospital sheet. "Is that what Jesus would have done to someone who came to him for prayer or forgiveness?" She cocked her elbows out and adopted a false baritone. " 'Hey, Peter. Do me a solid. Tell those cripples I'm not feeling well.' " She tossed her imitation and continued. "Nuns shouldn't hold grudges."

"Yeah, and we shouldn't curse or drink or lie or masturbate. But you can bet your ass we've done them all more than once," Eve-lyn said. Evelyn was tempted to point out

Maria's own vices — the bag of Hershey kisses she kept in her bedside table, soft porn disguised as paperback novels, or her predilection for online poker — but she knew it would injure her friend, and she had no interest in doing that.

Maria's voice softened and her expression lost any trace of joviality. Sibling relationships were dear to her. She'd grown up with three lively and protective brothers, and had lost all of them within the last three decades. "Enough is enough. You were shot, for God's sake. If this experience has taught you anything, it should be that time is ticking. We don't have forever. Your sister is here. Talk to her."

Evelyn stared at the ceiling tiles and blinked away tears. One trickled down her temple and into her ear. She wondered what Sean would tell her to do, how he would react if another Fanning showed up. Surely he wouldn't turn away a visitor. "Fine," she managed to say. But as Maria moved toward the door, she reached out for her arm. "Do you have a piece of gum? Feels like something turned over and died in here."

As Evelyn mashed peppermint Trident between her teeth, Maria slipped out of the room. Evelyn's heart began to pound, and she wasn't sure where to rest her stare.

Should she watch the door and greet her sister upon her arrival? And what the hell was she supposed to say?

She didn't have much time to agonize, because a round figure soon entered the light of the doorway.

Her auburn hair had silvered and her body, once a defined shape, had filled in around the edges. The skin of her face was waxy, with fine crisscross wrinkles, like netting. A deep line was carved between her eyebrows — the same line as that of the woman who raised her. It was strange to look at her sister and see an older version of her mother. Under the influence of painkillers, Evelyn was overcome at the sight of this person from a former life. She ached with longing for a childhood she hardly experienced, with regret for letting so much time slip by, and with that same old resentment.

Why couldn't life be simpler, better?

A sob surged up from Evelyn's belly and hit the back of her mouth like a wave crashing against a breakwater. Maureen's hand trembled up to her face, but she didn't come any closer. They cried on opposite sides of the room.

When Evelyn regained some composure, she pressed her face into her bedsheet and let one last ragged breath wrack her chest.

"How did you hear?" she asked, not letting her gaze linger on her sister for too long.

"An old nun, wearing nothing but a bathrobe, faces down a gangster to protect a house of abused women? You're all over the television. As soon as I heard, I called Johnny to find out where they'd taken you," she said, referring to Father John.

"Are news crews at Mercy House?" Evelyn asked, pushing herself up onto her elbows.

Maureen shrugged. "I don't know. I'm sorry. So, how are you feeling? Does it hurt much?"

"Not for now. They've got me pretty doped up."

They were quiet for a while. Finally, Maureen stepped closer. "It's been a long time."

"It has." Evelyn tugged at the sheet on her thighs. She knew she was setting a trap whose teeth might snap shut on both of them, but she couldn't help but ask, "Why do you think that is?"

Maureen scratched her temple, perhaps so her hand had something to do. "Oh, you know. It happens sometimes in big families. Too many people to keep track of. When you left, the church made it hard to stay in touch, and by the time the Vatican let you be more accessible, we'd gotten used to so

234

little communication. We'd grown apart."

"Out of sight, out of mind."

Maureen sighed. "It was the life you chose."

"Is that the story you tell yourself so you can sleep at night?"

"What on earth does that mean?"

"You think I decided to become a nun? Is that why you came here? So I can reassure you of that? Soothe your guilt?"

Maureen blinked rapidly, as if that could focus Evelyn's bewildering message. "Of course *you* decided to become a nun. Nobody took those vows for you."

"But it was you, all of you, who put me in the convent in the first place. Please, for once in your life, admit that. For the sake of my sanity."

Maureen placed her hands on her hips and her sweatered arms propped out like teapot handles. "All parents make wishes for their children. Maybe Daddy more than most. But nobody could have forced you to do anything you didn't want to do. I'm sorry if you're unhappy with the way your life turned out, but you need to stop blaming us. You're an old woman, for God's sake. You of all people should understand free will. For once in *your* life, take responsibility. Or at the very least, forgive. Or did they not teach you that at the convent?"

Evelyn turned her head and stared out the window. The clouds were gray and heavy. Another storm was coming. "Get out," she said.

"Evelyn, please. It's been so many years. Be reasonable, for once." Now not only did Maureen look like their mother, she sounded like their mother.

"Get out," Evelyn said again, this time with more bite. Her stare remained locked on the window, which was hazy with grime. Most rooms in this wing faced Fort Greene Park, a lovely tree-lined green space complete with tennis courts and a Doric column monument dedicated to American lives lost in British prison ships during the Revolution. But not Evelyn's; her window was opposite the graffiti-faced storefronts on Dekalb Avenue.

"Thanks for the reminder of why we don't talk," Maureen said, spitting the words. She spun around and doddered out of the room with as much fury as her advanced age would allow.

As the swish of Maureen's winter coat faded down the hallway, Evelyn's temper boiled over, and then diffused into sadness. She went to such lengths to change the lives of complete strangers — why couldn't she have changed her own life by holding her tongue for five goddamned minutes? Or why couldn't Maureen have humored her? For all Evelyn knew, it could be another thirty years before her next opportunity at reconciliation.

Evelyn hammered her fists into the cot at her sides. Then she balled the sheet in her hands, yanked it up toward her face, and stretched it over her brimming eyes. The moaning in her side grew, as if it too were exacerbated by the emotional experience, so she dropped the sheet and depressed the button for an influx of intravenous pain-killer, hoping it would numb the pain universally. She wished she could speak to Sean at that moment, hold his hand. Feel a connection with one family member. But since she couldn't, she lay back against her pillow and cried until she fell fast asleep.

CHAPTER 15

When her eyes parted two hours later, she cringed at the memory of her interaction with her sister, but was relieved to be distracted by a new presence in her room: Father John.

"Evelyn," Father John murmured as her eyes opened. He rested his large hand on top of hers. His touch was warm. His dark hair was flecked with flint around his ears and a permanent crease circled his neck, an indent from so much time spent bending his head in prayer. "You amaze me. I'm so proud of you."

Perhaps because her tear ducts had already been unsealed that morning, her eyes began to water once again. "I may have won that battle but what does it matter? I lost the war," she said.

His eyebrows lifted at the inside corners and angled down in a straight line toward his temples. "What's this, now?"

Her vision blurred and she pinched mucus from her nose. "Bishop Hawkins. He's going to shut down Mercy House."

Father John squeezed Evelyn's hands. "That can't be true."

She shook her head. "It is. He barged in looking for reasons, and he found them. He's going to recommend dissolving it when he meets with Cardinal Rode."

"But the cardinal will see the value in what you do."

"He won't believe the ends of Mercy House justify our means."

Every feature on Father's John's face was alive with fretfulness. "But you can modify your means."

Evelyn shifted her gaze back to the ceiling. "I don't think I can."

"I see . . . ," he said, trailing off. They sat for a moment, thinking and listening to the sounds of the hospital: heels clicking down the hall, a baby crying, a single laugh, nurses chatting, a patient coughing, a telephone ringing.

"And I doubt Bishop Hawkins will stop at Mercy House," Evelyn said, breaking their silence. "He won't stop until we're excommunicated."

Father John chuckled and patted her arm. "Now that isn't true. Even if that was his plan, I think you botched it."

She sniffed and looked over at him. Fine lines radiated from his eyes, which were the quiet cobalt of a blue morpho butterfly stilled on a leaf. "What do you mean?"

"He can't excommunicate a nun who shot a flamethrower at an infamous gang leader. You made headlines, Sister. You're a rock star. It'd be bad for business, and the Vatican is too smart for that. They know how to operate; heck, they're one of the oldest establishments around."

This news was some consolation.

If she could trust the Catholic Church, if she could trust what Father John said to be true, then the sisters' retirement was safe; they would remain in the order and would be taken care of when the time came. But without Mercy House, what would they do for work? St. Joseph of Mercy ran a foster house for children whose mothers were sent to prison. Perhaps they could join that team.

Another flood of exhaustion rolled over her body, submerging Evelyn from her toes to the crown of her head. She closed her eyes and nestled further into the pillow. "Thank you, Father. Thank you for coming. Now, go in peace."

The light in the room glowed amber the

next time Evelyn was stirred from sleep, as if the setting sun was a fire smoldering on the horizon, casting a soft luminescence onto Brooklyn.

As she reached for a sip of water, she heard, "She's awake. Gotta go," from the doorway, and turned to find Mother Superior leaning against the frame, her Blackberry phone tucked between her ear and her shoulder.

Mother Superior had a curly gray bob shorn around her ears and was almost elfin in size: barely five feet and weighing perhaps ninety pounds soaking wet. But what she lacked in stature she made up for in spirit. She was consistently doing multiple tasks at once: typing up a lesson plan while chatting on the phone, driving to a meeting while chatting on the phone, writing checks while — no surprise — chatting on the phone. In addition to managing just under two hundred nuns, she assisted in the operation of the church, and worked as an associate professor of religion at a local college.

"Sister Evelyn," she said, clipping the phone into her belt holster and advancing toward the hospital bed. "Sorry about that. Sister Jean Louise is on her last legs, I'm afraid. I was letting her family know it's time to come say goodbye."

"That's too bad," Evelyn said.

Mother Superior's head jutted a quick nod. "Yes, well, she's old."

"Aren't we all?"

"Yes, but Jean Louise is very old. You, on the other hand, are still sprightly. From what I hear, you're a regular Al Pacino; all you need is a machine gun."

"Yes. Say hello to my little friend: Lysol."

This might have been the first time Evelyn was actually looking up into Mother Superior's face. She smiled, and her eyes, which were already a bit sunken, were almost swallowed by her cheeks. "How did you even think to do that?"

Evelyn shrugged. "I saw it in a Facebook video."

"Thank the Blessed Mother for social media," Mother Superior said, and then her expression set. Enough with the pleasantries. It was time for business. "Evelyn, you were wonderful, and you should be applauded for your actions, but I'm afraid that's not the only reason I came to see you."

"The Hawk."

"Yes. The Hawk." Mother Superior's fingers laced in front of her, and she spoke primly. "You need to get used to the idea of closing this chapter of your life and beginning a new one."

"You mean, closing Mercy House?"

"Yes. I'm so grateful for your contributions at Mercy House, and I wish you didn't have to move on, but unfortunately, that is the case."

Evelyn gripped the railings of the hospital bed, grit her teeth against the pain in her side, and shimmied herself up to face her boss. "Mother Superior, please, do something. Don't let this happen. We do such good work there. You have to fight for us."

Mother Superior's eyebrows tightened. She was a tough cookie who approached her duties with a no-nonsense attitude; she wanted to get things done. But she also knew when to pick her battles and, sadly, in the case of the Catholic Church, there were many battles she realized she could never win. "You know I have. I did all I could. He isn't a reasonable man. His mind is made up. He's got you over a barrel," Mother Superior said, and Evelyn winced at the image. "Perhaps God is calling you elsewhere."

"This isn't an act of God. It's that serpent."

"That may be the case, but it doesn't make the facts any less true. I recommend you spend the next week getting your things in order: breaking the news to your residents, placing them in temporary housing if necessary, packing your things, et cetera."

Tears stung the back of Evelyn's throat. She swallowed them away. "Then what?"

"Sister Maria, Sister Josephine, and you are needed in the motherhouse. As you know, the sisters of our community are only getting older. They require more care and supervision than ever before."

Evelyn's heart sank. The motherhouse was essentially a nursing home for nuns, a holy hospice, stocked full of the type of cranky, conservative old women who were cold or even cruel to Evelyn when she first joined the convent. There would be Vatican I nuns who wished sisters still wore habits, kept their religious names, maintained silence, and stayed cloistered in convents. The place smelled of antiseptic and mothballs, and the hallways were peppered with elderly ladies, some bent over canes, others gripping walkers, their orthopedic shoes periodically squeaking against the linoleum floor. Working at the motherhouse meant wiping the asses of the cantankerous old-fashioned and then watching them croak. "What about at a hospital?"

"Your nursing license has long since expired."

"But there must be other social work I

could do? A homeless shelter? A foster home? A rehab facility? I can still make a difference out there." Her eyes searched Mother Superior's, begging.

"This *is* social work, and you *will* be making a difference. We have one hundred twenty women over the age of eighty-five who need you. The remaining seventy or so of us must work for a living to support the ones who can no longer earn an income. At sixty-nine, you have perhaps ten more working years in you. In our eyes, at least. But in the eyes of the world, you should have retired by now. No one will hire you at this age, Evelyn. Maybe an organization would take you on as a volunteer, but no one will pay you, and the sad fact is our order needs the wages. We have medical bills to pay, mouths to feed. Since you can't get a job, you must fill a position at one of our own organizations. The motherhouse has our only openings. We need women to administer drugs, clean bedpans, run errands, take the older sisters on walks, be on call in case of an emergency. That's where you three come in. I'm sorry, Evelyn. It isn't glamorous, but it is necessary."

"But Mother —" Evelyn grabbed her by the wrist.

Mother Superior looked down at their

contact and then back up at Evelyn. Her tone was soft but intentional. "The Lenten season is approaching. Consider this something to reflect on."

Evelyn dropped her hand back onto the bed. "I was already planning to give up sex for Lent."

"You shouldn't think of this placement as a negative thing, Evelyn. We are a family. Perhaps taking care of your elders will be a blessing. I know you and I will be grateful when a younger nun steps in to take care of us."

What younger nuns? Evelyn thought.

"I stopped by Mercy House on my way over here. The girls are doing fine. They wanted me to say hello. They are in awe of you. We all are," Mother Superior said. Then her phone rang the "Hallelujah" chorus. She angled the screen up so she could read the caller ID. "Sorry, Sister. I have to take this. May God speed your recovery," she said, and answered the phone as she left the room.

They are in awe of you. It was a nice idea, but Evelyn didn't know what wonder she really deserved. Yes, in the heat of the moment she took action, made a spectacle of herself, and with luck granted by God, it had worked. But people wouldn't be quite so amazed if her actions had an uglier, but equally likely, outcome. What if Angel's initial shots had killed Josephine or Maria? What if his bullet had busted the lock, and he forced himself in and onto the girls? What if her flamethrower had lit the place on fire? There was a fine line between a hero and hurting someone.

And she *had* hurt someone. Angel had died.

Plus, she'd been brave in the moment, fueled by adrenaline. But she'd failed to be brave with the bishop.

The room telephone blared at her bedside, startling her from her thoughts. "Hello?" she said, picking up the handset.

"Is this Sister Evelyn Fanning?" a male voice asked from the other end.

"Didn't your mother teach you to introduce yourself before asking questions?"

The man laughed. "She did, and I apologize. This is Derek Harding, a reporter from the *New York Times*. I've been covering the Vatican's apostolic visitation over the last couple months."

"I've read your work," Evelyn said. And she had. Any media coverage about the Vatican's investigation had been because of this reporter's initial interest and probing pieces. "I've enjoyed your articles."

"That's kind of you to say. I heard about you on the news this morning. I am a fan of your work as well. I was wondering if I could ask you a few questions, maybe bring my photographer along."

Evelyn's lips opened to reject the offer. She didn't want the attention, didn't want to worry about how grungy she'd look in a photo or how stupid she'd sound in a quote. But then, mouth agape, she stopped herself.

"I think we can arrange something. Can you stop by the hospital tomorrow at ten in the morning?"

Once Evelyn tracked down the bishop's cell phone number, she couldn't decide if it was surprise or displeasure that she detected in his tone.

"I was sorry to hear about your accident, Sister. Perhaps this is God's way of advising you to play by the rules," he said.

Judgment danced triumphantly behind his transparent veil of sympathy. She wanted to scream, to lambaste him. *God didn't shoot me, you arrogant piece of no-good, holier-than-thou, evil snake devil shit!* Instead, she said, "The *New York Times* would like a photo of the both of us. Can you stop by tomorrow morning?"

The bishop paused. She strained to hear a

hint of his train of thought. "I'm not sure any good would come from our meeting with a reporter."

Damn right. She tugged on her bedsheet. "I wasn't too thrilled about it myself, but the Church has gotten some bad press lately, especially regarding mistreatment of the sisters, and I thought we all might benefit from the media capturing a nun and a bishop smiling together. I might not be your biggest fan, but I still love the Church."

"Alleged mistreatment of nuns," he said. "And this reporter . . . he asked for me?"

Evelyn rolled her eyes. Typical, aroused by the lightest ego stroke. "He must have heard you are in town, and wants a quote from the bishop sent to New York by the cardinal."

"Perhaps it'd be best if you didn't talk to the media without my presence, anyway. What time, then?"

The hospital room had darkened after the setting sun, and the muted television affixed to the wall flickered on a rerun of *I Love Lucy.* She could almost hear the audience laugh track. Evelyn smiled. "Nine thirty."

The bishop arrived the next morning with his hair combed and slicked back. He carried a Starbucks cup in each hand. Did he

249

think a measly cup of coffee would be enough? A java-shaped olive branch? It was barely a whisper of goodness against the air horn of his wickedness.

Even so, she forced herself to say, "Thank you for the coffee, Bishop."

He instinctively pulled the cups into his chest. "The extra one is for the reporter." His eyes scanned the room until landing on the wall clock. "Ten minutes to spare until our appointment. I arrived a bit early to ensure you were not left unchaperoned."

An ember of rage burned in her stomach. "Then we have plenty of time for our discussion."

His attention had drifted up to the television, where an animated weatherman bounced before a map of the United States. A beat after she spoke, the bishop's gaze floated back to Evelyn and he blinked himself into the conversation. "Pardon me?"

She focused on the uneaten bowl of cereal on her bedside table, the cornflakes fat and limp with milk. "The reason I asked you here this morning was to strike a bargain."

His eyes narrowed. "Tread lightly, Sister. You're already on thin ice."

Nerves trembled in her belly and she took a deep breath to still them. "If you close Mercy House, I will tell this *Times* reporter what you did to me."

His mouth jerked, and with that movement something passed over his features — something like shame. He managed to steady himself, but not before Evelyn caught that fleeting regret, and the recognition of it twisted yarns of relief and revulsion together inside her. When he spoke, his tone was calculating. "And what, pray tell, did I do to you?"

"Don't play dumb."

"Sister, I can assure you I have no idea —"

Her eyes flashed up to his and her voice was full, despite a tremble. "This has been pressure-cooking inside me for years. If you make me say it, I swear to you, I will shout it."

He took a step closer. She didn't want to smell him, his sour breath and musty privilege. He leaned forward and she shrank away involuntarily. The cardiac monitor bleeped Evelyn's heart rate, and she feared it might quicken. His forehead wrinkled into four little rolls. The skin at the center was dry and flaked, perhaps from exposure to the winter air. His eyebrows were bushy with the odd long hair branching in the wrong direction.

"It wasn't just me in that room," he said,

his voice quavering, his eyes wild like those of a cornered animal about to fight. "We both committed a sin."

Evelyn searched his owlish features. Her voice was barely above a whisper when she said, "You can't really believe that."

He cleared his throat, flattened his shirt against his chest with one palm, and stepped back. "You think you are so clever. You think you've stored away this ace in the hole. Sister, your ace is nothing. I have an entire deck."

She licked her chapped lips and felt the soreness of a few thin slices where they'd split. She remembered Lucia's injured mouth, and the mouths of the many other women who'd arrived at Mercy House after men had tried to slap their words back down their throats. "I know what my secret is worth, and I am prepared to reveal it if you don't walk away from Mercy House."

He stepped closer. "I think you won't say a word."

"And why is that?"

A faint smile tickled the corners of his mouth. "Oh, Sister, you should know by now. I'm untouchable. But I promise you this. If you blab your big fat mouth, if you say one negative utterance about me, you'll destroy the life of Father John, a man with a history of, let's say, getting friendly with other priests."

"You are such a liar," Evelyn said, but her skin began to tingle, and her saliva tasted metallic.

"Am I? So he hasn't been seen in Astoria leaving the clergy house of Father Sal in the middle of the night? He wasn't caught at not one, but two retreats, literally with his pants around his ankles? He doesn't have pornography on the church's computer? He's a homosexual, Sister. A fairy. The Catholic Church has kept it quiet because he's also a valued priest. But if you say so much as one word against my good name, I promise you this: the Vatican will silence your claims. I am a bishop. Nothing will be done to me. But I will make Father John fall on the sword to divert attention. Testimony will be surfaced. Stories will be exaggerated. He'll be made to look depraved. A sex fiend. It doesn't take much these days for the media to latch onto a priest headline and run with it. He'll be humiliated first, and ultimately excommunicated. Is that what you want for your friend, Sister? Is that what you want to do to a decent man of God?"

Evelyn had noticed a bond between John and Sal. When they spoke, they bent toward each other, practically touching foreheads. And once, when John made a comment, Sal threw his head back with laughter, and John looked so pleased with himself, so proud for having amused his friend. Heat prickled her chest and her throat tightened. "You wouldn't do this."

"We both know I would."

Even if Father John was gay, what did it matter? Evelyn herself had had moments of temptation, was guilty of her own sins. They all were. He wasn't hurting anybody, and it didn't lessen his contributions as a priest. It certainly was no reason to dishonor a person, to excommunicate him. But she knew what the Catholic Church was capable of. And she knew what it was to live with shame. Father John didn't deserve that. "Please," she said.

And with that, the bishop knew he had her. He raised his coffee cups into a shrug. "You are the one making this decision, Sister. It is up to you."

Evelyn's breathing quickened. "I want you to get out."

"Sister —"

"Leave."

"I need to know we are in agreement."

"Yes, you've won. Okay? You are untouchable. Now get the hell out."

The bishop lowered his shoulders, relaxing. "I pray for your recovery, Sister. And here, since it seems I won't be seeing the reporter after all, enjoy this coffee — on me." He placed the cup on her bedside table.

He slipped through the doorway, but his memory remained as a sour taste in Evelyn's mouth. She listened to the sound of his loafers disappear down the hall. He had beaten her. He would always beat her. She had committed herself to a life of defenselessness. The life of a nun.

She remembered Holy Saturday of 1980, when a nun in Ohio had been slain: choked to death, stabbed in a ritualistic pattern, and then sexually violated. Her body was found in a sacristy — just like the one in which Evelyn had been repeatedly raped. Nobody was charged for her murder until 2006, when the state finally convicted her priest. The case had been reopened after two decades when that same priest was accused of ritualized sexual assault. It turned out he had been the prime suspect back in 1980 — the letter opener used to stab the nun was found in his office — but the church had so much influence on that community, and all the police investigators were Catholic, so the priest had been protected.

He, a murderer, continued to serve the community and congregation for over twenty years. He was finally convicted for the barbaric slaying, but sentenced to just fifteen years in prison, with the possibility of parole after ten. Only ten years of imprisonment for stabbing the nun with a letter opener thirty-one times, carving an inverted crucifix over her heart, and anointing her with her own blood. Only ten years for then defiling that nun, postmortem, with an altar cross.

Then there was the study submitted to the Vatican by Sister Maura O'Donohue in 1994. Twenty-nine nuns were impregnated in a single African congregation. Because the surrounding population had a high incidence of HIV, priests considered nuns safe from disease and raped them. In many cases, when a nun became pregnant, the priest insisted on an abortion. The study was supposed to remain confidential but was leaked in 2001. Nearly a decade after it became public, the Vatican still seemed to have done nothing about it.

Where was the justice? Where was God for those women?

Evelyn ran her hands up and down the hospital sheet that covered her legs. She thought of the first time Hawkins grazed his fingertips along her hip. If she'd slapped his hand away then, maybe it would have stopped. And when he heaved her habit above her waist, if she had screamed loud enough for somebody to hear, or if she had reported him after any of the following violations, maybe they would have punished him. Who knows how many men, women, or children he had hurt since then. Maybe she could have prevented it. But all evidence seemed to suggest, when it came to priests, the truth rarely mattered.

Evelyn pulled back her arm and smacked the Starbucks cup off the table. It crashed to the floor and spewed foam and creamy coffee across the tile below. While she seethed, the plastic lid floated like a stick in a river until the pool thinned and it stilled.

Evelyn watched the second hand tick around the face of the wall clock. The reporter was due any moment, and the pieces of her new plan were still arranging themselves in her mind. She couldn't fail — not again. The future of Mercy House women depended on her.

The man was scrawny, below average height, and bald, with ginger-brown hair rimming his head like a withered Christmas wreath. A leather messenger bag was strapped across his chest and perched on his hip.

"Derek Harding," he said as an introduction. He paused in confusion when he saw the spilled coffee, but sidestepped it and extended his hand.

Evelyn tucked her confrontation with the Hawk into a part of her brain she could access later. She couldn't reveal any hostility; she had to play the role of the sweet nun, the faithful and obedient servant, the do-gooder. She assembled her features into a welcoming expression. "How kind of you to stop in."

Derek wore perfectly round tortoiseshell glasses and a tartan shirt buttoned up to the throat. He gestured to a nearby chair and raised his eyebrows, asking permission. When Evelyn nodded her consent, he dragged the chair forward. After he took a seat, he pulled a notepad from his bag and balanced it on a crossed knee.

"Before we discuss the incident with Angel Perez, which of course I'm eager to hear about, was that Bishop Hawkins I just saw leaving the parking lot?"

The memory of the conversation rattled in its cage. Evelyn's mouth was dry and foul tasting, but her lips curved into a smile to disguise what was within. "It was."

"I know he's on the East Coast on behalf of Cardinal Rode to investigate nuns, in what some people are referring to as the nun-quisition. What was he doing here at the hospital?"

One negative utterance. One word against my good name.

She had to leave the truth of the Hawk out of it. She had to find another entry point. "Checking in on me. He's been quite attentive."

"Has he made his way to visiting your order yet?"

"He has."

"Has he stopped in to see you and the others at Mercy House?"

"Yes, we've all been blessed with his presence," she said, surprised by how convincingly she was able to mask her sarcasm.

He cocked his head to the side. "Don't you feel a sense of betrayal by the Catholic Church, or resentment in regard to your dealings with Bishop Hawkins?"

She blinked, innocent, doe-eyed. "Why on earth would I feel that way?"

"You've devoted your life to service, and in fact you've proven you're willing to lay your life down for your mission and your community. I just thought, for that reason, you might begrudge that the institution

259

you've given your life to is now investigating you as if you've done something wrong." He inched forward on his seat and leaned toward her. "You can be honest with me. Maybe I can help you. I'm not afraid of the Catholic Church."

Lucky you, Evelyn thought. She wondered where his passion for the Vatican visitation story came from; did Derek love Catholicism or hate it? Was he mentored by a priest and wanted to preserve the sanctity of the position, or was he abused by one? Was he tutored by nurturing nuns? Or did he have no experience with Catholicism, and viewed it as a fantasy that required debunking? Perhaps it didn't matter. Evelyn had spent a lifetime without an income, having to piece together scraps of life's cloth to make a workable quilt. She'd learned to be resourceful and, as she lay on the hospital bed, a hole gouged out of her hip, her home and purpose about to be yanked out from under her, Derek Harding was her only resource.

"You know, Mr. Harding," she said, "there may in fact be a way you can help me."

CHAPTER 16

On the drive to Mercy House from the hospital, Sister Maria sat beside Evelyn in the back of the taxi and clasped Evelyn's hand in her lap. The leather seats were split at the seams and revealed pale stuffing within. The car smelled like falafel and cinnamon sticks, which, after several days of bland hospital food, was not an unwelcome combination. They cruised through the streets of Clinton Hill — Bedford-Stuyvesant's attractive sister who went on to marry into money — while Maria hummed "Amazing Grace" absentmindedly. As they drove, the glow of streetlights blinked and highlighted Maria's face in soft halos. It struck Evelyn how angelic her friend looked and sounded, but before she let herself get sentimental, she tossed the notion up to her painkillers.

Leaves canopied Lafayette Avenue in every other season, but, in winter, the trees' skeletal branches rounded like a series of wedding arches. Snow blackened by exhaust hugged the curb. They passed the stone Cadman Congregational Church, so charming in its Romanesque style Evelyn thought it would be better suited in a forest than on a city street.

The driver slowed to a stop at a red light that burned in the darkness of evening, and the cane Evelyn had propped against the window fell on her knee. Back at the hospital, when Evelyn showed Maria her new accessory, Maria had said, "Don't you worry about its plainness. We'll doll it up with ribbons. Oh! We can Bedazzle it." Plainness was nowhere near the top of Evelyn's worry list.

On the next block was the Underwood Park playground, with swing sets, benches, and three jungle gyms constructed of hardy plastic and green metal poles — a far cry from Bed-Stuy parks, in which tree roots had raised walkways and loose screws made equipment a hazard for children. Once, it took the city almost four months to remove a fallen tree limb from a sandbox. Pristine three-story redbrick row houses sat opposite Underwood Park, the owners of which, Evelyn was sure, wouldn't be made to wait four months for anything.

The Bed-Stuy border was three blocks away now, and petite town houses with varying facades, like a collection of muted Easter eggs, were interrupted by twenty-five-story apartment buildings and ninety-nine-cent stores.

It felt good to be going home.

She prayed her new plan would work and that this place could remain home.

As they approached Chauncey Street, and the driver's hands crossed over one another to make the turn, Maria squeezed Evelyn's fingers tight enough that her bones scraped, and Maria's features puckered, as if she were trying to contain a sneeze. Before Evelyn could ask what in the world was going on, she saw for herself.

After the electric Christmas candles had been taken down, wrapped up, and set away for the following year, all the windows in all the houses up and down the block were relit. They looked like fireflies flickering in so many jars. Resplendent, like the glory of human goodness leading Evelyn home. It took her breath away.

"They did it for you," Maria said. "The girls, but the neighbors too. We all just wanted to share our gratitude."

Evelyn's eyes teared. She wondered if this was what it was like for a victim of abuse to find the magic of Chauncey Street during the holidays and wished she made the street glitter all year round. "This," she began, and cleared her throat of emotion in order to continue, "this really is something."

Maria also struggled to steady her voice. "I'm grateful we get the chance to see the street dressed in lights again. Back in December, we didn't know this Christmas was our last here."

Evelyn turned to her friend, whose cheeks glistened in the night. "We need to talk about that, about Mercy House closing."

Maria smiled and patted Evelyn's knee. "Not now. Tonight is a celebration."

Evelyn stabbed the asphalt with the foot of her cane and let Maria brace her elbow as she unloaded from the taxi. She paused at the bottom of Mercy House's stoop, intimidated by the task of climbing the stairs, but also caught off-guard by the oblong copper stain on the top step, where the concrete had absorbed her blood. She was reminded then that she had been shot, but her life had been spared. Her stare dropped to the sidewalk below them where she found a similar discoloration spotlighted by the streetlamp — Angel's blood.

"Ready?" Maria asked.

Instead of pressing down on her cane, she

leaned into her friend, although she could tell Maria struggled under the added weight.

"Welcome home, Sister," Joylette called from her fire escape, where she clasped a steaming mug close to her face. "It's good to see you on your feet."

Evelyn waved back. "It's good to be seen."

By the time they reached the front door, Evelyn was sucking air through her teeth. The ache radiated from her side; it was time for another pill and a nap before the fire. Maria patted her coat in search of her keys while Evelyn anticipated the smell of the house: muffins, hairspray, burning wood, and light sweat — a welcome change from the disinfectant of the hospital. When Maria finally located her keys, they jingled in the lock, and a smile tugged on her mouth.

"What's so funny now?" Evelyn asked.

Maria glanced up at her and puffed out her cheeks to mangle the grin. "A lot of things are funny."

Then she pulled open the door to reveal the residents huddled together on the other side, wearing party hats, blowing noisemakers, and holding up a makeshift banner of taped-together printer paper, each page a letter, that read "Our SHE-ro!"

"Surprise!" Josephine said from behind the crowd with a prim finger wave.

Evelyn clutched her pounding chest. "Mother of God, I didn't survive a shooting just to die of a heart attack."

For dinner they ate Evelyn's favorite meal: tomato bacon grilled cheese sandwiches with a side of overnight dill pickles from Simon's Brisket House in Crown Heights. The pickles were cucumber-green and crisp, and Evelyn savored their fresh salty brine alongside the grease and fat of the grilled cheese. Why was it that God made sin so heavenly?

"This won't do my figure any favors," Desiree said. She held a half-eaten sandwich in one hand and traced the side of her torso with the other.

"Now you can charge people extra. More bounce per ounce," Lucia said. Her face was almost entirely clear of bruising, and her hair, still wet from a shower, hung in ringlets and dampened the shoulders of her shirt. The waist of her sweatpants was rolled over twice so it circled her hips, exposing an inch of skin between her pants and her shirt. She opened a cabinet, grabbed a glass, filled it at the sink, and then took a seat beside Desiree — her new buddy, apparently. She looked comfortable in the kitchen of Mercy House, among the other women. She looked at home. This was usually one of Evelyn's most satisfying moments, when the once-defensive resident began to assimilate. It proved their system was working, that progress was being made, and that it was possible to heal, grow, and rehabilitate. This time, though, it proved exactly what was at stake — what she, and now Derek Harding, were fighting to save.

"Damn straight. I'm like a Cadillac. This ride is built for comfort." Desiree swiveled her hips and then took a comically large bite of her sandwich.

"More like a Lincoln Town Car. Room for the whole family," Lucia said and slapped Desiree's backside.

Desiree stuck a finger in Lucia's face. "I draw the line at the wrinkly asses of grandpas and grandmas." She stilled in her position and then rotated slowly toward where the nuns leaned against the counter. "No offense to you, Sisters."

"That was wildly inappropriate, Desiree," Josephine said, but without any conviction.

"Yes, it was. Because my ass still looks good," Evelyn added. After a beat of stunned silence, the girls broke into laughter.

"Besides, how many grandmas do you know who would do what Sister did?"

Katrina asked in her high-pitched voice. Her spine curved, as it typically did when she spoke in a group. But her eyelids, streaked with vibrant purple, suggested a different sort of confidence. Her grilled cheese was torn into pieces and scattered across her plate. She was more of a carrot sticks and couscous eater.

Desiree gestured emphatically toward Katrina. "True, true." Her enthusiastic affirmation inspired Katrina to straighten slightly. "Homegirl is more like Sarah Connor from *The Terminator*."

"Or Ripley from *Alien*," Esther added.

Mei-Li brightened at the opportunity to apply her breadth of film knowledge. "Or Lara Croft."

"Or Dirty Harry," Maria piped in. Then she raised her hand like a gun and pointed it at Josephine, who stepped back uncomfortably. Maria squinted and said with a gravelly voice, " 'You've gotta ask yourself one question: "Do I feel lucky?" Well, do you, punk?' " Pleased with herself, a giggle bubbled up from her belly, and the edges of her smile were almost lost in her round cheeks.

Desiree shook her hand in the air, as if to clear the Dirty Harry impression like she was erasing a drawing on an Etch A Sketch.

"Fuck Dirty Harry. He's a racist."

Maria raised her eyebrows and promptly lowered her handgun. "I didn't realize that. My apologies."

While Evelyn wished she could enjoy the praise, her attention strayed to poor Lucia, whose ex-lover had been the villain in this presumed action sequence. She chewed a pickle with slow, deliberate crunches and stared at a pile of ketchup on her plate.

Evelyn clapped her hands together. "Enough about me. Catch me up on you. I see Desiree and Lucia made fast friends. What else have I missed around here?" Katrina raised her hand up by her shoulder, and Evelyn urged her on. "Go ahead. This isn't fourth period history class."

Katrina smiled and tucked her hand back down by her side. "Well, Mei-Li has some news," she said, and turned to her left, where she found her friend blushing. Katrina gripped her earbuds and tugged them gently against her neck. "Sorry. I didn't mean to embarrass you. It's just that we're so proud, and Sister will be excited."

Evelyn waited for Mei-Li to divulge the information, but when she only sat in her chair, smiling awkwardly, Evelyn prompted her. "Well?"

Mei-Li met Evelyn's gaze. Her smile was

tight. "I got the receptionist job I applied for."

"Hey, that's wonderful!" Evelyn held her hand out for a high-five, which Mei-Li obliged, although somewhat languidly. "Aren't you happy?"

"Yes, happy," she nodded, but her fingers clamped the chair's seat at her sides, perhaps fighting off the compulsion to spring up and away, to find a secluded place to spew her trilingual profanities. "And terrified."

Evelyn stepped forward. She felt protective, as if one of her young had caught the eye of a predator. "What scares you?"

Mei-Li glanced around the room, uneasy to be at the center of attention. "The doctors at the practice seem perfectly nice, but what if they aren't? And what about any male patients? What if someone reminds me of him, my uncle? I'm worried having a job will mean I can support myself and you'll tell me I should go out on my own, but what if I'm scared after work and I come home to nobody?" Her voice became strained, and she dabbed her eyes with her sweatshirt sleeves. "I don't want to be scared, but I am. I don't want to be alone, but I will be. And I don't want to leave here yet."

Evelyn knew fear was a weed, a thorny

vine that wrapped itself around your limbs. It paralyzed you from the outside and then entrenched itself in your insides, digging through your skin, stretching and coiling in your guts until it strangled your organs. And although it was impossible, she wished more than anything that she could wrestle Mei-Li's fear on her behalf, prune it back, and untangle it from her heart and lungs so that she could breathe freely once again.

"It's okay to be afraid," Esther said, reaching across the table to place her hand on top of Mei-Li's. Her thumb stroked Mei-Li's knuckles and her voice was soothing. "I'm afraid too. But do not worry. They won't kick you out of Mercy House. Isn't that right, Sisters?"

"My poor dears, Mercy House is closing!" The confession burst from Sister Maria, and then she covered her mournful face with her hands. She turned to Josephine and separated her fingers just enough to see through them. "I'm sorry, I know we agreed to make tonight a celebration, but I just couldn't keep it in any longer."

Josephine rolled her eyes. "Yes, who could have expected you to withstand such intense interrogation?"

"We're closing?" Mei-Li's small voice shot above the stunned expressions of the resi-

dents, surprisingly charged, a small explo-
sion.

"It's because of that jizz-face bishop,"
Desiree said and slapped the table. The
corkscrew coils of her hair vibrated and the
dishes clattered, causing Katrina to wince
and grab both of her earbuds in tight fists.

"Woah, woah," Evelyn said and pushed
her palms out against the swelling strife.
"There has been talk of closing Mercy
House, yes, but nothing is official yet. And
I'm not going to let that happen. I promise
you. I have a plan."

Sister Maria dried her eyes with her
sleeves. "You do?"

Lucia folded her arms over her chest and
popped a hip. "You might be hot shit with a
Lysol can, but when it comes to Bishop Bi-
cho Pequeño, your plans have been pretty
lame so far."

"That may be true. But hear me out." Evelyn felt the energy of her proposition like an
electric current beneath her skin. "A journalist has agreed to run a piece about Mercy
House in the *New York Times*. As far as he
knows, the church is closing us down because they can't afford to run our operation. And that's all he needs to know. He's
coming in the morning to interview you
girls and share your stories — anonymously,

272

of course — in an effort to raise money. Between food, utilities, property taxes, and insurance, that's what? Two thousand dollars a month? Twenty-four thousand to keep us open for a year? We can raise that. We just need to brainstorm a fundraiser or two the public can get behind and advertise the hell out of it. Even if we don't raise it, even if we don't come close, the money isn't really the point. Once the public is on our side, working to keep this place afloat, rooting for us, the Church can't get away with being against us."

"Raise our voices so that, if silenced, the community will hear the difference," Josephine said, nodding.

"I only know one good way to make money, but I'm happy to teach ya'll." Desiree gripped her chin and surveyed the other residents, nodding, assessing. "With this group, we can make twenty-four thousand in a weekend. We got almost every type of fetish."

Evelyn patted Desiree's back. "I applaud your enthusiasm, Des," she said. "But let's keep brainstorming."

CHAPTER 17

February 16, 2010
MERCY HOUSE, A LIFELINE FOR
MANY, NOW NEEDS SAVING

It looks like any other brick row house in the neighborhood. If you weren't searching for the angel doorknocker, its signature piece, you might miss it entirely. In fact, you could live in Bedford-Stuyvesant your entire life, you could walk down Chauncey Street every day on your way to work, and never know it existed. That's how unassuming Mercy House — a haven for any woman who needs it — is.

Mercy House was founded in 1984 by three nuns of the Sisters of St. Joseph of Mercy. Since then, it has served hundreds of women in search of safety and rehabilitation through its open-door policy.

As Sister Evelyn described it, "We strive to remind these incredible women, though

274

they were victims of violence or emotional abuse, that that is not their identity. They are strong. They've been through the worst life can throw at you and survived. They can handle anything now. Their potential is limitless. Though their pasts cannot be changed, their future is up to them."

Sister Maria added, "And we spoil them when we can — my cookies are a house favorite, if I do say so myself. Our residents have suffered and they are such beautiful souls. They deserve every last chocolate chip."

But due to a shrinking attendance, and with it, donors, the Catholic Church is struggling to keep facilities like Mercy House afloat. The sisters of Mercy House and its current residents have only one month to raise their operational costs — a whopping $24,000 — before the church must repurpose the house into a more affordable, or perhaps even lucrative venture.

"I don't blame the Church," said Sister Josephine. "If they don't have the money, they don't have the money. It's just a shame to imagine all of this good work coming to an end, especially if it can be prevented."

And so, in order to continue its 25-year tradition of silently serving the community, Mercy House is finally speaking up and asking for something in return: the financial and moral support of Bedford-Stuyvesant, Brooklyn, and beyond.

But as Denise*, a current resident of Mercy House, noted, "Nothing in this world comes free. We know that, so we ain't about to go around asking for handouts. We aren't beggars. In fact, I myself am an entrepreneur, so I'm looking at this like a business. What can we provide that is so valuable, people with deep pockets want to throw money at it?"

Melissa*, another resident, continued, "As a group, we strategized a three-pronged approach to our fundraising effort, which we thought was fitting. Like the Trinity, you know? We'll all play our part, capitalize on our skill sets. The sisters have encouraged us all along to identify our own strengths. That hasn't come easy to me, and doesn't come easy to a lot of women who have experienced what we've experienced. But I'm getting better. And since I can acknowledge that I'm orga-

*Names have been changed to protect the identities of the individuals.

nized, I'll manage the project."

Denise jumped back in to share her part. "I'm director of marketing, of course. Not employing this mouth would be a wasted resource, especially since the sisters refuse to use some of my other talents. But I also thought up one of those prongs my girl Melissa mentioned. See, I'm kind of an expert on local playgrounds; I know they're hella bootleg, especially in Bed-Stuy. So for every $10 raised, I'll spend an hour pulling weeds, cleaning litter, sanding splinters from equipment, planting flowers. Beautifying the [expletive] out of it. I don't get on my knees and sweat for nothing. When I do, I mean business. If people pledge enough, by the time I'm done with Bed-Stuy playgrounds, I promise, you'll swear you're in Brooklyn Heights."

The second fundraising effort is being designed and executed by a teenager by the name of Kelly*. "When my mind is going places I don't want it going, my hands distract it by knitting. I'm knitting all day long. I know the bamboo, herringbone, and tree of life stitches. I can basketweave and diamond honeycomb. I knit until my fingers ache and my back tightens from so many hours hunched over the work. I knit until I feel everywhere but my feelings. This hobby might cause early-onset arthritis, but at least my mind will be at ease — and I'll never be short a scarf! Given all the beanies and mittens piling up in my room, so many I started stuffing them into pillowcases and sleeping on them, it seemed natural to offer them up in order to save Mercy House. So there will be knitwear for every part of your body, in every size and color of the rainbow, in every stitch I'm fluent in, available for purchase — if you're interested and like what you see, that is."

The last of their so-called trinity of prongs is the contribution of Elise*, a Mercy House resident and immigrant from the Caribbean. She said, "The sisters administer to us in a variety of ways, but one of Sister Maria's favorite techniques is through baking. I've learned there is something healing about every step in the process: combining dry ingredients and mixing in wet ones; preheating the oven; waiting while everything solidifies inside and the sweet scent spreads throughout the house, calling each of us down to the kitchen; the warmth of the item in your hands; the pleasure of finally indulging with one another. There is comfort in its simplicity and joy. I'd like to apply what

I've learned from Sister Maria in order to help Mercy House, with a cultural addition. I revisit my home country when I cook the food of its people, and I offer a taste of it to those who have never visited by sharing its flavors. In addition to pledging for an hour of Denise's playground work or buying a one-of-a-kind Kelly craft, you can also order a box of homemade Haitian treats, including tablet cocoye, a crunchy coconut cookie; *konparet,* a ginger, coconut, and cinnamon sweet bread; and bonbon sirop, a dark sugarcane and spice cake. The good people at Rite Spice Caribbean Restaurant have agreed to deliver on our behalf."

And finally, the newest resident of Mercy House, Lydia*, will provide the platform for donating and purchasing. "I took this class once in high school, back when I was still going every day, before I realized it was kind of a waste of my time. I mean, who needs to know what year some old as [expletive] king in some country no one cares about created a tax that pissed off his people? When am I ever going to use that random fact in real life? You think people ask about that kind of thing on the B23? Anyway, the class was called web design or something like that. We had to make fake sites as a final project. The teacher was nice, but she was right out of college and kind of a pushover, so we all built sites to sell drugs or guns or some other illegal [expletive], just to rile her up. It was funny, but I learned something too. So I'm in charge of building the website and running the books. There's a lot of stuff I don't know, but you can learn almost anything from YouTube. That's where I learned how to contour your chest with foundation to make everything look a size bigger. My mom loves that trick. Anyway, visit Save MercyHouse.com. And don't be cheap."

"Listen to them. Aren't they incredible?" Sister Evelyn said.

If you believe in the mission of Mercy House and would like its doors to remain open, you have one month to support its cause. And, in the words of Lydia, don't be cheap.

CHAPTER 18

The morning the *Times* was scheduled to publish the article, Evelyn was at the newsstand first thing, and arrived back at Mercy House to the girls' chatter in the kitchen. They were awake earlier than usual, pouring orange juice and boiling water for tea while Esther fried eggs and Lucia took orders for the extent of her cooking expertise: wheat bread, toasted or untoasted.

When the front door closed behind Evelyn, Desiree scurried down the hall, her hands reaching for the paper. "Are we famous yet? Are there photographers outside?"

Evelyn surrendered the goods. "Yeah, I just fended off the advances of Russell Crowe."

Desiree studied Evelyn, her lips pursed. Then she flicked her wrist and snatched the paper. "Now I know you're lying. No one alive would fend off Mr. Crowe."

Back in the kitchen, Desiree read the article out loud, and impersonated each of the nuns and residents as she recited their quotations. When she used her airy voice for Katrina's portion, Katrina whispered to Mei-Li, "Do I really sound like that?" and Mei-Li shook her head, although she did.

Esther reassured her, "Don't worry. She made me sound Jamaican."

There wasn't time to bask in the warmth of their newly acquired stardom. They had work to do, and they knew it.

After breakfast, everyone broke off to tackle her own task. Esther zested a lime for konparet; Katrina set up Maria and Josephine for their first knitting projects; Desiree and Lucia, their faces lit by the glow of a laptop screen, finalized SaveMercyHouse.com; and Mei-Li discussed tasks with each branch, created a calendar of deadlines, and taped it to a kitchen cabinet.

And though she should have been delighted by the camaraderie and dedication, Evelyn sensed him coming like a thunderstorm. It wouldn't be long now.

The bishop barged in just before ten o'clock that morning. Evelyn had disabled the door alarm so he wouldn't startle the women, but they were alerted of his presence when he collided with the coatrack she'd shifted into his path. The women and girls stilled and looked at one another.

"It's all right," Evelyn said. "The word is out. What can he do now?"

The bishop was breathless when he reached the kitchen. His overcoat was open, revealing a black clergy shirt and white collar, stained by a spot of coffee, perhaps. Evelyn wondered who removed spots from his vestments now. She hoped it was him; she hoped the bleach burned his fingers.

His hands were empty, though she knew he clutched the newspaper in spirit — that's why he was there.

Father John emerged from behind the bishop and lifted his palm in a sheepish greeting. That, she wasn't expecting. Although it made perfect sense. With Father John present, there was so much Evelyn couldn't say.

The bishop's nostrils flared with every inhale. "It is time for confession."

Something else she didn't expect. It seemed the bishop could still surprise her after all. "Now?" St. Joseph of Mercy Church normally didn't hold confession hours on Tuesdays.

There were eight other people in the room, but he spoke as if only to her. "I told you you'd return to the sacraments. That begins this instant."

Evelyn gestured to the women, mid-task. "I'm afraid now is not a good time. We are in the middle of important work. Maybe you heard we are raising funds to keep Mercy House open."

The sleeves of his coat ended just above his knuckles; he gripped his hands into fists. "I insist."

"Surely you can spare an hour for confession, Sister. It's a sacred sacrament, after all." Father John's features were waxy. He scratched his temple in such a way that she knew he didn't have a physical itch, just a persisting anxiety. Evelyn wondered what he thought of the newspaper article published that morning, and what the conversation was like that led the bishop to storm their row house, Father John reluctantly in tow.

Evelyn knew what the bishop was after with this strategy; he wasn't as slick as he thought. Inside a confessional booth, she'd feel the pressure of thousands of years of tradition, the pressure of her faith, the pressure of her life's vows, to be truthful. It was as close as the bishop could get to interrogation with a lie detector.

Though she didn't want to be subjected to such scrutiny, and she was disgusted that the Hawk would use a sacrament as a manipulation tactic, more than anything else, she wanted him out of her kitchen, away from the residents it was her duty to protect. She thought of a pet rabbit she had as a girl, an adorable four-pound Holland Lop with floppy brown ears and matching speckles around its nose. Evelyn named her Easter. It was a timid little thing that froze whenever it was held by anybody but Evelyn. One night, her father came home drunk, as he often did. Evelyn was only twelve, but even then she knew she would be a nun and could never have children of her own. She was cradling Easter, singing her an Irish lullaby her dad used to sing. Across the apartment, her father stumbled and knocked into the china cabinet that held their mismatched dishes. It crashed to the floor, shattering the glasses and ceramic ware. Easter's little chest was shaped like the prow of a ship, and beneath the fur and fragile sternum, her tiny heart hammered, as if fighting wildly to escape its anatomical cage. Evie cooed and stroked her ears. She knew Easter was terrified by the clangor, but she didn't know that, inside the palm of her hand, Easter was having a heart attack. Her rabbit died sometime that night.

In the kitchen, Evelyn was aware of her

heart beating, could feel it overworking; she thought she could hear it too, and hoped it wasn't loud enough for the bishop to realize how much he scared her.

She rolled her shoulders back and stood as tall as her squat form would allow. "I'd be happy to confess my sins. Penance is cleansing. It frees the spirit. We all should admit when we've done something wrong, don't you agree, Bishop?"

Father John's expression relaxed, but the bishop's smile was a tight fissure. "Through confession, the prodigal daughter returns to God."

"I will go with you, Sister." Esther spoke as solemnly as a loyal soldier, and wiped flour against the legs of her apron.

Maria struggled to untangle her fingers from the cat's cradle of her yarn. "Me too. I'm not too proud to admit gluttony has gotten the best of me this week. Month, really."

Desiree clicked her tongue against the roof of her mouth and leaned into the computer screen. "Shit, I've got work to do."

There was a chill in the sanctuary, a feeling of exposed stone. Although Evelyn had bundled in her Mets sweatshirt, coat, and a bulky scarf and hat set Katrina had knit for her, Evelyn shivered.

She loved the act of confession, or rather, she loved how it felt to have confessed, to kneel before God and admit all the ways in which she'd fallen short. And to be freed of those failings. To be forgiven was to be loved. Although the bishop's remark had dripped with sarcasm, she did view the act as one of a daughter supplicating before her father. A father who loved her purely and unconditionally.

But to be supplicant before the bishop, to balance the scales of lying — considered work of the devil — in God's house, inside a confessional of all places, designed for profession and atonement, while still protecting Mercy House . . . that would be something else entirely.

The bishop's footsteps echoed down the aisle ahead of the group.

Father John touched her elbow. Perplexity dug lines across his forehead. "Did you knowingly lie to the press, Sister?" he whispered.

Her dry lips separated, on the edge of a reply. But then she turned from him and followed the bishop.

The seventeenth-century confessional box was intricately carved from oak and stained dark brown. The priest's box was in the center, enclosed by a half door at the bottom, like one found at the end of a bar, and a fern-colored velvet curtain on top. The box was bookended by two penitent booths covered by long curtains, one for a parishioner in the midst of confession, and one for the parishioner on deck, who was meant to wait in a state of prayer and contemplation. This system was designed hundreds of years ago. Now, only two percent of Catholics attended confession on a regular basis; there was rarely a line, rarely a parishioner in either stall, never mind both.

Before she entered the left booth, Evelyn unwrapped her scarf and placed it and her hat on a nearby pew. She didn't want to bring Katrina's precious work with her, inside with him. Maria genuflected and crossed herself before sliding into a pew. Esther nodded at the sanctuary, acknowledging God, and followed Maria. They would be there, outside the booth. They would be there.

Evelyn used the bottom of her cane to nudge the curtain aside.

Inside the confessional the air smelled stale, like so many years of uttered sins, so many assigned penances. So many souls forgiven who went on to sin again.

The curtain effectively blocked daylight; it

was always the same time of day in a confessional. She knew the interior by heart. Normally, she dropped onto the red velvet of the kneeler. But that day, she sat on the bench; she would not lower herself before him.

She could make out the profile of his face behind the wooden grate that separated them. She could hear his ragged breathing behind it.

Evelyn waited for his greeting, the typical encouragement to trust in God. He remained silent, so she drew an invisible cross over her body. "Bless me, Father," she said, her voice strained, "for I have sinned. It has been five weeks since my last confession."

"Confess then. It is the only way to be absolved."

Had the bishop confessed his sins all those years ago? Did another holy man absolve him?

"I've been jealous of those who can walk without pain. I've been lazy; I slept until almost eight o'clock yesterday. I've hated my neighbor. And" — Evelyn paused, unsure if she should continue the way she was going. They both knew what he wanted to hear, and what was the point in pretending it wasn't true? — "And I lied to the newspaper reporter," she said. The bishop quieted on the other side of the divider, as if he was holding his breath. "I-I told him Mercy House has been open for twenty-five years, but really it's been twenty-six." She hurried into her closing prayer. "My God, I am sorry for my sins with all my heart. In choosing to do wrong and failing to do good, I have sinned against you whom I should love above all things. I firmly intend —"

The bishop interrupted her, sounding choked, "Those were all venial sins, Sister. I think you are forgetting a mortal sin. The gravest violation of God's law. If you do not confess it, you condemn yourself to hell."

"I've committed a mortal sin? That is news to me."

"You've insulted the Church, soiled its reputation, and therefore insulted God himself. Blasphemy. It is a crime against your faith."

"I don't see it that way."

"If you do not confess, I cannot offer penance, and your sins cannot be forgiven."

"I guess I'll take my chances." Evelyn cupped her knees with her palms and prepared to push herself to her feet, through the inevitable sear at the place the bullet had so recently ruptured her skin. But as she leaned forward, and her face passed

290

before the screen, the bishop propelled forward so only the thin grate separated them, his purple-larva lips almost kissing the wood. She gasped at his sudden presence. When he spoke, he hissed, and she felt the wet heat of his words.

"Now that you've launched this little PR campaign, you think you're safe. You think I can't touch you. But I can, and I will. I promise you that. What you've done at Mercy House is despicable. A disgrace to your vows. If other nuns see you go unpunished, they'll think they can get away with anything, toss doctrine aside at their whim. I won't allow that."

She recoiled from him involuntarily. "Why don't you just let this go? Haven't you punished me enough?"

His finger jabbed the grate and his words sounded as if they'd been dragged through gravel. "It was your responsibility to maintain custody of your eyes. But you taunted me. You begged for it, you whore." His next inhale rattled. "If you refer to that time again, Sister, and try to rewrite history, Father John will be ruined. So shut your fat disgusting mouth. And end this Mercy House nonsense or I will end it for you."

The curtain whipped across the priest compartment; the half door opened and then thudded shut. While the click of his heels reverberated off the cathedral ceilings, getting further from her with every step, Evelyn closed her eyes and leaned back against the wood of her booth. Her hand trembled as she lifted it to her chest and felt the wild palpitation of her heart; she had to remind herself that women did not die from fear alone.

CHAPTER 19

Each morning, the residents of Mercy House woke with purpose. They didn't groan against the sun streaming through the blinds. They didn't turn over and pull their covers tight against their shoulders. They rose. They brushed their teeth and brewed coffee. They got to work. Because there were sweaters to knit, dough to knead, orders to fulfill, gardens to weed, playground equipment to sand, accounts to balance, and marketing messages to post on social media platforms. And there was only so much time.

Each night, when they nodded off on the living room armchairs before a fire, or when they laid their worn bodies down in bed, their minds ticked through all that had been accomplished that day, and all there was still to do the next.

They were raising money. Lots of it. By the third week, they'd raised almost twenty thousand dollars, nearly hitting their goal — mostly as a result of donations made by people around the country, around the world, even. But more important than the funds was the effect the process and their success was having on the residents. Evelyn could see it in the way they held their bodies. Their arms fell from their chests. They stood tall, open — vulnerable. They laughed without tucking their chins. They touched one another on the knee, hand, or back. They talked to strangers. They joked more readily, expressed ideas, and took initiatives, risks of the heart. They were becoming more confident. This new mission — it was healing them.

But the money was important too. Evelyn was certain, inside their one-month deadline, they'd earn enough to fund Mercy House operations costs for the year. With that in the bank, how could the Catholic Church publicly justify shutting them down?

She felt like her shoulders had been hitched up since the bishop arrived, and the fact of the money earned was almost enough to make her neck muscles unclench. But then she'd hear his growl from the other side of the confessional booth. *End this Mercy House nonsense or I will end it for you.*

And the fibers of her muscles constricted almost tight enough to choke her.

Mother Superior's text arrived on the eve of their last fundraising day.

They were in the kitchen, sipping sparkling cider out of chipped mugs, celebrating having officially exceeded their goal.

Desiree had her arm slung over Mei-Li's shoulders and was drinking the last dregs of cider straight from the bottle. "I used to think this girl should hook. She'd clean up with those Asian-fetish horndogs on Wall Street. But the CEO of this fundraiser shouldn't hook. Girl should run Wall Street."

The last batch of Esther's delicacies was baking in the oven, filling the room with honeyed warmth, like the girls and sisters were living inside a cooling gingerbread house. Maria was wrapped proudly in the scarf she'd finally finished, which Katrina had encouraged her to keep for all her hard work, but they all knew the real reason was that it was unsellable, oblong and patchy with dropped stitches. Lucia intermittently pressed the refresh button on the Mercy House website and announced when another donation trickled in. She'd so enjoyed launching and running the site, she said she might even go back to school, or at least take the GED test so she could enroll in a community college course on web design.

Evelyn lifted a spoon and was about to tap it against the ceramic of her "What Would Jesus Brew?" mug, about to launch into a speech about the impressive talents, dedication, and growth of each of the young women in the room, when her phone buzzed in her jeans.

Mother Superior was programmed into Evelyn's phone as "Big Momma." The message read: "Turn on Channel 2. Now."

The buzz ricocheted around the room as the other sisters received and read the same text. They looked at one another, and Evelyn could see her own concern reflected back at her.

The television was on a table in the corner of the living room. Evelyn felt like her stomach contained choppy waters. She gripped the remote and punched the set on while the sisters gathered beside her. The residents, bewildered, followed close behind.

There he was, the Hawk, on the local news, bent over a three-headed microphone, wearing a black house cassock with a magenta-trimmed shoulder cape and buttons encased in matching silk, a zucchetto, and a heavy chain with a crucifix the size of a man's hand lying on his chest.

The red banner at the bottom of the screen read, "Bishop Announces Sale of Local Shelter Mercy House to Save International Orphanages."

"Holy shit," Mei-Li whispered behind Evelyn.

And she was right. He was a steaming piece of holy shit.

"It gives me no pleasure to report that the church must sell Mercy House. While it has been an indispensible service to this community for just over twenty-five years, our resources are being called elsewhere. There are ten orphanages throughout Latin America at risk of closing. They desperately need funds, and the sale of Mercy House will allow us to save these orphanages from the brink. We will be able to continue housing and placing thousands of God's children from third-world countries like Nicaragua, Honduras, Guatemala, and Ecuador," he said, pronouncing the names with an exaggerated Spanish accent. "Although we are saddened to see this chapter of our outreach closing, it is for the greater good, and the women of Mercy House understand that." From the television screen, he peered straight into their living room, and Evelyn felt the pierce of his stare, as if he were speaking directly to her. With this broadcast, he was seeing her PR campaign and raising it to another, heart-wrenching level. Ten orphanages to her one women's shelter. Camera flashes blinked and shutters sounded like window blinds being suddenly dropped.

"We applaud the women for their hard work raising money the last month, but unfortunately they did not raise nearly enough to match the price of the house. The funds they did raise will be used to place the current residents in alternate housing, and they've generously agreed to donate the rest to the children of our Catholic orphanages."

"Like hell we did." Desiree's objection pealed at the top of her register. "I'm homeless too."

Evelyn's mouth dried. The Hawk had let the young women in her care apply all their passion, all their hopes, into fundraising for an entire month, knowing he could sell the house whether or not they succeeded. In fact, he probably viewed their success as all the more satisfying; now he could show them just how little their hard work mattered — just how little *they* mattered.

The row house would be sold out from under them. Now, rather than being repurposed as a Church mission, used as a home for children whose mothers were imprisoned, or to shelter, feed, and nurture homeless families, Mercy House would be peddled to the highest bidder. It would be converted into cash, and she knew just how the Catholic Church often allocated their cash. The sale could be used to support the lavish lifestyles of so many holy men, with their fancy cars, watches, rings, and vacation retreats, a penchant for luxury reinforced by their top gun, the boss, Pope Benedict XVI — the Prada Priest, named for his infamous bloodred loafers. Or worse, in a matter of months, Mercy House could be used to silence the cry of victims abused by priests, or to retain lawyers who defended pedophiles and other dangerous men camouflaged by sacred vestments. Men like the one glowing on the screen in Evelyn's living room.

The thought of her Mercy House being closed by wicked men, and liquidated to subsidize their bad habits, made outrage swell in Evelyn like rising floodwaters. She didn't see an escape. She was helpless against the tide; she would surely drown.

Her thumb jabbed the power button and the television winked black.

■ ■ ■ ■

Evelyn dreamed she was being chased down the street of her childhood home; she recognized it from the decorative cornices topping the three-story buildings and the trolley tracks at the end of the block. The street was deserted, empty of pedestrians, cars, or any other signs that people had inhabited the apartments in the recent past. Evelyn was dropped into the scene mid-chase. She didn't know what she had done to anger her perpetrator, or who he even was, but she knew he was only several feet behind her, and she was petrified. Her legs gave out from under her. She fell to the concrete, and her body became paralyzed. She couldn't push herself up. She couldn't crawl forward. She couldn't even scream for help. She was frozen. Helpless. Then his fingers laced through her hair.

The dream cut to Mercy House. Its rooms were vacant — shadowed, dusty, and frigid. She was troubled by the absence of the house's inhabitants. She searched the first floor and then the second, screaming the names of the residents and the nuns, but nobody answered. She climbed into the attic and found it bare, save for a note taped to a plank in the middle of the floor. She knew the note explained what had occurred in the house, but she couldn't read what it said. All she understood was that they were gone, all of them.

The final scene was in the convent in upstate New York where she trained to be a nun. She sat cross-legged on the floor in the darkened visitation room. Before her was a small crowd of people seated in chairs. Their faces were too shadowed to recognize, but their presence was both familiar and strange. She felt their anger, and suspected they were members of her family. "Why are you here? What do you want from me?" she asked. "You abandoned me. I was hurt and you didn't see it. You didn't see me. I'm the one who should feel wronged." And when no one responded, she begged, "Say something!" She felt judgment emanating from them, pricking her like so many fishing hooks slicing through the surface of a lake. Finally, one silhouette rose from its seat. Her heart palpitated; she simultaneously dreaded the person's words and was desperate for them. As she anticipated the message, she leaned forward and her lips parted. "And what did you do?" a voice asked. It didn't sound like her father, but somehow she knew it was him. Then all the figures disappeared at once. The chairs were suddenly empty.

Evelyn gasped herself back into consciousness. Adrenaline coursed through her veins and dread swam in her stomach. Her eyelids were fat with tears and the fine skin at her temple stuck lightly to her pillowcase.

As she shifted in bed, the flesh of her underarm scraped against something sharp. Confused, she patted around her sheets and unearthed the foreign object, the crucifix that had hung over her bed for so many years. She remembered, then, eyeing it before turning in the night before. She'd unhooked it from the wall and brought it into bed with her. Wooden nails protruded from Christ's hands and feet, there were deep slices in his torso where he was whipped, and a crown of thorns bloodied his head. She'd nestled into her pillow and gazed into the agonized face of Jesus, head hanging with eyes cast toward the heavens.

She clutched the crucifix to her chest and stared at the dark shapes dancing across her ceiling like shadow puppets expressing the story of a battle. She gazed down at Jesus dying in her arms and stroked his bloodied face. "I know what you're thinking. Enough bellyaching and self-pity. 'I can do all this through him who gives me strength.' That

302

includes kicking the ass of an asshole."

It was three in the morning, but sleep didn't feel as important as it used to. She tugged her Mets sweatshirt over her head and tiptoed down the hall so as not to wake anybody.

Downstairs, a soft light emanated from the kitchen.

"What are you doing awake?" she asked Lucia, who was bowed over the laptop, her new altar, and the only source of light on downstairs. "I admire your work ethic, but I'm afraid tinkering with that website is wasted effort now."

Without looking, Lucia reached her hand inside the gaping mouth of a bag of Lay's, a provision they'd kept in constant supply since her arrival, pulled out a handful of chips, and crunched down on them. "It's not that," she said from around her mouthful.

"What, then?"

Lucia chewed, swallowed, and then her chin lifted to Evelyn; for the first time, her eyes weren't edged with thick black lines. She wasn't wearing any makeup at all, in fact. Her face looked scrubbed clean. A fresh start. She was beautiful. "I was thinking. My *tío* Adolfo? He's a real dickhead, but he's also kind of a genius. He's been living up here a long time, even longer than my mom, and he's never paid a dime on rent. Not a dime. He just wanders around, looking for empty spots, and when he finds one, he moves in. When the landlord finally realizes someone broke the locks and is camped out, Adolfo says he's a tenant who just hasn't paid rent. Everyone knows he's a piece of shit intruder who got way too comfortable, but, by then, there's no difference. It's the same fucking thing. It's mad expensive to evict a tenant because you have to get lawyers and go to court, so the landlords end up paying my good-for-nothing tío to leave a house he shouldn't have been in in the first place. One sucker paid forty grand to get his ass out. Adolfo took the cash, moved into an empty apartment across the street, and didn't work a day that year." Lucia leaned against the back of her chair and crossed her arms over her chest. "We're already here, Sister. If we decide to stay, how are they gonna force us out?"

"Lucia," Evelyn said, lifting her eyes to the ceiling and shaking her head. "You've inherited at least one quality from your uncle. You're kind of a genius too." She dragged a chair around to share a view of the screen. "Move over."

They spent hours researching squatters' rights in New York City. At around five o'clock, Esther descended the stairs, put a kettle on for tea, and set out sliced bananas for snacking while Lucia rested her head in her arms and took a brief nap.

Evelyn explained her understanding of the laws to Esther, to get her perspective as well as to hear the thoughts out loud, to test them against her own ears. By the time the rest of the residents made their way downstairs, later than usual, their motivation having been extinguished by the bishop's announcement, Evelyn was rounding the bend on confidence. Its edges were becoming more and more defined.

Katrina stirred Lucky Charms around her bowl. The artificial coloring created a faint rainbow swirl in the milk. "I don't mean to bring up a sore subject, but have they told us yet when we have to leave the house?" she asked.

"They haven't," Evelyn said and took a sip of her hot coffee. After she swallowed she said, "But I wouldn't pack your bags just yet."

This time Evelyn waited for the bishop outside.

She knew he'd come for his victory lap, to

305

preen that his publicity was more outrageous and would capture a wider audience. That he'd outsmarted her yet again. Evelyn didn't know what drew him to the priesthood, if he had had a happy childhood, or who was dearest to him in this world, but she knew him well enough to expect his arrival. So she took her coffee onto the front stoop and sat — ears pricked, alert — like a guard dog. This time, she wouldn't let him inside her walls.

Sure enough, half an hour later, a shiny black sedan, one of the pristine cars from a private taxi fleet used by businessmen, pulled to the curb in front of Mercy House and, though she couldn't see the passenger through the tinted window, she recognized the tassels on the bishop's loafers when they lowered onto the sidewalk. He closed the door behind him, but the car remained, idling. He must have told the driver to wait, that this — showboating, intimidation, a pronouncement of Mercy House's life expectancy — whatever *this* was, wouldn't take long.

The sky was fat with clouds. The weather forecast predicted snow and, from the looks of it, it would be the type of storm that drops a silencing blanket. But the refrigerator was stocked and the sisters still had plenty of sidewalk salt. They were prepared.

As the bishop approached, he smiled falsely and pulled leather gloves over his hands; the fabric caught on his obtrusive amethyst ring. "Good morning, Sister. You look tired. Did you have a difficult evening?"

She gripped her mug around its waist and grazed her thumb over the rough edge of a chip. "I was kept awake by some interesting reading."

"*The Constitution of Dominican Sisters,* I hope," he said, referring to the mission and rulebook of a conservative order of nuns, the kind he and Pope Benedict admired. "Those are women who understand how to serve God."

"No, actually. New York state's adverse possession laws." The long hairs of his eyebrows climbed his forehead. He thought he had her pinned, but she wasn't done fighting yet. She wrestled her excitement; she had to deliver this next blow calmly, strategically. "It turns out, if someone publicly moves into a property they don't own, inhabits that property for at least ten years, and pays its property taxes, they are legally eligible for the title. The law was made so a property would not sit idle. And while the Catholic Church has owned this house, we have been the ones putting it to good use all this time. Paying property taxes, making improvements. The law says this house is now ours to own."

He sniffed, unperturbed. But something had hardened beneath his cool expression. "You *are* the Catholic Church. You have done everything on its behalf. The law does not apply."

"That will be for the courts to decide, which could take a year to sort out. Until then, you can't evict us. We aren't going anywhere."

"Stop this before it starts. If you don't, you will regret it." His smile was waxy and his tone was instilled with false, almost creepy, cheer.

"My life's regrets tend to be what I didn't say or do. Not what I've done. So I'll be honest, Your Excellency, I don't expect to add this to the list."

The screen door rasped open at the row house to Evelyn's left, and Dr. Saha stepped onto his front porch. He nodded to her, crossed his arms over his chest, and looked beyond her and the bishop, as if he were surveying the block, as if this was part of his morning routine. It wasn't. Evelyn knew, with a rush of affection, that he was there for her.

The bishop's eyes darted to her neighbor

briefly, measuring the man's interference, and then he jutted his chin to the side, like a snake dislocating its jaw. He stepped closer to Evelyn and seethed harsh words beneath his breath. "You have forced my hand, Evelyn. Once again. What happens next you've brought on yourself." Then he reeled around and disappeared into the car without looking back.

"Everything okay, Sister?" Dr. Saha called. The car pulled away. What did the bishop mean? What would happen next? She watched the car until it turned and was out of sight. "I suppose we'll have to wait and see."

Chapter 20

The Hawk didn't strike right away. He waited long enough for Evelyn to think maybe he'd given up; maybe he was bluffing and didn't really have another move to play. He waited for her to get comfortable.

It was the middle of March, and everyone was settling back into their preinvestigation routine. Evelyn was ministering to the streets, Maria was performing Reiki and other counseling services, Josephine was writing a new grant, and the residents were imagining, and even preparing for, life beyond their temporary home. Especially Mei-Li, who, boosted by her fundraising role, had accepted the receptionist position as an entry point into the business world. Once she saved enough money, she intended to rent an apartment and convince her mother to move in with her.

The women were conducting a GIA meeting in the living room when Mother Superior knocked on the door. The sisters recognized her spindly shape through the front window, and all three rose to greet her.

In the entryway, Mother Superior massaged the cold from her hands. "Father John would like to speak to us," she said.

"I've got homemade granola bars in the oven. Let me just ask one of the ladies to listen for the beep," Sister Maria said.

"No, just Evelyn and myself," Mother Superior responded. She eyed Evelyn and her lips thinned into a line. "You should steel yourself, Sister. As you know, there's no mask to his emotions. He's the kind of man you want at your poker table, not in your foxhole. It isn't good news." Mother Superior's phone buzzed in the belt holster beneath her coat. Her mouth pulled to the left reluctantly, but she didn't answer the call. She didn't even check the caller ID before she pinched the device's sides to silence it.

Evelyn had never seen her miss a call. "Where is he?"

"The motherhouse."

They rode in silence in the back of a yellow cab. The motherhouse was a stunning building in the Clinton Hill district of Brooklyn. It benefited from architectural details including dentil moulding and round arches adorning every window. From the street, it looked like a landmark, a structure of historical importance. But inside, it more nearly resembled a convalescent home.

When Evelyn reached for the door handle, Mother Superior leaned over and laid her palm flat on Evelyn's knee. Her eyes were magnified behind her glasses. "Not for nothing, Sister, but I have to say I do not approve of how you've handled the news of Mercy House closing. I understand your disappointment. It's always difficult when important chapters in our lives end, especially when we view it as premature. You've been brave and strong in your reactions, yes, but you've also been childish. I told you we were moving you to the motherhouse back when you were in the hospital, and since then you have metaphorically stomped your feet and thrown a tantrum. You agreed to be part of something larger when you took your vows. That requires sacrifice, and it requires acquiescing to your superiors, like any employee to her boss. It means not always getting what you want in order to serve the larger community. You've made your residents a priority, which is admirable. But you've neglected your fellow sisters in the process. This is a vulnerable time for women religious, and your insolent actions are not helping our cause. I wouldn't be surprised if Father John brought us here to demand you relocate to the motherhouse, as I ordered you to do months ago. This makes me look bad, Evelyn. It makes me look as if I have no control over my order. It makes it seem like a man must get involved for the responsibilities of my job to be properly executed. I love you, but I don't appreciate how you've made me — us all — look. I know Mercy House is important to you and to the neighborhood. I know you have issues with the bishop. He isn't my favorite person either. But the Catholic Church is struggling financially, and I don't think it's outrageous to believe they need the money for other, more wide-serving, missions. It's time to say good-bye and move on. I hope you'll listen to Father John more than you've listened to me."

While Mother Superior passed her credit card through the cab's payment machine and typed in a tip, Evelyn stared at the place on her jeans where Mother Superior's bony hand had been. Mother Superior's perspective demanded Evelyn reinterpret everything about the last few months. Was she just being a brat, making a fuss because things weren't going her way? Was it possible selling Mercy House wasn't simply a ploy made by the Hawk to punish her and force the sisters and residents out? Was he following orders from those above him? She'd been so focused on the bishop as her enemy, she hadn't considered how her defiant actions might be affecting her friends outside Mercy House, like Mother Superior, and perhaps even Father John. It was possible that, inside the motherhouse, she might encounter another ally who had experienced the consequences of her behavior and was disappointed.

"Come on, Sister Lysol. Let's get this over with." Mother Superior winked and pushed her door open.

Evelyn felt like a giant hurrying down the hallway next to Mother Superior. It was impossible to avoid feeling oafish beside her boss's shrunken form, especially as she lumbered along with her cane.

The motherhouse chapel was situated on the far end of the first floor and resembled a hospital meditation room. The lights were dim and the walls were painted eggshell, offering a warm and peaceful alcove in which to pray. A collection of cushioned chairs faced a maple lectern and a simple altar draped with white linen. The room was windowless, but both side walls featured stained glass light boxes to simulate the reverent atmosphere of a sanctuary.

It was in this space that they found Father John, hunched over in a chair at the front of the room, his fingers kneading his thighs. Evelyn's stomach tightened at the sight of him.

Mother Superior closed the chapel door behind them, and its echo startled Father John into alertness. He pushed himself to his feet, began to approach the women, and then stopped, thinking better of it. He gestured to the empty chairs beside him and then ran both hands through his thicket of salt-and-pepper hair, which splayed out from the sides of his head.

"Please, take a seat." The women followed his directions, and Father John smiled weakly. Then he shook his head, and gazed over their heads at the stained glass cross. "I can't believe I have to say what I have to say," he said, his words strained and followed by a false laugh. "I just can't believe it."

"Whether you can believe it or not, if you have to say it, you may as well go ahead and say it," Mother Superior said evenly.

This was it. Despite all Evelyn's hard work, all her strategies, she was about to hear a decree to abandon Mercy House and live out her days in this purgatory. And what could she say to Father John about it? What could she do? It was easier to imagine battling the bishop, but how would she fight her friends?

Father John's stare dropped down to Mother Superior. "I suppose you're right." When his attention floated to Evelyn, his expression broke from disbelief into sorrow. His eyes watered and he swallowed. "Sister Evelyn Fanning. It has come to our attention that you advised and assisted a woman under the care of Mercy House to obtain an abortion." In his next blink, tears slid down his cheeks. "Because of this crime against the Catholic Church, you have sustained a *latae sententiae,* an automatic excommunication." He couldn't bear to look at her anymore, and his stare dropped to his feet. "They say you must leave immediately."

Evelyn's eyelids fell shut and her ears began to ring. Ever since the Hawk had arrived, she'd felt like a nail being hammered over and over again. He wouldn't stop until he'd flattened her completely. Now he had.

She felt the brush of Mother Superior's leg as her boss jumped to her feet, and then she heard Mother Superior's screeches at Father John as well as his equally stressed replies. But Evelyn couldn't concentrate on what was being said. Her thoughts swirled and sizzled. She'd given her entire life to the Catholic Church. She was sixty-nine years old. Seventy, soon. Where was she to go? How was she to survive, homeless and destitute? She had nowhere to live, no job, and no money. She was no more secure than Miss Linda, with her plastic bags and peeling sneakers.

Evelyn worried she'd be sick right there in the chapel.

"It is beyond my control. You must know that!" Father John yelled. He was openly weeping now, and despite this show of emotion, or perhaps because of it, Evelyn's blood ran with acrimony. This was her moment for despair. It was because of his sins she wasn't able to blackmail Bishop Hawkins in the first place. And perhaps that was why the bishop was having Father John deliver the news: the irony. The painful, painful irony.

"Never, in sixty years, have I ever known a nun in this order to be excommunicated. Surely there must be another way," Mother Superior said with deflating passion.

"How could you have done this, Evelyn?" Father John implored, his voice cracking. "You knew it was wrong. You knew the risks. You knew." He was getting off scot-free and

317

had no right to cry.

Evelyn gripped the crook of her cane, pressed its foot into the floor, and heaved herself up. She rested her hand on Mother Superior's frail shoulder and glowered at Father John. His eyes widened, surprised and affronted at being the object of her ire. "I know I am not the only religious person to commit a crime against the Church. In fact, I'm not even the only one in this room," she said from the back of her throat. "But what's done is done. There's no sense fighting it. Mother Superior, you have to accept the reality. We are outmatched, and we always will be."

Evelyn craved spirits, the perfect medicine for when your own spirits were low. Good spirits: fill yourself up. Or better: holy spirits. *Let the holy spirits wash over you.* The ad campaigns wrote themselves.

As she traveled the streets of Brooklyn back to Mercy House, the memory of alcohol's sharp, almost punishing, taste made her mouth water. She longed for the magic with which it dulled pain, the way it blurred the edges of her world. And at that moment, there was so much she'd like to blur. The craving taunted her, seduced her as she imagined the serpent seduced Eve.

And lead us not into temptation, but deliver us from the evil one.

She eyed Harry's Discount Liquor Store as the cab passed it, and took note of each additional store on the route. How easy it would be to enter any number of those shops, triggering the chime that announced a customer's arrival. She would walk the aisles like anybody else restocking their home supply or preparing for a party. The owner wouldn't know she was a nun. Or, rather, an ex-nun. An alcoholic ex-nun at that. She'd be just like anybody else. And without Mercy House, without the title "Sister" preceding her name, that's exactly what she was now. Whiskey had been a constant in a time when there was little else to rely upon. She may not have much now — a vocation, income, savings, home, community — but she still had more than she did then: the friendships of Maria and Josephine, the responsibility for the residents. She didn't want to disappoint them.

Still, despair radiated from her heart through her limbs. She felt heavy, sodden, like a waterlogged willow tree, bent over, weeping into the ground, its branches stressed to the point of breaking.

She hadn't experienced such a shift in identity since Vatican II took away their habits in the late 1960s. The long black wool had reminded Evelyn of her commitment, and it created community. But the Vatican stripped them of that, first into a modified habit, and then no required uniform at all. Most nuns — especially the younger ones — found it liberating. They could assimilate with their congregation. But many found it confusing — without the clothing of nuns, other boundaries blurred as well.

Evelyn had disliked the freedom. She felt naked without her full-length robes, without being able to wrap herself in the symbol of what she was supposed to be.

But like an animal tossed into the wild, she'd survived. She found a new pack with the women of Mercy House.

Until a predator zeroed in on her herd, forcing them all to scatter.

Now she was alone. Singled out. She heard the thundering hooves of the hunter behind her. She smelled the acid of adrenaline in his sweat. And although she'd keep running as fast as her old body would take her, she had a feeling it wouldn't be long before he caught her in his teeth.

She ascended the Mercy House stairs, not Sister Evelyn Fanning, just Evelyn Fanning. Not a nun, just an old woman. She paused at the angel doorknocker. Its lips were parted as if asking God a question with no answer.

Inside, the girls were in the midst of chores: dusting, sweeping, scrubbing countertops, and cleaning windows. They were playing one of Katrina's Fleetwood Mac albums off the laptop. Desiree was lipsyncing "Gypsy," using the broom handle as a microphone. When she saw Evelyn in the doorway, she slammed the laptop shut to silence the song.

"Sister, what happened to you? You look like you seen dead people."

"I'm not . . . I've been . . ." Evelyn struggled for the words. Called by her shaking voice, everyone abandoned their tasks. When she saw Maria at the top of the stairs and Josephine rounding the doorway of the kitchen, she spoke to them, desperately. "They excommunicated me."

"Holy shit," Maria said, out of character. Then she rushed down the stairs and threw her arms around Evelyn. She smelled of peppermint and wool.

"It's a disgrace. We can't allow it." Josephine stood rigid, a cobra prepared to strike.

"Excommuni— What does that mean?" Lucia asked.

"It means," Evelyn said, and threw her arms up, "I'm not a nun anymore."

"Because of . . ." Josephine's voice trailed off but her eyes finished the sentence by looking in Esther's direction.

Evelyn didn't want Esther to feel any responsibility, because of course it wasn't her fault. She answered quickly, "Yes."

Mei Li said, "We have to fight."

"There is nothing to do. It's done." And although Evelyn knew it was true, to see them outraged on her behalf made her feel, at least temporarily, less alone.

Josephine shook her head, still incensed. "It shouldn't just be you. Maria and I are equally guilty. We should take the blame along with you."

But Evelyn couldn't allow them to do that. Josephine had already saved her once. She remembered her friend all those years ago, standing in the kitchen the morning Evelyn had forgotten about the assassination of Martin Luther King Jr. She remembered Maria joining Josephine in the weeks that followed, both taking turns rubbing her back as she vomited, dabbing her forehead with a cool washcloth, praying over her, and dutifully, painfully, denying Evelyn one last drink, no matter how she begged for it. They accompanied her to meetings. They celebrated her eventual sobriety. And, whenever Evelyn encountered times of stress over the next forty years, they reminded her of her coping tools. They didn't let her struggle with addiction on her own. Now, decades later, they were still standing steadfastly by her. *It shouldn't just be you.* Evelyn smiled and shook her head. "Let it be me."

"I can't believe it's come to this. That the jerk actually took it this far," Maria said, her eyes brimming.

"That man is a . . ." — Mei-Li searched for the right word — "a *svolach.* A fucking svolach."

Lucia crossed her arms over her chest. "A mamabicho."

"Evil," Esther added.

"A motherfucking asshole-licking dick sniffer," Desiree said, finishing the chorus.

"Yes, well." Evelyn coughed to clear a clot of emotion from her throat. "I suppose I better collect my things. Take stock. Figure out my next step."

Mei-Li's forehead furrowed. "Where are you going?"

"I don't know yet," Evelyn answered.

"Why are you going anywhere?" Katrina asked.

"Because. I'm no longer . . . everything is different now."

Lucia's face was etched with conviction. "You were already squatting here against the wishes of that bastard. What's changed? Now you aren't a nun. So what? Neither are we."

Desiree snorted. "Far from it."

Maria took Evelyn's hand and squeezed. "Stay. We've still got work to do."

That night, before Evelyn lay atop her covers to wait until it was no longer the day she was excommunicated, there was a knock on her bedroom door. She opened it to Katrina standing in the hallway, wearing her pink nightdress.

"What's the matter, dear?" Evelyn asked.

"I just wanted to say . . . I just wanted you to know . . ." Katrina shook her head at her own inarticulation. She toed a dark spot on the wood floor before her. Finally, she looked up. "You aren't alone. We all had our own bishop," she said. "And he might still have us if it wasn't for you."

Evelyn never told anybody in Mercy House the full extent of her relationship with the bishop, but it seemed she didn't have to. The residents understood it implicitly.

Chapter 21

Katrina

A child should be raised. Simple as that. I knew I was missing something being shuffled around the foster care system, tossed from one temporary house to another. Something necessary. So I searched for a family to raise me, like that little bird in *Are You My Mother?*, a children's book one of my foster parents kept around the house to — I don't know — mock us, maybe. After years of hunting, I finally found my tribe on CDs I checked out from the library and refused to return: Joni Mitchell, Janis Joplin, Stevie Nicks, Fiona Apple. I found mothers and aunts and sisters. I had no use for fathers or uncles or brothers; I'd had enough of them already.

There was Allen, who sat by my bed while I was sleeping and touched himself. Larry, who removed the locks from the bathroom doors so he could walk in while I was using the toilet. Martin, who said my foster brother grabbed my breasts because I looked like I wanted it. Frank, who seemed nice at first, but ended up being the worst one. He convinced me I was a target, that men couldn't resist a childlike voice coming out of such plump lips. But he promised I'd be safe if I slept in his room. He'd take the couch. Then he got tired of the couch.

Through all this, I wore cargo pants so I could carry my family around in my pocket, snapped inside a CD player I found on the side of the road on top of a pile of castoffs. I hooked in my earbuds and pressed play in the morning when I wanted to forget what had happened in the night; over dinner when I needed to escape the hungry watch of everybody around the table; on the school bus, amongst kids who were still kids, who didn't know what I knew. I pressed play whenever I needed to hear from my musical family. Mother Joni plucked her acoustic guitar and shifted from her chest voice to her head croon.

And then there was my sister, Fiona Apple.

Once, when riding the F train from Queens, through Manhattan, down to Brooklyn, and back up again, anything to avoid going "home," I was switching Fleetwood Mac's *Rumours* to Fiona Apple's *Tidal,* and the train bumped. The *Tidal* disc slipped from my fingers and rolled along the subway floor. I clasped *Rumours* in the closed player for safe-keeping and chased down *Tidal,* which had clattered, to my relief, facedown, saving the iridescent back from scratching. Just as I reached for it, the train hit a bend. A woman stumbled backward, and her stiletto heel pierced the CD like a dagger to a heart.

"No, no, no." I knelt beside it, gathered it in my hands, and held it against my chest. But it was too late; the CD had cracked.

My library account was blacklisted from so many overdue items, so the next day I took a bus to RadioShack and slipped a new copy of *Tidal* inside my jacket. When the alarms triggered at the exit, I ran.

I'd do anything for Fiona, even shoplift. Because we weren't just family, we were kindred spirits. She was raped in Harlem when she was twelve years old, and then developed an eating disorder to punish the body she thought of as bait.

My body was bait too. That's what Martin and Frank said. I was asking for it. I was just the right combination of innocent and sensual. Like a nymph. Men lost control around me. It wasn't their fault. They were defenseless against their instincts. I was responsible for parading my sexuality in front of them, for looking at them like I was asking for it, for sleeping in their beds. How else could I explain this type of thing happening to me over and over? I was the constant in every scenario. It was me. I made people do bad things.

Fiona knew the truth when she sang about bad girls and delicate men.

Her songs were electric, plugged in. She flipped the switch from her lowest register to a falsetto, added vibration, and laced her sound with emotion. She controlled her voice expertly, maybe because she'd learned long ago it was the only thing she could control.

I met Sister Evelyn on the subway. It was fall, and all of New York City was trading miniskirts for leggings, and sandals for knee-high leather boots. Except me.

A man in an orange hoodie pulled over a flat-brimmed Rangers cap slid onto the bench next to me. His mouth moved in my peripheral vision, but Aunt Janis was singing at full blast. I pretended I didn't notice and prayed for him to leave.

I felt a tug as he plucked out the earbud closest to him. He leaned in close. "Why don't you give me a smile? You're too pretty to frown," he said. I thought of Allen and Larry, Martin and Frank. I wasn't sure how I'd enticed this man, but obviously I had. All of my muscles constricted as my body did its best to turn to stone. "Relax, beautiful. I'm just saying hello. I'm not gonna bite." It was early afternoon, but he smelled of corn chips and cheap beer. Tears stung my eyes.

"She'll smile when there's something to smile about. And I guess you aren't it," an old lady said as she elbowed her way through standing passengers. When she reached us she waved the Rangers fan away. "Now move it along."

"Are you her bodyguard?" he asked with a mocking laugh and turned to me, as if I might be in on his joke. When I didn't react, he continued to egg her on. "What, you gonna hit me?"

Her eyebrows rose, a challenge. "Stick around and find out."

He pushed himself to his feet, and for a moment I thought he wanted a fight. Then he said, "She isn't pretty enough for this bullshit," and shoved his way through the subway car.

The woman waited for him to gain some distance before she asked me, "You okay?" I nodded, and she asked, "Where you headed?"

"Home," I said. I don't know what made me clarify, why I felt I could or should share something extra with her, but I added, "My foster home."

She considered me for a moment, and then she said, "Well, if you ever need a different home, you can find it at Mercy House."

A month later, I took Sister Evelyn up on her offer and ran away from Frank in order to wait out the last few months before I turned eighteen and was free from the foster care system. I went to Mercy House, not to protect myself, but to protect others from me.

My first night on Chauncey Street, I woke mid-scream from the kind of night terrors I'd been having regularly for years, probably waking the whole house with me.

Mei-Li roomed with me then. She did her best, sitting on the edge of my bed and touching my arm, trying to stir me from my terrible sleep, but I thought she was him, and that just made me shriek louder. Mei-Li returned to her bed, away from me, and I didn't blame her.

Then I heard Sister's voice outside the door. She knew not to come into my room. People always came into my room.

"Katrina. You had a nightmare. But it's okay. You're safe," she said from the hall, as if she woke up to someone sobbing and screaming bloody murder every night. "And you know, now that I'm here, I've been meaning to ask you something, but I always seem to forget. Now is as good a time as any, I suppose. So, tell me, what's your favorite movie?"

Hot tears fell from my eyes and my heart still pounded like a medieval drum calling for war. I wasn't in the frame of mind to swap small talk. "What?"

"I'm so busy, I don't have the chance to watch many movies, but lately I've had a hankering, and I'm looking for recommendations. So, do you have a favorite?"

"I don't know."

"Just one you like, then."

"I don't know. Maybe *Ratatouille?*"

"Oh, is that good? I think I saw advertisements back when it first came out in theaters. What's it about again?"

By the time I finished telling Sister about Remy, the cute little rat who followed his dream of becoming a chef in Paris, I felt calmer. Not calm, but calmer. And of course that was the whole point. Because she'd seen *Ratatouille.* Everyone had seen *Ratatouille.*

How many nights did we end up that way, me curled up on one side of the door and Sister Evelyn on the other? Six? Nine? She was the first stranger I had trusted in a very long time. The first person at all, really.

Eventually, I opened the door and joined her on the other side. Some nights, Sister brought colored pencils and paper; she knew I liked to create pretty things, to counteract the world's ugly stuff.

A couple weeks into my stay, sitting shoulder to shoulder with Sister Evelyn on the hallway floor at two in the morning, I confessed my wrongdoings, the list of men I'd tempted.

She looked so sad that night. So tired and sad. Instead of assigning me prayers for penance like a priest might, she swore I had no reason to feel shame. The constant in the equation of abuse wasn't me. It was bad men with little accountability. I was young, eager for love, and homeless. I was at their mercy. And they took advantage of that. They knew they could do anything to me, and the odds were they wouldn't get caught. There'd be no proof. Even if I told, which they figured I wasn't brave enough to do, the system was too unwieldy to keep track of accusations without proof.

She said, "This started when you were ten

years old, Katrina. Ten years old. There is not a nightgown short enough to make you the tempter. This is not your fault. You didn't seduce them. You couldn't. Some people are just evil. And you've had the misfortune of crossing paths with a few. But you didn't do anything wrong. You don't deserve to shut yourself off from people. To be alone. You deserve to be safe. You deserve to love and to be loved."

CHAPTER 22

Bishop Hawkins took control of Evelyn's story by issuing a press release to *National Catholic Reporter, Christian Today,* and *National Catholic Register,* all of which published the story the next day. The Hawk must have known secular news would follow, perhaps with their own liberal biases, but at least his perspective would be the first version told. And Evelyn's heroics with the gangster wouldn't be enough to absolve her of the crime he broadcasted.

Nun Excommunicated After Convincing at
Least One Woman to Kill Her Baby.

By the time Evelyn woke the next morning, her email inbox was full of hate mail. The messages she received were fueled by odium, and their content often made it clear the author hadn't read beyond the headlines.

"You are evil, and you will pay for these sins in the next life."

"That poor woman and her beautiful little baby! He could have grown up to be the greatest president to ever live. Or the pope!"

"It's vermin like you that is wrong with this world. Liberal commie, go back to where you came from."

"Hitler! Demon! Burn in hell!"

"The KKK knows what you done. That's the Ku Klux Klan, killer bitch. Sleep with one eye open."

"She trusted you! You disguised yourself as a religious figure, but you're nothing but Satan in a habit! Shame on you."

Evelyn found the last one particularly careless, since it'd been forty years since she'd worn a habit.

Interspersed among the hate, there were a few positive messages too.

"Nun of the year!"

"An advocate of female reproductive rights."

"Thank you for bravely making the world a better place."

And while Evelyn hardly believed she was nun of the year, she also hoped she wasn't as evil as some of the emails suggested. If she were lucky, she would come to believe she fell somewhere in the middle.

A fire crackled in the living room, licking the interior of the chimney with orange and red tongues, leaving a trail of soot saliva behind. Esther sat in the armchair closest to the flames and gripped the *National Catholic Register* in her hands. Her foot alternately flexed and pointed. "Someone stuck this through the mail slot," she said. Her expression was quietly grim. "They decimate you in here. Because of me."

Evelyn hovered a couple feet behind Esther. She leaned forward with both hands on her cane. "You weren't the only one."

"But I was the one that got you caught. It was my journal that served as proof."

"He would have found something else, some other reason. This is what he wanted all along. He wasn't going to stop."

Esther folded the paper carefully and laid it on her lap. "Why did you do it?"

"It's what you wanted." Outside, a garbage truck rumbled and clanged over a pothole. Evelyn stepped forward and lowered her voice, not wanting the girls in the other rooms to hear. "All those years ago, when the bishop . . . I've never been in your position. Even if I *had* been, I still wouldn't know what it was like to be you. Only you understand your own experience." That was the closest she'd ever come to talking about her trauma to anybody but Eloise. It made her tremble with nerves, maybe a little exhilaration too — the glimpse of freedom from her secret. But this wasn't about her. It was about Esther. She stepped back. "It wasn't my place to tell you what was wrong. It wasn't my place to know."

"Do you think it was wrong?"

"I'm contending with many decades of indoctrination," she said, but she hadn't answered the question, and Esther didn't appear satisfied with her diversion. Evelyn sighed. "My brain and my heart have different answers."

"Which do you listen to?"

"When it comes to Mercy House? My heart. Always."

Esther's finger traced the newspaper headline at her knee, pausing over the word "excommunicated." "Still, your life is forever changed. I feel responsible."

"Don't. I would do it again."

A car with a broken muffler clanked and coughed, making itself known along the street. Evelyn turned to the window at the sound and saw a dark-haired woman carry a bundle up their walkway, abandon it on their porch, and dash back down the steps to the car, which ran loudly idle.

"Holy Mother Mary," Evelyn said, already limping toward the entryway. "I think that woman just left a baby." When she opened the door and saw what the woman had delivered, a shrill groan roiled from her belly.

A steak knife was stuck into the baby's chest. Its body and the swaddling blankets were all doused in a red so deep it was almost black. Evelyn's wound roared as she dropped to her knees on the stoop and groped for the baby's vitals. But as her heart pounded in her ears and her fingers brushed the baby's neck, she realized with a start that this was not a real infant. It was only a doll.

She tried to close the front door behind her, to shield this gruesome image from the girls running down the hall, but their hands reached out and pushed and blocked the way. Evelyn shifted her body in front of the doll, but not before Mei-Li screamed and Esther's mouth and eyes were opened by horror.

"It's just a doll," Evelyn said. "It's fake." She noticed then that there was a note pinned to the blanket. *Eye for an eye,* it read. *Kill and be killed.*

"What sick fuck?" Desiree asked, craning around the doorway to search the streets. "This is some Hester Prynne–level hate."

"Go back inside," Evelyn said. "This isn't real." But the terror that still flowed through her veins felt authentic. Though the baby wasn't real, the threat was.

Although the doll was just a prop, Evelyn couldn't carry it any other way than cradled against her chest. She circled around to the alley beside the row house and reluctantly deposited it into a trash barrel, resisting the urge to apologize to it, to kiss its forehead.

Maria and Josephine had gathered the residents in the living room. Esther was especially shaken. Her arms wrapped and rewrapped around the front of her body, as if searching for a comforting position. She bit her thumbnail. Then scratched her jaw. Then crossed her legs.

Seeing her, it was clear what Evelyn had to do. She inhaled and exhaled long and slow, the way Maria instructed the residents to breathe during meditation. When she spoke, her words were even. "I'm moving out this afternoon."

Protests mounted from the girls and hovered in the room like the whipping blades of a helicopter. Evelyn lifted her palms against the noise.

"The bishop used our campaign against me. We fought for visibility so the community would know about us and our mission. Now that they know our story, when news of my excommunication spreads, and the reason for it, the crazies know where to find me. The house will become a target. A target meant for me, but you'll be collateral damage. And I won't have that. I'm going to leave, at least temporarily, until this all settles down. It's the only way to ensure your safety."

"But where will you go?" Josephine asked.

It was a good question. Since Evelyn had left home fifty years before, her entire world had been made up of rosary beads, vows, and service to others — of being a nun. Now that she was no longer welcome in that world, and had no safety net of her own, she'd be forced to ask for help from people in her life before the convent.

She might as well begin with the only person she'd kept in touch with.

Sleepy Hollow Correctional Facility was surrounded by a twenty-foot-tall concrete wall topped by loops of barbed wire, and prison guards stood in towers at the wall's four corners. It looked like a fortress, an ecosystem just as intent on keeping people out as it was keeping inmates in. No matter how many times Evelyn had approached this facility over the years, as soon as the gravel agitated beneath her tires and the intimidating facade came into focus, she shuddered. And it didn't help her nerves on this day to know the convent in which she was formed was a mere thirty minutes away. It was kind of poetic, really. She began her identity as a nun in this neighborhood, and when it ended, this is where she returned.

Evelyn had rented a car for the day for far too large a percentage of her net worth and arrived at the gate ten minutes before visitation hour began. "Just in time. I was about to lock up the entrance. Lucky you," a female detention officer said gruffly, before letting her pass through.

There was a famous colloquial expression adopted from Proverbs that rang in Evelyn's mind: Pride goeth before a fall. It bothered Evelyn that it failed to outline what, exactly, happened *after* the fall. What happened to Cain after he slayed his brother Abel? Yes, he moved to another land, married, and had a son, Enoch — but what happened to his heart, his humanity? What became of Lot after he slept with his daugh-

341

ters? How did he live with himself? And how did Pontius Pilate survive having allowed the crowd to crucify Jesus of Nazareth, King of the Jews?

Certainly, though not to the extent of those biblical figures, Evelyn had fallen in her own way; she lay prostrate on the figurative muddy ground. And yet here she was, at a goddamned maximum-security prison in the Hudson Valley, still at the mercy of her pride, still avoiding asking for help from the family that could actually provide it. Instead, she was seeking out the one sibling who had nothing tangible to offer her.

So, what goeth after a fall?

Or, God forbid, had she not yet finished falling?

She sat at her typical seat in the visiting room and, after ten minutes of waiting, her rear chilling on the metal chair, her fingers drumming against the table's surface to distract herself, her brother Sean shuffled through the door. An orange jumpsuit billowed on his shriveled figure. He certainly resembled a Fanning, but at eighty-five he was now decades older than their father had been at his death. Sean's nose was long, his ears were as large as conch shells, his hair had turned to dove feathers, and white whiskers prickled his jaw. His bones could no longer hold his stature erect, and so he hunched and padded across the room, his progress restricted by his chained ankles.

A little piece of Evelyn's heart broke every time she saw this frail prisoner, her brother, withering away in a jumpsuit, knowing he was behind bars in the dangerous company of young, muscled convicts. Sometimes she imagined what they could do to him, how they could take advantage of their feeble peer. Thieving, physical abuse, sex crimes — it would all be effortless. Sean would be in agony without their pulses ever elevating.

Normally, as a matter of survival, she blotted those images from her thoughts. But today, she just didn't have the strength. Everything inside her felt crushed, shattered into shards, like a dropped box of glass Christmas ornaments, ruined and rattling, their fragmented contents made worthless. And so tears streamed freely down her cheeks.

She gestured at her brother's shackled wrists. "Is that really necessary?" she asked the prison guard who stood at the door, a three-hundred-pound beefcake with a buzzed head and a roll of extra skin at his nape. "Is he posing a threat to anybody in this room? Doesn't anybody around here have a speck of goddamned decency?"

"Ma'am, lower your voice," the guard warned.

Evelyn stood as Sean reached her table and she braced his elbow as he lowered himself into a seat. She dared the prison guard to reprimand her for touching an inmate. He watched them steadily, but didn't say a word. Perhaps he had some decency after all.

"I thought, with your hip, you weren't supposed to drive long distances for another couple weeks," Sean said after he'd caught his breath. She'd written him a letter detailing the reason she would miss that month's visit. She knew what it was like not to have visitors, to lose contact with family, and didn't want Sean to think she'd forgotten him, or that he wasn't worth the trip.

"Sean," she said, struggling to properly order her words. "If you do a bad thing for a good reason, is the reason enough to make your actions right?"

His light blue eyes seemed to have shrunk, sinking into the depths of his skull, hidden behind the drooping flaps of his eyelids. "It depends how bad the thing is, and how good your reason."

Evelyn nodded and pressed her eyes closed. "The reason was good. I think it was." Sobs welled in her belly, and she strained against their force.

"Spud," Sean said, softly, using a term of endearment that was as old as she was. He leaned forward and placed his hand as close to hers as he could without actually touching her. "What happened?"

The sweet sound of her nickname rocked through her. No matter her age, she felt like a small girl beside him. She laid her forearms down on the table, leaned forward, and rested her cheek on her sleeve so she could still look sideways and see her brother. "I'm not a nun anymore."

His eyes widened. "You quit?"

She smiled sadly and shook her head. In her next blink, a tear rolled over her nose and dropped onto her arm. "They kicked me out."

"Why?"

"Because I did something terrible."

"I doubt that."

"I did," she said, although she still wasn't sure if this was true. "I've killed."

His eyes narrowed as he studied her, and then he sat back in his chair and chuckled. "Like hell you have."

Evelyn prickled, surprised by his reaction to her grave words, but a cloud of relief also formed in her gut. "I have according to the Catholic Church."

"Well to hell with them."

In her fragile state, she couldn't trust her own judgment anymore; it swung from one end to the other, like a loose pendulum. She felt lightened by his confidence in her. She sniffed, sat up, and wiped her nose with her sleeve. "Whether they are right or wrong doesn't matter. It doesn't change the fact that they don't want me anymore." She hung her head and then looked up at him, her face damp with tears. "I have nowhere to go. I don't know what to do. Tell me what to do."

His forehead wrinkled and his mouth tightened. "Do you have money?" he asked, and she shook her head. "A friend outside the convent. Someone you can call?" She shook her head again. "Then I think we both know what you have to do." Evelyn nodded, and Sean reached out and squeezed her wrist, prison guard be damned. "Who knows? Maybe you'll finally get the chance to choose your own life."

The sun was nearly blinding as she exited the prison that had been so devoid of natural light. She squinted against it and thought about what her brother had said about choice, free will — supposedly God's greatest gift to humanity.

As she hobbled toward her car, a voice

called behind her, "Sister." She turned instinctively, forgetting that the title no longer fit. It was an African American prison guard, one who had been friendly to her in the past, and courteous to her brother. His jogging slowed as he approached her, but he was still breathless. "Sister, I'd like to ask you a favor. My mother came down with pneumonia. She may not have long. Would you light a candle for her?"

His eyes were so wide, so pleading. She reached for him, but then her hand fell to her side. "Yes," she said. "Of course."

Evelyn was lucky she had her siblings' numbers stored in her cell phone; she figured she'd better make use of the device before the church deactivated it.

Evelyn shivered in the front seat of her rental car and raked her hands up and down her thighs. The phone rang three times before a thin voice answered. "Hello?"

"Fay? It's Evelyn. Evie. Your sister."

Silence dragged tortuously. Evelyn thought of her eldest sister sitting opposite her in the motherhouse visitation room, delivering the news of Sean's crime. She wished her sister had been more loving in that moment, that she'd been more sisterly. That they could have been together in their grief. But perhaps Fay wished the same of Evelyn. When Fay finally responded, her tone was distant, aloof. "What a surprise."

"I know. I'm sorry to call so suddenly, out of nowhere. It's just that, I — I need some help."

"From the way Maureen described her visit to your hospital room, it sounded as if you are doing quite fine on your own."

Evelyn closed her eyes. It seemed they wouldn't be making this easy on her, but then again, had she expected them to? Had she earned their kindness? "My situation has changed. You see . . . they . . . I'm . . ." Evelyn's fingers whitened around her knee. "I'm not a nun anymore."

"Oh?" Fay's surprise was her first sincere response.

"They asked me to leave, and I can't stay on Chauncey Street. So, the thing is, I have nowhere to go."

"I see."

Outside, a seagull soared on wind currents. They were miles from the Hudson River, even further from a body of saltwater. Unlikely things happened all the time. "And I was hoping you might not mind some company for a while."

On the other end of the line, Fay burst into laughter, which quickly dissolved into hacking coughs. Evelyn winced at the sound and pulled the phone an inch away from her ear. Evelyn imagined Fay smoking in a dark bedroom, propped up against her headboard, her ample body taking up most of the mattress space. Her sister finally said, "If you ever bothered to ask, Evie, you might know that isn't possible. I'm in an assisted living facility now. Have been for almost five years. Five years, my dear. Needless to say, they don't allow overnight guests."

"Oh, all right. I understand."

"Yes, and for old times' sake, let me spare you from any further embarrassment. Patty, your other older sister — remember her? She lives with her daughter now. I doubt that's a viable possibility. And Luke, the brother who *isn't* a cold-blooded killer? The brother you don't speak to? He moved to Florida with his second wife, Janice. A terrible woman, mind you, but she owns a condo on the beach, so at least there's that." She paused in her rant, and when she spoke again, something had deepened in her voice, made it more complex; perhaps it was intensified by a layer of compassion, by the unending loyalty built into familial bonds. "Your best bet is Maureen. She lives in a three-bedroom ranch in New Jersey. She has the space, anyway. I can't speak to her other hesitations. After your recent spat, I imagine she was last on your list to call, but there you have it."

Evelyn's tears collected at the back of her throat. "Okay. Thank you, Fay. And, listen" — Evelyn took a deep breath that was rattled by her tears — "I'm sorry I've never been in touch. I've been . . . angry. So angry. And it's possible you didn't deserve all that anger."

Fay's voice was lower, quieter. "The years have gone by now, Evie."

She screwed her eyes shut and nodded. "I know."

"We all had children you could have known and loved. Grandchildren too."

"I know."

Fay sighed into the phone. "Listen, I'm only an hour from Maureen. Maybe once you get settled you can stop by. It'd be nice to see you before we meet our Maker."

Evelyn sniffed and swallowed down tears. "I'd like that."

"Okay, then. Good luck to you."

Evelyn pressed the button to end the call. She clutched the phone against her breast and remembered Fay as a young woman, laughing too loud at the neighbor's joke, tossing her hair and leaning forward to expose her cleavage. She married that neighbor, but he'd died too young — in his fifties — from a heart attack. And Evelyn wasn't there to console her sister. She was more intent on helping strangers than comforting her own flesh and blood, all because she'd believed her family hadn't done right by her. Evelyn wondered how Fay had handled the death of her husband at such a young age, if she still grieved for him so many years later. And Evelyn wept. She wept for her sister, and she wept for the many years of relationships she'd squandered. Maybe she deserved to be alone. And she would continue to collect her punishment. After her sobs evened, she dialed the next number.

"Maureen, it's Evelyn."

"Hello, Evelyn." Her sister's tone was one of tempered irritation.

Evelyn hurried ahead before she lost the courage. "I know you have no reason to help me. You were good to visit me in the hospital and I was cruel to you. I've avoided you, Patty, Fay, and Luke all these years. It was petty of me. I could have buried the hatchet, but I didn't, and for the rest of my life I will regret what I've lost by ignoring you. I don't know what heartache you've suffered over the years because I've never been there for you, and so I understand if you don't want to be there for me now. But I have no one else to turn to, so I have to ask you this favor." She took a deep breath and continued, "They've excommunicated me. I need a place to stay. Do you have room for me in your house? In your life?"

Maureen paused and Evelyn imagined her on the other end of the line absorbing that flood of information. Would she smile spitefully? Would she roll her eyes in annoyance? Would she sympathize? "Do you have transportation?" she asked.

The rental car was due back that night. She couldn't afford to renew it another day. "I'm afraid not."

"I see," Maureen said, and Evelyn felt her chances drifting away, a raft floating out to sea. Then her sister continued, "I'd come get you now, but I don't drive very well at night. My eyes aren't what they used to be and it'll get dark soon."

Relief surged up from Evelyn's belly with almost enough force to make her laugh. Maureen would take her in. She had a place to stay. It was nothing short of a miracle. "I'm fine for tonight. I can stay on Chauncey Street, where I've been living."

"Should I pick you up there tomorrow morning, say ten o'clock?"

Evelyn imagined Maureen's car pulling up to the sidewalk outside Mercy House. The goodbye scene. "It'll be easier for you to get me at the church. Thank you, Maureen. Truly."

"All right. Hang tight. And Evelyn?"

"Yes?"

Maureen sniffed. "About us. Our past. The whole thing."

Evelyn held her breath. "Yes?"

"We all played our part."

The line disconnected and, as tears streamed down her face, Evelyn allowed herself to laugh, out of nerves and gratitude. She wiped her face with her palms and took several calming breaths. Everything would be, if not great, then at least all right. She may have been beaten down, but she would survive it.

CHAPTER 23

Evelyn didn't sleep that night. She was kept awake by all the unknown that stretched before her like an unlit road, and by Desiree's throaty snoring down the hall. But the restlessness made it easier to get out of bed before the others, to exit Mercy House while it was still dark. The old Irish goodbye.

Only Joylette, smoking a cigarette on her balcony across the street in the early hours of the morning, saw Evelyn leave. While she inched the front door closed, careful not to disturb the house, Joylette called to her. "Sister, what's with the tote?"

Evelyn looked to her overnight bag as if seeing it for the first time. When she answered, she tried not to raise her voice enough to wake anyone inside Mercy House. "It appears I'm leaving. For a while, anyway."

"How am I going to look down from my fire escape and not see you there?"

Evelyn forced a smile and a shrug. "You'll survive. We all do." Then her fingertips caressed the cheek of the angel on their doorknocker, and she turned away.

The air was cold and wet, the kind of atmosphere that sank through skin and into bones. She pulled the collar of her coat tight.

She used too large a percentage of her remaining petty funds to buy two coffees and two bagels with cream cheese from Abdul at the corner bodega and crossed the avenue to St. Joseph of Mercy Church. Her sister wouldn't be there for a couple hours. Until then, she sat down beside Miss Linda on the bus stop bench outside the church, and handed the woman half of her purchases.

"Light and sweet," Miss Linda said after the first sip of coffee. Her eyelids fluttered with pleasure. "You remembered."

"You know the church is always open. You don't have to be out in the cold. You can sit inside."

"Same goes for you, don't it?"

A train rattled in the distance. Evelyn carried her paper cup to her lips and the coffee slid down her throat like warm salve. "I suppose it does."

"Seems like we're both just fine where we are then."

As the sky lightened with morning and storeowners hauled open their metal gates, Evelyn's pocket began to buzz with a barrage of texts. She imagined the sisters and residents checking her room, finding the covers of her bed pulled taut, her crucifix missing from the wall.

"Where you at?"
"Popo, you didn't leave, did you?"
"How could you just ghost? No goodbye? After everything??"

And then, from Josephine, "Evelyn. We are worried and you aren't responding. Just tell me this. Are you drinking again?"
To her, Evelyn typed back, "Not yet."

When Maureen was twenty minutes late, Evelyn told herself there was always traffic on I-78. After forty minutes, she called her sister's phone. No answer. After an hour, she accepted the reality. Maureen had changed her mind. She didn't want to come to her sister's rescue. She didn't owe Evelyn anything.

With this realization, Evelyn slapped her knees and turned to Miss Linda, sounding stiffly upbeat. "I'm going to call some women's shelters, see if they have room.

Would you like me to ask on your behalf as well?"

Miss Linda's eyebrows rose, but she spared Evelyn the embarrassment of asking why she had nowhere else to go. "No," Miss Linda answered. "I've got my place."

Just then, the window of a maroon mini-van cranked opened and revealed Maureen's face. "I'm sorry. I left late. Then the Holland Tunnel was a parking lot. And I forgot my phone at home. I always do that. I should glue the thing to my car key." She waddled around the car to Evelyn and paused at the sight of Miss Linda. Then Maureen touched Evelyn's elbow in greeting, and Evelyn misread the gesture as the beginnings of a hug. She leaned in to embrace her older sister, sensed the miscommunication, and wrenched back upright.

The car ride to Morristown was mostly quiet, sprinkled with honking horns, engine revs, and small talk. Evelyn asked about Maureen's children, Patrick, Samuel, and Eileen, whom Evelyn mistakenly called Elaine and she had to be corrected. Maureen volunteered a description of her grandchildren: the ten-year-old girl who had been pretty all her life but was beginning to enter an awkward phase, the artsy eight-year-old boy they worried might be gay, the six-year-old who was intelligent for her age, and the two-year-old rascal they already knew was a troublemaker. "But not in any real sense," Maureen had said to qualify, flashing Evelyn a meaningful look. "Not like, criminally."

Evelyn caught her reassurance — either to Evelyn, herself, or both — that although violence might run in their blood, her grandson didn't inherit it, he'd been spared. He was benignly mischievous, not a convict in the making, like their older brother. But Evelyn was too preoccupied with an earlier descriptor, another quality Maureen mentioned that might run in the family. "The eight-year-old, your artsy one," Evelyn said, steadying her stare on the skyscrapers of midtown Manhattan lingering in her side mirror. "If he *is* gay, would that be so bad?"

Maureen scoffed and her hands shifted on the wheel. "Hard to believe they excommunicated you."

Evelyn tried not to spend too much energy interpreting Maureen's behavior. Did providing only one pillow symbolize her stinginess with forgiveness? Was the Bible on the bedside table considerate of Evelyn's recent culture or a passive aggressive attack on her excommunication? Evelyn was encouraged by the bundle of fresh carnations in a glass vase on her dresser but discouraged by the dresser drawers and closet still being chock-full of Maureen's belongings — as if to say, *Don't get too comfortable. You aren't staying for long.*

Maureen clanked around the kitchen — she never had been light on her feet. Although, perhaps she was being intentionally noisy, trying to make herself known like a hiker shaking a bear bell in the woods. The question was: Was she alerting Evelyn to her whereabouts so that Evelyn would join her or so that Evelyn would avoid her? But Evelyn had ignored her sister long enough. Perhaps it was time to try something different.

As Evelyn entered the kitchen, her sister's back was to her. Maureen turned on the faucet, filled her miniature two-cup coffeepot, and emptied the water into the machine. "Coffee?" she asked, without turning.

"Sure. Thank you."

"Do you drink Dunkin'?"

"I'm not picky."

Evelyn's gaze wandered. So much could be learned from a person by surveying her kitchen, and when it came to her sister, Evelyn knew so little; she would have to be a quick study. The space looked as if it hadn't been updated since the 1960s. A tea towel featuring a cartoon granny and the words "Grandma's Kitchen" was laced through the oven door handle. It was hard for Evelyn to accept that her sister was a grandmother — she'd barely even known her as a mother. But further evidence covered the top door of her refrigerator-freezer. Affixed by a plastic four-leaf clover magnet was a laminated collage of family pictures: Maureen and her children and grandchildren at barbecues, beachside vacations, making silly faces over birthday cakes, baptisms, graduations — happy occasions spanning perhaps forty years. Forty years Evelyn had missed — she'd *chosen* to miss.

Evelyn scanned the collection for images of Maureen's husband but she didn't find any. There were no other signs of him in the house and Maureen hadn't yet mentioned his name. Evelyn would have to wait for the right time to ask about his story.

At the center of the kitchen table, a ceramic saltshaker rooster kissed a ceramic peppershaker chicken. Also on the table was that morning's edition of the *New York Times,* folded open to the New York section. Her stare locked on the headline: "Nun Excommunicated for Allowing Abortion of Raped Woman."

Evelyn's stomach tightened. Damn, news traveled fast.

"Anything good in the paper?" Evelyn asked.

Maureen stilled for a moment at the counter but then continued to fumble in the cabinet for mugs. "I guess that depends what you consider good," she said, a chill in her voice.

Evelyn rolled her eyes. "And what do you consider good, Maureen?"

The mugs clicked against the countertop. "Who am I to say? I'm not God."

"You may not be saying anything, but it sure feels like you have an opinion." The coffeemaker hissed and dripped. Steam seeped from the lid. "It wasn't an easy decision," Evelyn said, squeezing her arms. "But it was the right one."

Maureen placed her palms down on the counter and leaned into them, hunching her shoulders. Her voice was restrained when she said, "You are always so sure you're right, Evelyn. Aren't you?"

Evelyn's nostrils flared. In the past, she would have chosen to flee over facing her family's coldness. Evading was easier than challenging. But, in the past, she had somewhere else to go.

"And what would you have done? Would you have forced a young woman to carry around a reminder of the worst moment of her life, let it reshape her body and her brain, and then wreak havoc as she birthed it? Don't you think she would have terminated the pregnancy on her own? At least this way she didn't have to be lonely and ashamed. At least this way she didn't think about ending it irresponsibly, about hurting herself."

Maureen spun around. Anger etched her face. "You were a nun. Her spiritual guardian. Maybe if you convinced her it could be a blessing in disguise, she wouldn't have done it. Now this family is disgraced — again. As if one murderer wasn't enough."

Evelyn leveled her stare. "It isn't the same thing," she said, but heat flared up her neck.

"Seems the same to me."

"What was I supposed to do?"

"I don't know. Ask God for guidance? Talk to a priest? Maybe if you weren't so self-righteous as to consider yourself infallible, that baby would still be alive today."

"I'm infallible? The homeless excommunicated nun? No, my dear. I'm afraid I'm wrong quite often. More often than I'd like. I was wrong to think this arrangement might turn out to be a good thing. I was wrong to hope the Catholic Church could ever be just and reasonable. And I was wrong to listen to you people all those years ago, because look where it landed me. In your damn guest room!"

"Not this again. You didn't do it for us. You did it because you were Daddy's little angel, weren't you? I wanted his approval too, just as much as you. But did he ask me? No, I was passed right over. I wasn't good enough. You were his nun in the making! And you ate it up. You loved all the attention until it turned out it was more fun preparing to be a nun than actually being one. That's why you got so mad at us. Because nobody fawned over you at the convent. Nobody praised you for all your sacrifice, because everyone there was in the same boat. They were all self-righteous martyrs. And you realized you didn't want to be that, you just wanted people to *believe* you were that, for people to treat you like God's chosen one. So don't blame us because the party wasn't as fun as planning for it. Nobody ever stopped you from calling it quits. Take some goddamned responsibility."

Evelyn pressed her eyes closed. Every September, on the Feast of Saint Michael, she knelt between her daddy and her big brother Sean in front of their icon of the patron saint of warriors, and her daddy lit a candle and thanked the saint, once again, for his son's life and for the life of the daughter whose commitment saved it. In those moments, and in the many other moments throughout the year that her father honored the sacrifice she'd agreed to, she felt almost holy herself. Where was Maureen in those memories? Evelyn couldn't picture her sister. Perhaps her ego had been so large, it filled her vision. It seemed they'd been fated by names given at birth: she was Aibhlín, the wished-for child. And Maureen, from the Irish Máire, meant "bitter."

Evelyn collected herself and then lowered her voice. "I wasn't mad because it was hard. I loved being a nun, eventually. I was mad because as soon as I was out of the house, I was out of all your lives. You didn't even care . . . didn't even notice . . ."

"Notice what?" Maureen demanded.

Evelyn's throat tightened. She shook her head. "Never mind."

Maureen shifted her weight from one foot to the other and seemed to soften. "Okay. We didn't visit often during the seven years or whatever it took for you to become a nun. But after that, you were able to contact us too, and you didn't visit for the next forty years."

A thud against the front door caused the sisters to pause their argument; they studied each other's faces as if their expressions might hold the answer to the source of the sound. Maureen broke away first to investigate and Evelyn followed.

Lying askew on the front stoop was a small black plastic bag, the top knotted closed.

"Eat shit, baby killer!" The shout came from a heavyset bald man hanging out the window of a white pickup truck idling in front of the house. He drifted back into the truck and then emerged again, another bag dangling from his fingers.

Evelyn yanked Maureen's arm. Her sister shifted back just in time for the next missile of what Evelyn could pray was only dog feces to smack against the doorway. Although she wasn't hit, Maureen yelped.

First Mercy House, now Maureen's house. The hate was following Evelyn, and she sensed it wouldn't stop. "I should leave. I'll find somewhere else to go."

Maureen's eyes glinted with rage. At first Evelyn thought the fury was directed at her, and her pulse quickened. Then Maureen's hulking form advanced onto the stoop. She bent to retrieve the most recent projectile and whipped it at her side. Then she slung the poop at the truck like David hurling a steaming, stinking stone at Goliath. "You eat shit, asshole!" she screamed.

Although it landed on the sidewalk, her toss got close enough to make the man flinch. His features twisted with ugly hate. Then his chin retreated into his neck and pitched forward as he hocked a gob of mucus onto her lawn, and followed that up by spitting the word "Bitch."

"Real clever," Maureen said. She leaned over and pinched the remaining bag between her thumb and forefinger. "You get this load from your shit-for-brains?"

The man's lip curled. His body disappeared into the cab, but his arm shot out to deliver a blunt middle finger as punctuation. The truck's tires squealed as he sped away.

The bag fell from Maureen's hand. She stepped back into the foyer, shut the door behind her, leaned against it, and closed her eyes. Her chest was heaving from exertion or emotion or both.

Just as Evelyn was about to apologize for the trouble she'd accidentally dragged across state lines, Maureen's shoulders rose, slowly, like a construction crane hoisting a steel beam. When they reached a certain height, she couldn't repress the urge any longer. Her hand covered her mouth, but laughter choked out of her throat, and her shoulders juddered along with it.

Relief bloomed and bubbled out of Evelyn's own mouth. The sisters laughed together over the absurd tension, Maureen's unlikely reaction, and the joy of their immediate forged alliance.

When Maureen's mirth settled, she dabbed her eyes with her sleeve and exhaled her last laugh as an audible sigh. Then she turned to Evelyn. Her head tilted and her chin crinkled as she considered her sister. When she spoke, her voice was soft with seriousness. "I dumped Wayne's ass ages ago. We never officially divorced, mind you, but the only way we are wed is on paper. I'm sure that's not what God had in mind when he designed marriage. I guess I'm not exactly the perfect Catholic girl either."

Evelyn nodded, gratefully. She reached out until her fingertips grazed her sister's wrist. "I'm sorry things didn't work out the way we planned."

"Me too." The words were fragile, prone to shattering.

Evelyn hesitated to soil their first sincere moment, but something tickled at the back of her mind, and she knew this might be her only chance to satisfy that itch. Despite her trepidation, she scratched it. "Let me just say this one thing and then I swear we can drop it. What you said about Sean earlier . . . he isn't a murderer. He is a good person who saw a lot of bad things, and maybe because of those things, in a moment of insanity, he did something unspeakable. But he is still a good person, a veteran, and our brother. And just as I was unfair to snub you all these years, maybe, just maybe, you were unfair to him."

Maureen was still smiling from their recent amusement, but her lips stiffened. When she spoke, she sounded tired, like she wanted to lie down right after she got this last bit out. "And maybe, just maybe, there's a part of you that doesn't believe all that hooey. Maybe you dedicated your life to mending the damage done by violent men because your brother was a violent man, and that shames you the same exact way it shames me."

Her words were blows that knocked the breath from Evelyn's gut. She had memorized and was comforted by her own narrative of their family history. She and Sean were the good guys, the misunderstood, slighted exiles. Her other siblings were the coldhearted villains. But, with a single remark, Maureen had recast the story.

And yet Maureen didn't know everything. She didn't know what else might have motivated Evelyn's mission against assault. She didn't know about another character who, Evelyn realized with dread, demonstrated a similar darkness to that of her own blood.

A machine sizzled from the kitchen, wheezed to finish its cycle, and beeped. Maureen said, "The coffee is ready."

CHAPTER 24

Evelyn was beginning to go stir-crazy at her sister's house when the doorbell rang, and Maureen's footsteps echoed down the hall.

"Johnny? Is that you? Lord, I haven't seen you in ages! What a pleasant surprise. Come in, come in."

Sitting at her laptop (also purchased by the church, but it'd be a cold day in hell before she'd return it), Evelyn became very aware of her breathing. It was amplified and labored, like the sound of a horse exhaling. On her keyboard, a stray silver hair curled itself around the numbers 4, 5, 6, and 7, parenthesizing exactly what she was feeling: "$%^&." Evelyn snorted, and hoped God was chuckling with her.

She pushed herself to her feet as soundlessly as possible, tiptoed to her bedroom door, and pressed her ear against it. Her sister and Father John caught each other up on the last several decades. The priest sounded disinterested, or distracted, but he still filled Maureen in on the death of his parents and his work with the parish. Maureen shared news of her offspring.

After several minutes of small talk, Father John said, "Well, it is so nice to see you, Maureen. But is Evelyn around? I'd like to speak to her privately, if that's okay."

"Oh, of course. I'm sorry to have gotten in your way," she said, perturbed.

"Not at all. It was a pleasure catching up with you," he said pleasantly, as if he was oblivious to her snipe.

"I may have to wake her. She sleeps a lot."

Evelyn made a face from her side of the door. What a shrew her sister could be. Then she ran her fingers through her hair and cleared her throat. She didn't want him to take her sister's word for it and assume she had nothing better to do than nap in the middle of the day — although that was indeed the case.

Evelyn opened the door just as Maureen was poised to knock. "Father John came for a visit and he'd like to say hello to you while he's here."

"You don't say."

Evelyn followed Maureen down the hall and into the living room, where Father John sat on the couch, his ankle crossed over his knee. Maureen bent down and grasped his hand. "So nice to see you," she said, more emphatically than before. "Come back soon." Then she continued down the hall to her bedroom, where Evelyn was certain she would snoop from behind a partially closed door.

Father John unfolded his long legs and stood. He had been searching for her gaze ever since she entered the room, and she continued to evade him.

"How are you doing?" he asked, and his tone was so warm and sympathetic it made tears sting her eyes.

She flashed a fake smile. "Just peachy."

"Sister Ev—" he began, and then paused and corrected himself. "Evelyn."

The revision pierced her. She suddenly wanted him out of this living room, this house, this state. She didn't want a reminder of all that she'd had and lost standing in the ruins of what remained. She focused her stare on her sister's mantel, on the photo trail of family history, another life Evelyn lacked.

"What are you doing here, Father?"

"Let's sit, shall we?" He returned to the couch and, after a moment of hesitation, Evelyn reluctantly settled into the armchair opposite him. "Something has been nagging me, and it'll drive me nuts until I clear the air. When I told you the . . . bad news, in the motherhouse chapel, you said, 'I am not the only religious person in this room to commit a crime against the Church.' What did you mean by that, exactly?" He grasped his thighs and kneaded them.

She toyed with a fabric pill on the arm of her chair. "Jesus said to John, 'Come forth and receive eternal life.' But he came fifth and received a toaster."

"Evelyn."

"I guess you've heard that one a million times already."

"Evelyn," he said, more sternly.

She finally looked up at him. "You came all this way because you know what I meant."

"I really don't. Were you, uh, referring to me?" he asked, casually lilting his words.

Evelyn steadied her voice. "I was."

An anxious smile pulled at his mouth. "And what is the crime you think I've committed?"

She stared up at the ceiling fan; a thin layer of dust coated the edges of the blades. At a certain age, she supposed, it just wasn't worth climbing onto a step stool. Evelyn said, "Let's just forget this."

He leaned forward and clasped his hands

together. "Evelyn, please."

His gaze was steady and pleading. If he just wanted reassurances, she wished he would man up and ask for her confidence directly. "Fine. I know. I know your secret."

He cocked his head and his smile tightened. "What secret might that be?"

"I know about your . . ." Her eyes scanned the room as she searched for the word. Her stare finally settled on Father John. "Proclivity."

He sniffed. "Proclivity? For what?"

She sat back in her chair and crossed her arms over her chest. So it would have to be this way. "For men, Father. Your proclivity for men."

He stiffened and lowered his voice. "Evelyn, that is a serious accusation. And a misguided one." He stole a glimpse down the hall toward Maureen's bedroom. "Whatever gave you that idea?"

His discomfort softened Evelyn. She knew what it was to be ashamed of feelings, of actions — to be terrified of yourself. "Bishop Hawkins told me," she said, gently. "He told me about your relationship with Father Sal, and your activities at those retreats."

"Well, that is ridiculous." He forced out a laugh. "Those are lies."

"He wasn't lying."

"It isn't true."

"Father John, please. Look at me. Look where I am, what I've become. If you can't be honest with me, who can you be honest with?"

"Why —" Father John coughed and repositioned himself on the couch. He glanced up at Evelyn, and then looked down at his feet. When he spoke again, it was in a whisper. "Why would he tell you those things?"

"Because he's an asshole."

"That may be true, but he wouldn't divulge something so significant, so damaging, for no reason at all. Unless —" His stare traveled up to meet Evelyn's. His eyes were rounded. "Is he after me, Evelyn? Am I next?"

"No."

"How can you be so sure?"

"Because —" She recalled the bishop's twisted, crazed expression as he threatened her. *He'll be humiliated first, and ultimately excommunicated. Is that what you want for your friend, Sister?* All so she'd keep her mouth closed about the bishop's terrible actions. "Because he didn't give me that information because he wants *you* out. He gave me that information because he wanted *me* out."

"What do you mean?"

"Just trust me. As far as I know, you're safe."

"Evelyn." He closed his eyes and took a deep breath. When he opened them, he was calmer, restored. "He told you something inculpating about me, and you say it's because he wanted *you* out. Well, I don't want to have had anything to do with your excommunication. You are a good person, and you were a great nun. I want to know how I am involved, or, perhaps, to blame." He leaned forward to reach across the coffee table and touched Evelyn's knee. Then he slowly retracted his arm. "Please, tell me."

She exhaled all her breath and tried to keep her explanation light. "You aren't to blame. I had something on Hawkins, and I thought I could use it to keep Mercy House open."

"And?"

"And he had a stronger hand."

"He used what he knew about me against you?" he said. Evelyn shrugged. Silence hung between them for a moment before he asked, "What did you have on him?"

She shot him a look. "That isn't any of your business."

His head bobbed and his hands worked

each other. "You're right, of course. But, if you'd like to tell me, I'd like to listen."

Evelyn crossed her legs, turned her body away from him, and looked out the window. Several ravens were still pecking meanly at the last crumbs of bread Maureen had thrown to them earlier that morning. Evelyn couldn't stand that daily routine of her sister's. She'd told her, *A group of ravens is called an unkindness, Maureen. An unkindness.* "It was so long ago, it doesn't matter anymore." Evelyn resented herself for it, but her voice wavered halfway through.

"It appears that maybe it does. Maybe it matters very much." His compassion detached something inside her. It floated up her torso and gathered as a knot in her throat. She bit her tongue to distract herself from tears, and her face fought to keep its composure. "Did he hurt somebody?" Father John whispered. She lowered in her seat and turned her face into the arm of the chair. "Did he hurt you?" Tears welled in her eyes and crackled at the back of her throat. Her fist rose up to cover her quivering mouth. Father John again reached across the table, but this time lay his hand on Evelyn's knee. He waited patiently in that position until Evelyn's whimpers passed. "You don't have to tell me what happened, but I beg you to listen to me. If he hurt you or anybody else, I don't want to be the reason he gets away with it."

She swiped at her tears quickly, as if he might not notice if only she worked fast. His forehead was lined with concern. She swallowed. "But he'll do to you what he did to me."

He shook his head. "I couldn't live with myself if I thought he used my sins to hide his own. If they excommunicate me as a result of the truth you tell, so be it."

Evelyn considered his words like rosary beads between her fingers. Even if she decided against exposing the bishop, it was something just to know she *could,* that she had Father John's blessing. It was something to know that such goodness still existed. She pushed her heavy body up in the chair. "Father, your secret, you called it your 'sins.' Is that really what you consider it?"

He smiled sadly. "Some days I do," he said, nodding. Then he turned his palms up toward the heavens. "On better days, I consider it my humanity."

CHAPTER 25

Easter Sunday awoke sleepily, a chilly forty-three degrees with gray skies. But as it stretched its arms and yawned, pockets of blue broke through the clouds to promise the day would be brighter, if Evelyn could just hold on. She had been waiting for this morning since her meeting with Father John.

Holy Week had passed as it was meant to — in quiet reflection. She attended the Mass of the Lord's Supper on Holy Thursday to honor Christ's farewell to his disciples, knowing some would betray him by morning. But when it was time for Maureen's priest to wash the feet of his congregants, Evelyn remained seated. She couldn't stand to have a priest stoop before her, touch bare skin that was so often covered, and feign subservience she presumed he didn't feel. From afar, she wondered what he might be repenting during that week of self-examination and penitence, if he had done anything truly despicable. She wondered if she was capable of asking for forgiveness when she still wasn't willing to give it. She didn't have her feet washed, but she did take Communion — although, as an excommunicated nun, she should have been deprived of the sacrament. *To hell with that,* she thought. It was her rite.

On Good Friday, she circled the nave of Morristown's Church of the Visitation, sat in a pew before each Station of the Cross, recited the appropriate prayers, and meditated on the events they represented. Jesus was condemned and forced to carry his cross. He fell three times. He was stripped of clothes, nailed, suffered, and died. Along the way, he was joined by women: his mother, who offered compassion; Veronica, who wiped his face; and the group from Jerusalem, whose sadness inspired Jesus to minister to them, to be true to his calling, even at the end. And he was helped by a man too — Simon, who carried his cross.

The Stations of the Cross depictions were mosaics, glass shards created by accident, arranged and bonded to create something beautiful, maybe even more striking than the original.

Although she knew she wasn't supposed

to, Evelyn ran her index finger along a slice on Jesus's rib cage. Blood dripped along a sharp ridge. And she thought, *What wonders can be built from broken stuff.*

Now the day had come — Easter Sunday — and her stomach fluttered and knotted like a host of sparrows alternatively spreading their wings wide and huddling together in a feathery mass.

Evelyn wanted her sister to join her, but without understanding the magnitude of the request, Maureen insisted on attending Easter service with her children. She did, however, agree to lend Evie the car.

Knights took their trusty steeds into battle. Evelyn would take a Honda Odyssey. But if an Odyssey was good enough for Homer, she supposed it was good enough for her.

Church bells clattered and pealed in Bed-Stuy to announce the ten o'clock Mass, and Evelyn still hadn't found a parking spot. It seemed everybody was Catholic on Easter Sunday. The only empty space was marked handicapped, and though she would have qualified, Maureen didn't have a pass in her car. Sweat dampened Evelyn's shirt. She prayed it didn't blur the ink scrawled across the paper inside her front pocket.

She circled the block for a fourth time, and when she approached the still-empty handicapped spot, she swerved into it, parked, and tucked the crook of her cane over her review mirror so it swung where a pass would. "There, I'm handicapped. See?" she said to no one and limped unaided toward St. Joseph of Mercy Church.

Miss Linda sat in her signature place on the bus stop bench out front. She wore a Yankees baseball cap and white Jackie O sunglasses. "You're late," she said.

Evelyn huffed along. "Better late than never, and all that jazz."

The heavy oak doors had already been closed for the service. Evelyn gripped the metal pull. How many times had she stood in this very spot to greet parishioners on their way into Mass and to say farewell on their way out? How many services had she attended, assisted in? How many Sunday school and confirmation classes had she led? How many times had she opened that door as if opening the door to her own home? A lifetime's worth. And now she was back. This was her encore. She heaved the door open.

To her dismay, the creak and subsequent slam of the door announced her arrival to the packed pews. Several congregants, perhaps desperate for distraction, turned to look. Those who recognized her as the excommunicated nun, the infamous Sister Abortion, whispered to their neighbors, and the murmurs spread like a burning match dropped in a puddle of kerosene. Soon the entire place was lit.

Father John stood at the top of the chancel stairs wearing white robes to reflect the light of resurrection. He spread his arms and looked down the aisle, directly at Evelyn, smiled, and then lifted his attention to the entire congregation. "Brothers and sisters, let us acknowledge our sins, and so prepare ourselves to celebrate the sacred mysteries."

Most of the congregation reluctantly faced forward and together recited, "I confess to almighty God, and to you, my brothers and sisters, that I have greatly sinned . . ."

Several clusters of people remained rotated in their seats, watching Evelyn. Theirs were mostly friendly faces, including Joylette beside her three strapping teenage boys and Sister Maria and Sister Josephine, too close to the front for Evelyn to join them. Maria waved, and though Evelyn meant to return the gesture, she couldn't. Her brain was too busy talking down her sympathetic nervous system, which perceived this return to all that had rejected her as a threat to her survival. *Close the adrenaline floodgates,* her brain said. *Call off the evacuation plan. This isn't fight or flight. This is stay and speak.*

"You waiting for a mailed invitation? Sit with us."

Directly to Evelyn's right, in the back row, Desiree sat beside all the residents of Mercy House: Lucia, Esther, Mei-Li, and Katrina. It was like a multitude of heavenly host appearing to Evelyn to say: *Glory to God in the highest. And peace to his people on earth.*

Their presence laid a steady hand on her nerves. Her body stilled; her adrenaline factory shut down. She lowered herself into the pew.

Desiree wore a hot pink bandage dress that cut deeply down her chest, wrapped around every bend and bow of her belly, and ended abruptly across her thighs. "You like my Easter finest?" she asked in barely a whisper while her hands outlined her sides. "God wants to admire the shit He made.' " She pressed the sides of her breasts together so that they rose like leavened bread, and her eyes lifted toward the ceiling. "He's got the best view."

Evelyn patted Desiree's knee. "You look beautiful," she said. Then she leaned forward and extended her hand beyond Desiree. The other four women reached back.

Lucia's face, which had once been swollen and bruised, now looked fresh and strong. A gold pendant in the shape of Haiti glinted on Esther's chest, and her full lips were painted a more vibrant ruby than Evelyn remembered seeing her wear. Mei-Li wore a crisp white button-down shirt, collar pressed, and her hair was tied back in a neat, professional twist. Katrina's hair was streaked with additional highlights; pink strands were now lined up beside shades of purple, blue, and green, like in a unicorn's mane. But there was something else — for the first time since Evelyn had known her, Katrina wasn't wearing earbuds. Evelyn's fingers grazed theirs. "Good to see you, ladies."

When she straightened, she spotted a far less pleasant sight: Bishop Hawkins roosted on the sanctuary, in the ornate celebrant chair. He'd left to investigate another order but had returned on Easter to show stability and solidarity during this parish's time of uncertainty — a nun's excommunication was no trivial thing. Evelyn knew he'd be there, but shuddered to see him all the same.

If he'd seen her enter, which he undoubtedly had, he was ignoring her — convincingly. He'd had years of practice.

Little bundles of anxiety scaled the interior walls of her stomach. She focused her attention elsewhere in the sanctuary: the vaulted cathedral ceiling with clusters of arches meeting at a central point; morning light streaming through stained glass windows; the altar, set with pristine linens and candles, a table ready for a celebratory meal; behind the altar, a wooden Jesus nailed to his crucifix; evangelists carved into the front of the pulpit. The congregation said, "Lord, have mercy."

The Mass continued with readings from Acts, Psalms, and Colossians. When it was time for the Gospel, Bishop Hawkins ascended from his perch. He had donned a cream chasuble with a stripe of rich gold embroidery down the front. Evelyn couldn't make it out from where she sat, but it likely depicted a biblical scene. Such vestments cost thousands of dollars. She thought, *You can shroud a rodent in lavish garments, but it doesn't make him any less of a rodent.*

As he approached the pulpit, the congregation rose, but Evelyn remained seated. The residents followed her lead. Desiree's hand covered hers.

The bishop took a moment to survey the crowd before beginning, perhaps allotting extra time for the reluctant. He wanted everybody on their feet. Finally, he said, "A reading from the holy Gospel according to Luke," and then he made a big show of tracing crosses over his forehead, mouth, and heart.

Of course the bastard would choose Luke. It was the only version of the Easter story that belittled the women's discovery of the empty tomb, calling their testimony "nonsense," and allocated more airtime to the male experience.

Evelyn couldn't listen to the story. Not from his filthy mouth. She sat back against the pew and closed her ears to it, thinking, *Your time is coming.*

Once the Hawk finished reading, he said, "The Gospel of the Lord," and raised the book to his wormy lips. The congregation recited, "Glory to you, Lord Christ," but Evelyn just joined in for the final word.

The nave rustled and murmured as hundreds of people settled back into their seats. Bishop Hawkins returned to his place on the right side of the chancel and, on the left side, Father John pushed himself to his feet.

This is it. The climbers in Evelyn's gut lost their hold on her stomach wall and plummeted in a simultaneous free fall. *This is it.*

Father John gripped the edges of the pulpit and surveyed the crowd. "Happy

Easter," he said with a congenial smile.

"Happy Easter," they responded as one.

"This morning is going to be a bit unorthodox. Instead of preaching a homily with the same Easter message you've probably heard too many times, I've invited a dear friend of mine, and one of the most upright Catholics I've ever known, to offer testimony. I hope you will receive it as the disciples received the resurrection — as a new beginning, a new age. A *better* age. Brothers and sisters, I invite you to open your hearts to Evelyn Fanning."

A wildfire of murmurs reignited in the crowd and hundreds of people rotated in their seats to face Evelyn. Up in the chancel, the Hawk looked bewildered, a mole disturbed from slumber. His head darted from Father John to Evelyn and back. Finally he scurried to his feet. "No, no. I forbid it."

Father John held up his hand to stop the bishop, and spoke directly into the microphone. "What is it, Bishop, that you fear she'll say?"

"I fear nothing. Absolutely nothing. But these people should not be exposed to the drivel of a lunatic."

"Perhaps we should let them decide for themselves. Evelyn," Father John said, and gestured to the back of the nave. "Please."

Her legs wobbled as they balanced the weight of her body. She held the pew in front of her with one hand and pulled the paper from her pocket with the other. A sea of mystified faces gawked up at her; she'd never had the attention of so many. She shook the paper open and let her words fill her gaze.

"Ephesians 5:8–9 tells us, 'You used to be like people living in the dark, but now you are people of the light. So act like people of the light. Be good and honest and truthful.' God knows I haven't always been good. Or honest. I'm a work in progress, and even in my old age I'm still trying to be better.

"In that spirit, here is my truth: over forty years ago, when I first entered the order of the Sisters of St. Joseph of Mercy, Bishop Hawkins, who was then a priest, sexually assaulted and raped me on multiple occasions."

The crowd buzzed to life on the other side of her paper and, in her peripheral vision, Lucia grabbed the hands of Desiree and Esther. For fear of the bishop interjecting, extinguishing her speech before it really ignited, Evelyn forged ahead.

"When this sort of thing happens, and it still happens to one in five women, people ask, 'Why didn't she say something?' There are so many reasons. Here are mine: I was ashamed; I worried my vow of chastity had been stolen away, and if people knew, I'd be considered a lesser nun, a lesser woman, and wouldn't be allowed to take my vows. I didn't tell because I feared he wouldn't be removed and would hurt me or others as retribution. I didn't tell because it would make what happened real, and I wanted to pretend it away. I didn't tell because I was worried I wouldn't be believed, because he was a priest, and I was just a novice. I didn't tell because I was petrified people would presume I'd seduced him, that I'd invited it by being kind to him. I didn't tell because I knew that instead of asking the real question, 'Why did he do that terrible thing?' they'd ask irrelevant questions still asked of women today, 'If she didn't want it, why did she continue going into that room?'

"So, for over four decades, I have lived with the memory of what he did to me over and over again, and I haven't told a soul. It might surprise most people to learn you can live with such a history of violence. But it's no secret to the women I have met at Mercy House."

At that, Mei-Li shot to her feet. Then Desiree slapped her hands against the back of the pew in front of her and pulled herself up. Then Esther rose like a fist. Then Lucia. And Katrina. Now Evelyn was no longer facing this crowd and her greatest adversary alone. She was joined by a line of soldiers who had seen the belly of combat and had survived — a small but fierce army.

Evelyn continued, her voice fortified, "Women whom I can no longer help because Bishop Hawkins, in all his infinite malevolence, lobbied for my excommunication, and is fighting to shut Mercy House down.

"For all these years, I've kept silent. I still fear the consequences of speaking out. But for the sake of all the women Robert Hawkins has hurt, and all the women hurt by men like him, I can't be silent anymore. This man, standing up there in the sanctuary, wearing holy robes, reading sacred words, raped me. And everybody should know what God has known all along."

When Evelyn finished, she let the paper drop, revealing rows and rows of stunned expressions, and beyond them, Bishop Hawkins, leaning against the arm of the celebrant chair, glowering at her. She hoped he was trembling with rage, and maybe a bit of terror. Because now he stood in front of a mob of people who had heard the truth, and knew what kind of man was beneath those shrouds of expensive cloth.

It was as if a giant vacuum had sucked the sound out of the room. Evelyn might have worried she'd been deafened by the shock of the event if it weren't for a light scratching to her left, as if something, someone, was trying to dig his way out — or in.

Three rows from the back of the nave, Derek Harding, the *New York Times* journalist, scribbled madly against his notebook. When Evelyn had called him after her meeting with Father John, he'd sworn he would show up. "I wouldn't miss it, and that's the Gospel truth," he'd said. It seemed there was another man she could count on.

Triumphant, she discovered the bishop had followed her gaze. He was gaping at the reporter, aghast. He gripped excess chasuble fabric in his fists. Now Evelyn presumed it was *his* sympathetic nervous system that was in overdrive, pumping survival hormones, preparing for fight or flight. Finally, he spun toward the exterior wall and flew out the side door of the sanctuary, into the sacristy and beyond.

Evelyn felt as if the heavens might crack open. As if a team of trumpeters might tout from the rafters. As if a Baptist choir might appear from the narthex mid-hymn. This was her moment of reckoning; and she'd waited so long.

Desiree bellowed loud enough for her words to echo, "Sister can preach!" Evelyn suspected Desiree was not referring to her as a nun; still, it felt good to be called "Sister" again.

Father John leaned forward to speak into the microphone. "Thank you, Evelyn," he said, with the utmost solemnity. Then he addressed the entire congregation, "Now, let us stand for the Profession of Faith." The crowd, still a little shell-shocked, but beholden to obedience inside the church's walls, shuffled to their feet.

Evelyn didn't know what would happen to the Hawk now that she'd broken her silence. She didn't know if news of this incident would flood the media, if reporters would bang on Maureen's door and beg her for interviews, if more women like her would step forward, or if the story would fizzle out without fanfare. She couldn't predict whether this would be, like Father John hoped, the start of a new era in the Catholic Church, or whether Robert Hawkins would be transferred out of the spotlight and protected, like countless holy men before him.

The word "catholic" meant "broadminded, universal, liberal." Evelyn hoped the religion would become more faithful to its name. Because there was so much beauty in Catholicism — its rituals, its creed. She believed in divine mystery, charity, and mercy. She believed in salvation and in resurrection. And if the Church would just open its eyes, if it would listen to the cries of the people it served, she could believe in the future of the Catholic Church.

Desiree tapped Evelyn's shoulder, and she turned to see Mei-Li stooped across the other girls. Evelyn bent forward to meet her. Behind the hedge of hundreds of parishioners chanting the Apostles' Creed, Mei-Li said, just loud enough for Evelyn to hear, "Sister, you're one badass bitch."

CHAPTER 26

Father John dismissed Mass, and the congregation filed out of the pews and milled past Evelyn, some avoiding eye contact, but most offering her a smile of condolence, an acknowledging nod, or a hand squeeze.

An older nun Evelyn had never spoken to paused to shake her head and say, "I always knew he was an impostor. You could tell," before continuing out into the sunshine. Derek Harding communicated to Evelyn like he was a baseball coach, tapping his watch and then flashing a thumbs-up. When Joylette approached, her mouth firmed. She stroked Evelyn's cheek and then leaned in to whisper, "Honey, I get it. I wish I didn't but, like so many, I do."

Then just the core remained, those who had stood by Evelyn during her personal stations of the cross: the sisters, the residents, and Father John.

Maria nearly shoved Josephine out of the

way to reach Evelyn. "Johnny told us you were coming, but he didn't say why." She seized Evelyn so tightly, it was difficult to breathe.

"Careful there, Lenny," Evelyn struggled to say. Maria released her boa-constrictor hold and smiled apologetically.

Josephine still kept her distance. "If I'd known, I wouldn't have let that bastard near you," she said.

Evelyn nodded. "I know."

Maria dabbed her sleeve against her eyes. "You were so strong."

"Was I?" Evelyn asked, her voice breaking.

Josephine's chin dipped in response to Evelyn's doubt. Then she gathered her friend's soft body in her lean arms. "Of course you were."

Evelyn let herself be held. She closed her eyes and concentrated on Josephine patting her back and Maria rubbing her arm. They smelled like laundry detergent and baby powder, like home.

When the sisters stepped aside, Father John was waiting, his hands clasped before him. Despite the events of that morning, his expression appeared entirely at peace. Evelyn opened her mouth, although she wasn't quite sure what to say. How do you thank a man who was willing to become a living martyr on your behalf? There was a chance no consequence would befall him, that the Catholic Church would prefer to avoid more bad press, but he accepted the risk of all possibilities. She'd never known such a pure gesture of friendship. It was a gift from God. She began, "Johnny, I —"

He shook his head. "Please don't. I couldn't bear it. Not when your excommunication could have been avoided if not for me. So, for my sake, let's just . . ." He extended his hand to her, and she grasped it at once.

"This is sweet and all, but we were promised we'd get pizza if we came to church. So . . .," Desiree said.

Maria smiled at Evelyn. "Come on. Let's go home."

The girls streamed around the side of Mercy House to the back patio, where chairs were arranged around a folding table. The day had warmed and burned off the gray clouds of that morning, and everyone chatted and laughed loudly. They hooked Katrina's CD player up to speakers and swayed to Janis Joplin's "Call on Me" and Fleetwood Mac's "You Make Loving Fun." Katrina spewed the lyrics before they played so everybody could sing along. Sister Josephine's voice fell flat, but she sang with eyes squeezed shut and a palm pressed against her heart, as if the songs were her anthems.

After the second track, Desiree yanked out the CD player's cord. "That's two for the white people," she said. "Now who's got real music?"

Lucia plugged in her iPhone and Desiree scrolled through Lucia's music. She squinted and brought the phone closer to her eyes. "I can't even read most of this shit."

"That's because it's Spanish, *pendeja.*"

Finally Desiree found something she liked. "GS Boyz in the house!" she said and cranked the volume up. Electronic bleeps scattered over cymbals. Then the bass kicked in.

Side by side, Desiree and Lucia lunged and dipped their bent knees to the floor. "Come on, Esther," Lucia yelled. "Don't act like you don't know the stanky leg."

Esther crossed her arms over her chest. "I know no such thing."

Mei-Li tugged Katrina's arm to go join them, but Katrina planted herself more firmly in her chair. Sister Maria whacked her other arm. "If Josephine and I do it, no one will even notice you. They'll be too busy watching the old fools."

Evelyn wasn't sure she'd ever seen the sisters dance before. She would have guessed, of the two, Maria would demonstrate more rhythm. But, at least in this song, Josephine's lanky frame lent itself to the choreography. Her long limbs plunged and swiveled like the legs of an intoxicated flamingo, while Maria jerked awkwardly. Mei-Li joined the group, maybe in solidarity with poor Maria, and Lucia welcomed her with a whoop. Finally Katrina relented and offered them a subdued version of the dance, which they happily accepted. Esther nodded along from her seat.

Evelyn decided she'd spent too much time on the sidelines. "Brace yourselves," she said and began what felt like a lurching Charleston. She knew they were just being generous when they circled her, clapped, and chanted, "Go, Evie. Go, Evie."

The song faded, but before the other dancers could drift away, Lucia turned to the table. "Hey, DJ Esther. What's the hold up? Drop the fucking beat."

Esther raised a cautioning eyebrow, but obliged.

After "Crank That (Soulja Boy)," "Walk It Out," and "Lean Back," Esther thumbed past something that made her sit tall. "Watch out now," she said, "we're about to get funky." She placed the iPhone on the table and hurried over to the dancers. The music kicked in and her grin spread like a horizon. "I love 'Cha-Cha Slide.' "

When the residents finally settled back into their chairs, Maria collected several Easter baskets from where they were propped at the side of the house. "This may be corny, but I don't give a hoot."

Katrina, Esther, Lucia, and Mei-Li played along with the egg hunt, maybe out of nostalgia, or maybe just to humor Maria. They patrolled the small lot, peeking under bushes, listening to Maria's unimaginative clues of "Mei-Li, you're as cold as an ice cube," and "Esther, you're practically on fire," while Desiree gestured Evelyn aside.

"What you did today was pretty baller. I knew you had the willfulness of Scarlett O'Hara, but back there at the church? That was like Joan of Arc crusading."

Evelyn smiled. "I wonder where I learned to be so bold."

Embarrassed by the compliment, Desiree dropped her gaze to her sneakers, but by the time it flicked back up, she'd already cast her modesty aside. "I said Joan of Arc. I didn't say Desiree Martin. That level of audacity can't be taught."

"And I wouldn't dare try it."

She grinned, and one cheek dimpled; Desiree looked so young, so playful, despite all she'd been through. But she held wisdom in her eyes. "The last thing an old white lady needs is more flattery. I didn't come over here to tickle your ego. I came to say this: in case nobody ever told you what you repeated to us so many times it got annoying, you should hear it yourself: you deserve to love and to be loved. We all do. So don't settle for anything less." Before Evelyn could respond, Desiree stamped back to where the other girls were still hunting around the hedges. "Ya'll better have left some chocolate for me," she yelled. When she reached them, Mei-Li hooked an arm around her neck.

Maria approached Evelyn with a pink plastic egg propped between her thumb and index finger. "This one is special for you."

"Aren't I a little old for Easter eggs?"

"Too old? No. Too cranky? Maybe. Just open it."

Evelyn accepted the egg and shook it by her ear. Silence. "Sounds light in calories," she said. Then she cracked apart the plastic shell. Inside was a crumpled piece of paper. She unfolded it. "The Trenton Clubhouse," she read and waved the scrap like a tiny white flag. "What's this?"

"It's where Eloise works. You know that quote 'Coincidences are God's way of remaining anonymous'? She's just over an hour from your sister's house," Maria said. Evelyn shook her head, but Maria was insistent. "It's about time you revisit that part of your life, while you still can. Don't you think?"

July 17, 1967
Evelyn's feet ached as she and Eloise walked to the bus station from Newark Hospital in New Jersey. They'd spent the last four days caring for victims of the riots. Hospital beds were filled with people suffering broken bones, gunshot wounds, blunt force trauma, trampling, and stabbings. Evelyn and Eloise took temperatures, dressed and sewed lacerations, and administered medication, but they also held hands, called loved ones, recited scripture, and prayed.

Under the harsh summer sun, Evelyn was, for the first time, grateful for the revised habit. Her skirt hem now fell at her shins, allowing for a breeze to lap at her legs, and her shortened veil began at the crown of her head and ended at her shoulders. She often missed her old uniform like one misses an amputated limb, but for the past couple days at least, darting around hospital rooms without air conditioning, she was glad to be free from the burden of excess wool. And rumor had it, in another year's time, they would ditch the habit altogether.

Evelyn spotted the bus stop down the block. Every step toward it was a throbbing effort. How she longed to collapse on her humble cot in her humble oasis, free from the relentless cries of a burning city. But at least there was Eloise, a comfort she could take with her.

"I'm leaving the convent," Eloise said, and the words shot through Evelyn like a bullet, slicing decisively and burrowing until they hit bone. Evelyn stopped short and Eloise grabbed her wrist. "This world can be a more just and accepting place, don't you think? And I can help, but the church won't let me. So I have to leave. I'm sorry I didn't tell you sooner; I thought the feeling would pass. But now, after everything we witnessed this week, I know. God is calling me, and I'm going to answer."

"God already called you. He called you to be a nun," Evelyn said. Her words sounded as if they had ricocheted around her empty insides, losing their force before exiting her mouth.

Eloise let her arm drop to her side. "The world is changing. Even the Vatican admits that. We have to change with it."

"We are. We have," Evelyn said, gesturing to her attire.

"It hasn't changed enough," Eloise said. She sighed, and her stare drifted past Evelyn, as if trying to identify a sound in the distance. When her gaze returned, she asked, this time more quietly, "Will you come with me?"

Eloise's veil was darkened by sweat along her hairline. Her sapphire eyes were wide and fervent as they searched Evelyn's. Then her fingers floated up and tucked beneath Evelyn's chin. Eloise had held her when Evelyn fell apart. She spoke to Evelyn through the all-consuming hush. She created fun from nothing. They'd been together in the presence of death, in the presence of prayer, in the presence of God and camaraderie and loneliness. The last seven years had been the most challenging and fulfilling of Evelyn's life, and every shred of goodness she'd experienced in that time had been because of Eloise. Her friend. But more than that. Certainly more than that.

Eloise leaned in and brushed her lips against Evelyn's.

At first, the kiss felt like a psalm. The

sweetest hymn. Praise be to God. Evelyn felt a flutter in her chest, like a hummingbird flapping its wings. But then she heard Father Hawkins groaning in the sacristy. She felt him thrusting into her, cracking her in two: the before and the after. *Serving your priest is akin to serving your God. You tempted me, damn you.* A darkness rose up from Evelyn's toes. *You tempted me, damn you.* It spread throughout her body like a cancer and hardened beneath her skin. *You tempted me, damn you.* It clipped the hummingbird's wings and deprived it of light and oxygen. *You tempted me, damn you.*

Now, forever the biblical Eve, she'd tempted Eloise too.

Evelyn flinched and stepped back. Her saliva soured, as if she were about to be sick.

Eloise's eyebrows pulled together and her mouth dropped its faint smile. "I love you, Evelyn. And I thought . . . don't you feel . . . don't you love me?"

Evelyn shook her head, but she couldn't bring herself to speak.

"Yes you do. We love each other. We've always loved each other; we just couldn't do anything about it. But if we leave, we can. Don't you want that?"

Evelyn stared at the ground. She thought of earlier that year when Eloise first got a

405

record player. They lay side by side in Evelyn's bed, listening to Buddy Holly. Their hands brushed and neither of them pulled away. Then Eloise laced her fingers through Evelyn's. They held hands for ten minutes before they heard someone walking down the hall. Later, when Evelyn thought about that night, an electric pulse rushed to the place between her thighs. Sometimes she touched the pulsing bud until it bloomed into mortal sin. "No. I'm a nun."

"I know intimacy is complicated for you. I can be patient." Evelyn shook her head more forcefully. Eloise lowered her voice. "You've been hurt, but that doesn't mean it's all over. Evelyn, don't push me away. You deserve to love and to be loved."

Eloise reached for her and caressed her cheek, but Evelyn slapped her friend's hand away. "I said no."

Eloise retracted her arm, and her eyes rounded with the surprise of her friend's fierce anger. She cradled Evelyn's hand like a bird with a broken wing. "I guess I was wrong."

Evelyn quivered; she knew, even in that moment, that she'd just thrown away the most precious gift she'd ever be given.

If Evelyn had believed Eloise back then — if she hadn't considered herself damaged, disgraceful, a temptress — would she have left the convent and embraced the love her friend so generously offered? If she could have entrusted her emotional and physical selves with another person, who knows, maybe everything would have been different.

Eloise called and wrote letters for years, begging Evelyn to reconsider, then just to keep in touch. But without any response, the contact became sparser. A postcard from Latin America. A Christmas card. A brochure of her latest endeavor. A threaded bracelet a girl in the community center she ran taught her to weave — which Evelyn wore for a year before it shredded and snapped apart. After long enough, the communication evaporated altogether.

She wondered what Eloise looked like, if her hair had whitened or silvered, if she'd grown fat like Evelyn or skeletal like Josephine, if her skin was sagging or finely lined. Evelyn wondered if Eloise had seen the photo of her in the newspaper after she was shot, if Eloise had found her short haircut homely, or if her friend had identified the acumen of all her years and the

407

beauty that remained in her eyes. She wondered if Eloise had married, if her life had been happy, if there were people who loved her the way she deserved to be loved.

Standing in the backyard of Mercy House, Evelyn stared at the scrap of paper, and she considered Desiree's reminder: maybe she, too, deserved to be loved.

Trenton, New Jersey. What were the odds?

Just then, the deliveryman arrived and placed a stack of steaming pizzas at the center of the table.

"It's about fucking time," Desiree said. She elbowed her way to the front of the group and lifted a cardboard lid.

"Be nice," Lucia scolded, her gaze lingering on the man as he left.

Desiree noticed Lucia's interest and swatted the idea away. "That boy's too scrawny for you. You'd break him in half."

Lucia leaned sideways to watch him go. "That's just what I was thinking."

The girls distributed slices, ate past the point of fullness, and drank lukewarm Coca-Cola out of red plastic cups. And though Evelyn didn't know the next time they'd all be at Chauncey Street together again, it didn't feel like a last supper. It felt more like a resurrection.

CHAPTER 27

A report of Evelyn's confessional homily ran the next day in the *New York Times*. She knew because, on Monday morning, back at Maureen's house, her bedroom door creaked open. She rolled over and found her sister standing in a shaft of light, her face soft and wet with tears.

Evelyn's heart heavied, like an overfilled water balloon. She gestured for Maureen to come in. Tears streamed more freely down her sister's face. Maureen crawled into bed beside Evelyn, wrapped an arm over her stomach, and laid her head on her sister's shoulder. They lay side by side like that for a moment, two old women made tired by years of heartache and equally exhausting joy.

"I didn't know," Maureen whispered in the dark. She smelled of coffee and cinnamon toast.

Evelyn stared at the light slicing through

the space between the curtain and the window, where the morning sun pierced the darkness. "Nobody did."

"I wish you had told me, or any of us. We wouldn't have let you stay at the convent with him."

"I couldn't tell you. They censored my letters. And, well, you didn't visit."

Maureen's body ebbed as she cried. "I understand it now — your anger. I feel we've ruined you."

And there it was. The regret she'd been waiting a lifetime for. Why did she no longer want it? It was as if she'd spent forty years struggling to draw water from a well, and the moment a puddle began to collect, she felt compelled to pour it back into the earth. Maureen's tears moistened her nightshirt. She crossed her arm to caress the top of Maureen's head. "It's okay. I'm okay now."

"It isn't okay." Maureen sniffed and squeezed Evelyn closer. "And I don't know that you're okay either." Her voice sounded choked. "We've had our differences, I know. And I can't change that. But I'm here for you now. You're my sister, and I love you. I want you to know that."

There it was again, her identity — *sister.*

Evelyn tilted her head until it touched Maureen's and clamped her eyes shut, sending warm tears down her cheeks. Maybe she was okay and maybe she wasn't. But after all those years, someone in her family had heard her and understood. They'd finally exchanged small mercies, and Evelyn felt her resentment release in her chest like so many doves from a cage. *Thank you, Lord,* she thought.

And if she wasn't okay, maybe there was still time to fix that. "You know what might make up for it?" Evelyn said.

Maureen lifted her head from Evelyn's shoulder. "What?"

"If you lend me your car again."

The ride afforded Evelyn time to mull over her shame for shutting Eloise out of her life. The lovely gesture scorned in Newark, the letters unacknowledged, the phone calls unreturned.

Evelyn's habit of denying people was the greatest error of her life. She'd opened Mercy House twenty-five years earlier, but was only just beginning to truly understand mercy and its value to the person who bestows it. Because what good did it do her insides to hold onto old grudges, to cradle and nourish them over the years so they grew robust and mighty enough to become nearly an unrecognizable form of their original hurt, so they transformed into daunting formidable resentment? It did nothing but blacken her organs, like soot to the spirit. She had refused to forgive her more benign offenders — her family — while attempting to forget the one who truly wronged her.

But Eloise hadn't hurt Evelyn (except in leaving their convent cocoon). Evelyn had just *feared* she would. And she'd feared herself. So when Eloise reached out, when she so bravely offered herself up, Evelyn had rejected her.

These were Evelyn's mistakes, but she was old now, and didn't have time to dwell on mistakes.

The Trenton Clubhouse was beyond the riverfront district, the slice of the city that was actually beautiful and which featured the American Renaissance–style, gold-domed statehouse and the pillared city hall, the historic war memorial and the iconic battle monument, the blocks of quaint row houses. The nonprofit run by Eloise was located in East Trenton on St. Joes Avenue; Evelyn wondered if this was intentional on Eloise's part or just another one of those deific chances.

Crushed Styrofoam cups, napkins, broken

bottles, and empty cigarette packs littered the street. The row houses came in spurts of three or four, and the spaces between were overgrown with brush and leafless trees, as if to make a statement about wildness, or the persistence of life. The paint on the front of homes was peeling, and awnings were dreary and ripped. Weeds sprung up from cracks in the sidewalk. A streak of white spray paint ran across the bottom of three homes and then immediately ended at the fourth, as if the offender suddenly ran out of paint, or perhaps either feared or respected the last dwelling's inhabitants. There was a wooden sign over that entrance that read: Trenton Clubhouse. The door was propped open, even though some days still felt like winter.

Evelyn felt her soul rise up from her feet and through her limbs to fill the space in her head. Her body below was strictly mechanical, a world apart from herself. She climbed the front stairs and knocked as a formality on the propped door before entering.

The hallway opened into a living room that was deceptively large, having been bumped out into the backyard. Sunlight poured in through large windows, illuminating a collection of six adolescent boys and

413

girls gathered around a board game, giggling and shoving one another playfully, and a few others sitting with a middle-aged adult at a table by the back door, workbooks flopped open before them.

The floor creaked below Evelyn's feet. Several of the children glanced her way but continued with their game. The adult pushed herself to her feet. "Can I help you?"

"Yes, I'm — I'm looking for Eloise? Eloise Harper?"

Her head tilted to the side. "I'm sorry. You just missed her, quite literally. She'll be back tomorrow. Is there something I can help you with in the meantime?"

Evelyn's spirit floated down from her head, a balloon whose party had passed. She reoccupied her body again. Her thigh muscles were gelatinous and trembled beneath her bulk. Her hip ached. "No, that's all right. Never mind."

Outside, she gripped the railing and took care not to slip down the front steps, whose brick edges were crumbling.

"Hello, Evie."

The woman's voice rang in Evelyn's ears like a lullaby from a past life. It filled her with nostalgia, and with something else, a fondness, a sweet melody.

Although her hair had whitened and her

skin had paled and lined, although she looked frailer than her robust twenty-eight-year-old self, Eloise still emanated a glow, a youthful verve. She wore a colorful argyle scarf and thick cat-eye glasses. Her lips spread in a complicated smile, and her chin tensed with emotion.

"I saw you get out of your car. I should have said something. I just couldn't believe it. I couldn't believe it was you," she said and added a girlish shrug.

Evelyn saw her friend so clearly, it was as if they were standing in the hall of their convent on the Hudson River so many decades earlier. The delicate chin. The poise of a dancer who'd just stuck a calypso leap. And the bold sapphire eyes, which hadn't been altered by the years. Evelyn clasped the railing so that she wouldn't falter.

"Oh, Eloise," she said. The words were choked by a tangle of feeling. Her other arm extended all on its own, stretching out to touch her friend. Without hesitating, Eloise stepped forward, reached out to Evelyn, and took her hand. "I'm sorry," Evelyn said. "I am so, so sorry." Eloise's eyes watered. She looked up toward the heavens and dabbed her eyes with the back of her free hand. Tears stung Evelyn's eyes too but she did nothing to stall them — it had taken her sixty years to live honestly. In her next blink, they raced down her cheeks. "I'm sorry for pushing you away."

"It's all right."

"It isn't. It isn't." A sob rose up from Evelyn's belly. "All the time I wasted. All the years that have gone by."

Eloise squeezed her hand and looked back up at Evelyn. Her eyes had the power to break the space-time continuum, to bring the estranged into the here and now. "Let's not waste any more."

If grace was undeserved love, then perhaps here was proof of that — a love, a mercy, Evelyn hadn't earned. She couldn't help herself — a laugh effervesced through her open mouth like a champagne bubble. Evelyn didn't know what her future held — if the bishop would be punished, if she'd move back to Mercy House, if the Catholic Church would change — but her present, this exact moment, was a gift, a little drop of grace.

She stepped down onto the sidewalk and wrapped her arms around Eloise. Her friend's cheek, nipped by the crisp air, rested against her warm neck. It was like a dream. Eloise's scent was unfamiliar, but pleasant and comforting. Evelyn hadn't expected to smell lilac in such an inhospitable season.

She was inflated, made full by a great deal of hope. Hope that you were never too old to love someone, and to ask someone to love you. Hope that the truth of what the bishop did would not be ignored. Hope that Mercy House would continue operating. Hope that she still had good work left to do in this life.

Beyond the rundown row houses, the dusky sky blushed across the horizon like so many scattered carnation petals. When Evelyn was a child, joy was pure. Now it was shadowed by the complications of human existence: pain, worry, loss. But perhaps this contrast was what made joy sing. She held Eloise close enough to feel her heartbeat, and she thought, *How strange and mysterious, how divine this world could be.*

ACKNOWLEDGMENTS

The deeper I delve into the publishing world, the more I realize that books are not born of the author alone. They are a collaboration, and I am forever indebted to all my brilliant collaborators, who redirected and intensified this novel in so many necessary ways.

Thank you to my agents, Nicki Richesin and Wendy Sherman, who picked me up when I was on the verge of shredding this book (and my authoring aspirations along with it). Thank you to Amy Schumer, Kevin Kane, and Corinne Brinkerhoff, whose belief in the story and characters was not just the thrill of a lifetime, but a true launching point. Thank you to the good people at William Morrow, especially my editor, Lucia Macro, who took a chance on me, and Asanté Simons. Thank you to Ioanna Opidee and Jennifer Cinguina, invaluable readers and friends.

419

And of course, to the sisters of St. Joseph's College, especially Sister Suzanne Franck — thank you for the inspiration.

I also extend my gratitude to family and friends who never stopped asking, "How's the writing going?" manuscript after manuscript after godforsaken manuscript. Ten years is a long time to ask the same question knowing you're likely to hear the same dreary answer. Thank you for asking anyway. I'm especially appreciative for the love and support of my parents and brothers. I'm tempted to call us the Dillon Five. What do you think?

And to Phil, my collaborator in life. We got here together.

P.S. INSIGHTS,
INTERVIEWS & MORE . . .

■ ■ ■ ■

ABOUT THE BOOK

■ ■ ■ ■

INSPIRATION BEHIND
MERCY HOUSE

My husband and I worked at St. Joseph's College in Long Island for five years. I grew up Episcopalian and never had any personal interaction with nuns. My exposure was limited to media portrayals, specifically the kind brought to life by Whoopi Goldberg and the gang. Despite seeing (and loving) *Sister Act* countless times, I still imagined religious women were stiff and dull, that piousness meant sacrificing personality. Two months into my time at SJC, I attended a Christmas party where I witnessed a group of sisters on the dance floor rocking their hips and pumping their fists to "It's Raining Men." That moment was a delightful shattering of assumptions. I quickly learned that sisters aren't just rosary beads and chastity. They are secret chocolate stashes and sarcastic remarks made beneath their breath. They are rule benders. They brew beer like Sister Doris Engelhard in Germany and pitch perfect strikes like Sister Mary Jo Sobieck from Minnesota. They are fascinatingly human. When they aren't being superhuman, of course.

At SJC, religious sisters hold high-ranking full-time positions: provost, president, director of academic advising, professor. But they also work additional roles of service outside of the college, like running a house for children of imprisoned mothers, operating women's shelters, or taking shifts at the motherhouse. Most of these women are over the age of fifty. Many are in their seventies. Some are in their eighties. While the rest of their peer population are eyeing retirement or stopped working long ago, they churn out twelve- or thirteen-hour days for no salary whatsoever. I was inspired by their sacrifice, selflessness, and work ethic. This was while the apostolic visitation was winding down, and although none of them said as much, I got the impression that the Vatican didn't respect their commitment. In fact, they appeared to be searching for a reason to suppress or punish women religious. These sisters who had devoted themselves to others seemed to be underappreciated and even oppressed by the very institution to which they'd pledged their lives. Women religious were under interrogation, forced to prove they were good Catholics. Holy men should have been their strongest advocates but were actually their biggest critics, at the same time going to great lengths to protect the true criminals in their ranks: abusive priests.

While working at the college, I heard stories about sisters that moved me, some of which are referenced in the book, like the woman who slept overnight at a shelter to let in victims of abuse who arrived afterhours. Every time the doorbell rang, she groaned, but of course ultimately got up and answered the door. I found this to be so very . . . normal. Because they perform acts of altruistically mystical proportions, we forget that sisters are fallible people. I loved the scene so much I made it the opening of the novel — one of the few places that wasn't reworked through the revision process.

Another story: a male professor wanted to have his autistic son confirmed but was rejected by a priest who claimed his son was incapable of making such a decision. A sister held a secret ceremony. This is also mentioned in the novel.

I began writing this manuscript when we moved away from SJC. In some ways, it's a love letter to my time there and the women

427

I met and admired.

As I was researching the apostolic visitation and nun life, I continued to be stirred by holy women's passion for social justice, by how often they speak for those without a voice, and I was outraged by their mistreatment.

I read of a case in Africa during the 1980s in which twenty-nine nuns were pregnant in a single congregation. The village was suffering an AIDS crisis, and the nuns were considered safe partners, so the priests raped them. When many became pregnant, the priests forced them to have abortions. A nun sent a report detailing this to the Vatican in the 1990s. The report was leaked in 2001. There is no evidence to suggest the Vatican did anything in response to the report. This report is referenced in the book.

Also mentioned is a case in which a nun was murdered on her church altar by means of holy objects. The town was very Catholic and the priest had influence over the police. An investigation was conducted but no one was convicted. There was a similar murder ten years later. This time, after a proper investigation, the priest was found guilty of both crimes.

I read about a nun who was excommunicated in 2010 for allowing an abortion at her hospital that saved the mother's life. This was when I decided to have Sister Evelyn facilitate abortions in extreme situations.

And of course I came across the historical figures behind the apostolic visitation who are cited in the book: Cardinal Rode, who scorned (or feared) the increasing "feminist spirit" of women religious, and Pope Benedict XVI, whose conservative views earned him the title of God's Rottweiler, and whose infamous lavishness was in such contrast to the humble lives demanded of sisters.

Perhaps another influence on the conception of this novel was my great-aunt Peggy, who died in 2018. She was a nun, but left after the switch to Vatican II. Nobody knows why.

Those circumstances are so often left mysterious and unaddressed — and are irresistibly compelling. How could a writer in the family not be intrigued by such a scandal?

INTERVIEW WITH SISTER SUZANNE FRANCK, CSJ, PHD

*I had the pleasure of working for Sister Su-
zanne Franck at St. Joseph's College in Long
Island. She is a member of the Sisters of St.
Joseph, Brentwood, and graciously agreed to
reflect on aspects of her forty-year commitment to religious life.*

Alena Dillon: *What compelled you to
make a commitment to religious life?*

Sister Suzanne Franck: I grew up in a
practicing Catholic family with grandparents and parents who were committed to
their faith and kept God present in our lives.
They were very involved in all aspects of
parish life and so I became involved too.
Prayer was central in our daily lives and we
attended Mass every Sunday. I went to
Catholic school from kindergarten through
college and saw the lived reality of sisters as
faith-filled women giving service to so

431

many, always keeping God at their center.

With a strong faith and ministry foundation from birth, a desire to serve others, and my own experiences, particularly in high school, witnessing daily the joy, compassion, prayer, and generous presence of the sisters to students and others, I was drawn to religious life.

Alena: *Did you experience a calling at a particular moment?*

Sister Franck: I can't say that there was one particular moment when I knew religious life would be my path. It was more a constant nudge deep within, beginning in my last two years of high school and continuing into college. As a sophomore in college I decided to explore what a commitment to religious life would mean for me. I actually was thinking that if I found out more information I would learn that religious life was not the right choice.

I became part of a group of young women exploring possible candidacy with the Sisters of St. Joseph, and by senior year of college I knew. I had some concern as to the reactions of family and especially friends. Forty years later I know I made the right choice and have been blessed with people and opportunities in my life that continue to enrich, inspire, and challenge me.

Alena: *Why were you afraid to announce your decision to friends and family?*

Sister Franck: In the late 1970s, entering religious life was not a common choice. Among my friends, no one was discussing this as an option. I also had friends who were Jewish, Christian but not Catholic, and nonbelieving. So there was a concern that their lack of understanding would change our friendship. Then there was the concern of not wanting to disappoint my boyfriend.

I knew my parents were excited to some-day be grandparents and, since I had been dating the same guy for a while, there was an assumption that marriage would follow. Since I was the oldest of five, I took comfort in knowing that if I did enter religious life, I had many siblings that could (and did!) provide grandchildren. In fact, my sister became engaged and got married just before I entered the novitiate so that I could serve as her maid of honor.

In all cases, my fears were unfounded. Although many of my friends did not fully understand my choice, they supported me wholeheartedly and celebrated with and for me. My parents and grandparents were thrilled by my choice (an Irish family always wants one child to go into religious life!) and, along with my siblings, were very excited for this new venture in my life.

Since my boyfriend and his family were active in the same parish as my family, he was not totally surprised by my choice. Since he was at a college out of state, we had begun to experience life apart from each other. In the depths of my heart I knew entering religious life was the right choice for me and I am forever grateful that my family and friends saw my joy and supported me as I followed my passion.

Alena: *What are your favorite aspects of Catholicism?*

Sister Franck: My favorite aspects of Catholicism include the universality of the faith. Many scripture passages are the same for the Judaic, Islamic, and Christian traditions, uniting us in faith. The Eucharist is central to the Catholic faith and through worship and sharing the presence of Christ at the table we are strengthened and nourished for the journey. Prayer and song enrich and deepen our faith life and our relationship with God both individually and communally. The humanness of God in Jesus helps us to know the immanent God as well as the transcendent God.

Alena: *What is something that you wish was different for women religious?*

Sister Franck: In general, I would like to see more equality for all women, not only in the Church, but also in our world: in workplaces, in political arenas, et cetera. The place of women within the Catholic Church has advanced over the years but there are still imposed limitations regarding certain roles. The book of Genesis in the Hebrew scripture tells us that God created male and female in God's image — this is a belief we need to live out in all areas of our world.

Alena: *Do you think Vatican Council II was beneficial to sisters even though it seemed to prompt an exodus?*

Sister Franck: The changes within the Catholic Church brought about by Vatican Council II resulted in more inclusion, increasing the participation level of male laypeople initially, and eventually including women in a very limited capacity. Another wonderful change was the move from the traditional habit to the modified habit (the modified is the habit that I wore). In time, wearing the habit at all became a choice that each individual made for herself. Prayers and hymns were now prayed/sung in English (or the language of the location) and not only in Latin. The Eucharist was celebrated in the vernacular with the priest (presider) facing the congregation and people receiving Communion in the hand.

Women religious began to assume more leadership roles and have a greater voice, especially regarding aspects of the life of women religious. There was a greater sense of freedom and, for some, this new freedom led them to explore other avenues outside of religious life. The changes, some felt, resulted in a different type of religious life than what they had committed to at their entrance time. Benefits of Vatican Council II are still unfolding. There is more inclusion of sisters as well as other laypeople in the Church and more women are acknowledged as respected theologians.

Alena: *In what ways can the rest of society benefit from the example set by sisters' community life and emphasis on prayer?*

Sister Franck: In a world filled with

violence, unrest, and fear, prayer provides a solid foundation for knowing peace and hope. Prayer, both individual and communal, deepens the relationship with God and with others as you share together in the experience. Prayer also offers the opportunity to take time out of a busy schedule and remind us of the values and meaning of life, and the gift of God's presence to all humanity and in all creation.

Community life is the invitation to share the daily joys and struggles with others and draw together to commit to working for the common good. Our life in community gives witness to the power of working together — to accomplish more than one could imagine! Particularly in our American culture of being independent, the gift and value of being interdependent gets clouded. Vision is broadened, ideas are more creative, energy is increased, wisdom is deepened, and life is more joyful when one is united with others around a common good: experience, morals, and values. A life of communal living is not just for religious people, but should be practiced among family and friends, church communities, and organizations.

Alena: *Are women still entering the convent today? If so, what draws them to the religious life?*

Sister Franck: Throughout the world there are still women entering religious life, particularly in developing countries. In America, there are not large numbers entering religious life as they once did. I think women are drawn to religious life today for the same reasons they were long ago — love of God and desire to serve people in various ministries and to live a life of prayer in community.

Alena: *Do you think more women should consider such a vocation?*

Sister Franck: Religious congregations have opportunities for people to be connected with the charism and mission of a particular congregation, living in association with the religious group as an associate or an agrégée. This has broadened the number of people, both male and female, who are living out the values and vision of a religious group and giving witness to the message of God on a daily basis. In the Sisters of St. Joseph congregation, we also have the St. Joseph Worker Program, which invites young women, post-college to age thirty, to volunteer for a year at an agreed-upon site and live in community with the other St. Joseph Workers, committing to prayer and living the mission and charism of our congregation. It is through these partners in mission that the spirit of the Sisters of St. Joseph will live on into the future.

READING GROUP GUIDE

1. This novel takes place before the #MeToo movement gained traction in social media. How might the characters have benefited from the voices and ideals of those activists? In what ways would a shift in time have affected the plot?
2. Sister Evelyn is a heroic character, but she makes mistakes too. Were there any moments when you felt frustrated by her mind-set or actions?
3. There is a large emphasis on female characters and their relationships in this novel. Did you feel male characters (Father John, Bishop Hawkins, Evelyn's father, Sean, etc.) were presented fairly or unfairly?
4. How is the setting of Bed-Stuy important to the story? How might a different setting have affected the conflict and/or characters?
5. Evelyn's brother Sean demonstrates a his-

tory with violence, first in World War II and then when he murders his neighbor. What did you think of his character and in what ways do you think Sean's situation and the reasons behind his imprisonment influenced Evelyn's life's work? Do you think her forgiving attitude toward her brother is justified?

6. How did Evelyn's childhood and family relationships, particularly with her father, affect her life long-term?

7. Do you think Evelyn's actions in helping a young woman get an abortion were defensible? Do you think the Catholic Church was right to excommunicate Evelyn? Why or why not?

8. In what ways is heritage important to the characters, particularly Esther, Mei-Li, Lucia, and Evelyn herself?

9. How do issues of sexuality motivate character choices in this novel?

10. In what ways were you surprised by the attitudes and actions of the sisters? Did they challenge or reinforce your preconceived notions of women religious?

11. The nun population has been steadily decreasing since the 1960s. Do you think this is a shame, or do you find the calling to be outdated, unnecessary, or even counterproductive? Why are we still fasci-

nated by stories of women in the religious life?

12. How might the course of Evelyn's life have been altered had she not been sexually assaulted in the convent? Do you think she still would have gone on to help the women of Mercy House? If not, can a traumatic event ever be considered valuable if positive effects transpire because of it?

13. What is the importance of names in this book? Do you find names to be relevant in your life?

14. Each of the women who come to Mercy House gets her own voice and story but, save for Evelyn, none of the sisters do. Why do you think the author made this creative choice?

15. Did Evelyn truly have a calling, or was she solely influenced by her father's choices?

16. What do you imagine happens beyond the close of this book between Evelyn and Eloise, to the other sisters and residents of Mercy House, and to Mercy House itself?

ABOUT THE AUTHOR

Alena Dillon's work has appeared in *Slice* magazine, *The Rumpus,* and *The Seventh Wave,* among other publications. She earned her MFA from Fairfield University. This is her debut novel. She lives on the North Shore of Boston with her husband and son, and their black Labrador, Penny.

The employees of Thorndike Press hope you have enjoyed this Large Print book. All our Thorndike, Wheeler, and Kennebec Large Print titles are designed for easy reading, and all our books are made to last. Other Thorndike Press Large Print books are available at your library, through selected bookstores, or directly from us.

For information about titles, please call:
(800) 223-1244

or visit our website at:
gale.com/thorndike

To share your comments, please write:
Publisher
Thorndike Press
10 Water St., Suite 310
Waterville, ME 04901